INSENSIBLE
LOSS

ALSO BY LINDA L. RICHARDS

INSENSIBLE LOSS

A NOVEL

LINDA L. RICHARDS

OCEANVIEW ● PUBLISHING

SARASOTA, FLORIDA

"Battle not with monsters, lest ye become a monster, and if you gaze into the abyss, the abyss gazes also into you."

—FRIEDRICH NIETZSCHE

INSENSIBLE
LOSS

CHAPTER ONE

I AM GAZING into an abyss. When I plant my feet on the edge of the cliff, all I see is a canyon yawing below me. I see the canyon, and I see my feet, tightly laced into trail runners. Below and beyond my tidy feet, red rock can be seen everywhere, edges softened by millennia. And steep.

Arcadia Bluff. It has a gentle sound, this location. But the reality is anything but gentle. A rough rawness that would accommodate anything one pitched in that direction. Wild west. There's that, but also more. The secrets of an earth so raw and new, it doesn't know what it wants to be when it grows up.

It happens that the physical landscape matches what is going on in my heart, but this is mere coincidence. And anyway, everything is connected.

I am in a remote part of one of the largest national parks in the United States, and I am all alone, but for my dog.

Again, aside from that dog, I feel as if I have been alone for my whole life, but that isn't true. What *is* true: everyone I've ever loved is dead. Some of them by my hand.

All of that was before. Here is now.

I stand on Arcadia Bluff and the canyon below my feet seems to careen out endlessly. The aforementioned abyss. The red rock, dotted by trees and even the occasional cactus sprouting at odd angles because the perpendicular drop doesn't support normal growth.

In the distance, far below me, I see a sliver of silvery blue. Maybe it's a river or the edge of a lake, but when I look straight down, between my feet, I see nothing but rock and cactus and peril. It gives me a funny feeling in the pit of my stomach to look down, so I try to avoid doing that.

We drove in my old Volvo to get here, the dog and I. The car is dear to me. I've had it a long time and it performs elegantly. Like a tank. An elegant tank. It is a premium car, or it was, but now it is ancient. In good condition, but unremarkable, one of the things about it that I've always cherished: it doesn't draw comment. And no one would suspect that under the trunk's false bottom they would find two Bersa Thunder 380 handguns and a whole lot of cash. The car is now my home, my armory, and my bank. Who needs anything more?

Well, maybe I do. But never mind. The journey, that's the thing.

To get here, the path we traveled in that old Volvo is a forestry road. The road is marked on maps as little more than a trail. It is unpaved and unremarked. And putting it that way—the path we traveled—makes it sound like a destination. It wasn't that. It is just the place where, for the moment, we have ended up. When this moment is complete, we'll travel some more. Maybe come to something else. It's what we have now, this life made of almost nothing. As you will have guessed, this state of near nothing didn't happen overnight.

A while ago I left behind the hollowed-out shell of the life I had created. The sham. The farce. The life in which I lived while I processed all of my grief.

Tried to process all of my grief.

Do you know what I discovered? You don't process grief. It lives inside you, waiting for you to trot through the minefield that is life. Waiting for you to make just that one step and the grief explodes back into your face. If you were to process it—like cheese, like peanut butter—at a certain point it would be smooth and glossy and perfectly digestible. Consume it and forget it. But grief isn't like that. It waits around because all it actually wants is to bite you in the ass.

I sound bitter. The tonic in a vodka drink. I don't mean to, but there you are. Sometimes what you feel overrides everything you know.

After I left said reconstructed and hollowed-out life, I didn't know what to do with myself. I was basically—entirely?—homeless. My dog. And me. Homeless and aimless. I had my car. Several handguns. A few small things that I had come to treasure. And a whole whack of cash. The cash was necessary, because this is what I no longer possessed: any form of identification or credit cards. Or anything that said I was a person at all. I had simply disappeared. You mostly can't do that forever.

A myriad of small things will trip you up. You can't travel by air. You can't book a motel. You can't call an Uber. Or bank. When you start to think about it, there are more things you can't do than what you can. After a while you need a landing spot. And you need a plan.

But I'm getting ahead of myself. Here goes another run.

Once upon a time—like a fairytale—I was a mom. A wife. A cornerstone of my community. I had a house. A pebble-tech pool. A minivan with leather seats and televised communication. I had all of the accoutrements of suburbia, right down to the suburb. Tree-lined streets that I traveled to get to my job and take my kid to his school. I had attractive but not fiendishly manicured lawns. A home. That's what it was. My husband, my son. Me. We were a family. We had a home.

One day there was an accident. People were killed. My child. Ultimately my husband, too. I was unexpectedly alone. All I had was a whole bunch of mortgaged crap I hadn't even dreamed of wanting in the first place. After a while of being alone and having no money, I needed a new job and I started taking contracts to kill people.

You see how my narrative breaks down right there? I mean, everything was going along well, from a storytelling standpoint. I'd engaged your sympathy. Maybe even your interest. And then—boom!—I blow all that goodwill with a simple revelation. Yes. Killing people. For money. What kind of nice lady does that? No kind, that's what. But it lets you know at least part of why I run.

And so here we are. Standing on the edge of a cliff. And I'm not expecting to jump.

CHAPTER TWO

LATELY I'VE NOTICED that I have become afraid of the dark.

It doesn't make sense to me. I am aware of no new trauma that might have led to this condition.

Nyctophobia. I have read about it. I have googled, as they say. I've "done some research." So I know a little about the condition that currently plagues me. I've read that it is fairly normal or, at least, not uncommon. I've read, also, that fear is healthy. In our natural state, I guess, fear is what keeps us alive and safe.

For months, I have found myself waking from peaceful slumber to the endless black and the terror that ensues. The dog smells the fear, or at least that is what I guess. When I wake in this way, I can hear him rustling about as he comes to me. He lays his muzzle on whatever part of me he can reach: my hand or my arm or even a bit of toe. And he'll stay there like that, breathing quietly, until my demons have passed, or I turn on a light.

Usually, I turn on a light.

There are things you can do, that's what I've read, as well. And there is evolved language around it. You can deal with your triggers or work at desensitizing yourself to darkness. This sort of healthy self-examination has never been my forte, and so after a while, I come up with my own solution: I begin to sleep with the light on. It keeps the demons at bay.

All of this would probably be of more concern if we had a home anymore, the dog and I. But we don't. We are traveling, no destination in mind other than a vague and distant future that at present has no shape.

Every day, we cover many miles in the Volvo. The forestry roads in Arizona's Cathedral National Forest seem endless. The park itself seems endless, as well. We keep traveling, only occasionally surfacing for fuel or other supplies. We do that at small gas stations either within the park or just on the outskirts. Places that take cash and don't ask questions. Then we delve right back into the depths of the park. We just drive and drive and drive, stopping only for calls of the body, as well as those infrequent times when I run out of steam. At those times, since we are out—literally and actually—in the middle of nowhere, I just stop the car, then pitch the small tent that lives over top of the false bottom of the trunk. And then I try to rest.

The closest I ever get to actual rest is when the dog settles down somewhere near me, then gets to snoring peacefully. Something about that sound is hypnotic to me. I'll surf behind it until, under the spell of the simple, primal cadence, I fall asleep. In and out, in and out. I float away on a column of dog snores that lead to core sleep, when my subconscious scrambles to make up for time lost.

In the morning we pack up and head out again. Where are we going? Why? I don't have answers. I don't even have questions. All I know is that everything is behind me. I'm not hopeful about what is in front of me, but it's better than going back.

Everyone knows you can't go back.

CHAPTER THREE

THE THING ABOUT Cathedral National Forest is that it is everything. Many different types of terrain and altitudes and microclimates. And it is huge. It encompasses mountain ranges, deserts, a couple of lakes, even a few towns that are so small they are insignificant: perfect for my current mood.

Wild horses roam here. Herds of elk and white tail and mule deer. I've been told there are lynx and cougars, but from the cat family, I've only ever seen the occasional bobcat. There are coyotes and foxes and even—I've read about but have not seen—actual wolves.

There are birds of so many kinds I can't begin to recognize them. And the terrain is beautiful. Turquoise rivers, seasonal waterfalls, mountains, and valleys, all on nearly three million acres of land, which, when you think about it, is roughly the size of Montenegro, which is a whole *country* in Europe. It's a big park.

And though there are highways that run right through Cathedral National Forest, most of those three million acres are uninhabited and accessible only by air or forestry roads.

It is everything.

So we have been camping, if you can call it that. We have only that small tent plus not much protective gear, so I figure it's all risky as shit—but risk, right? What the hell. There is nothing left to lose. It is not the hottest season, or I wouldn't even bother with this. Camping in Southern Arizona in the hot season is no joke and no fun. Weather that can kill. But right now it is just the right temperature and the pleasantly warm days drop to a slightly refreshing cool at night. There might be better climates for this sort of behavior, but I don't know what they are.

I go out of my way to avoid encounters with other people. In my present mood, I want to be alone. I make an exception for the dog because he keeps his jokes and comments to himself.

There comes a time that we are so deeply into the forest that there are four days straight when we don't encounter anyone. The exception is when, the first night out, I spot a ranger in his truck. He seems to barely notice me, just tipping his hat and carrying on. Whatever he's looking out for, it isn't me.

Occasionally we are passed by a handful of off-road vehicles with model names like "Monster" and "Cheetah." These look more like dune buggies than cars, but there are no dunes here. Sport utility vehicles, maybe they're called. Four-wheelers. Whatever moniker they are known by, the vehicles all seem filled with yahoos looking intent on having a good time. Some of the vehicles have gun racks attached, holding rifle barrels skyward. Other racks support handguns; presumably meant to keep the guns within easy reach.

What are these guys—and the ones I see do all seem to be guys— what are they tearing off to bring down, I wonder? I feel sorry for the elk and mule deer that will fall to their brutal approaches. I imagine campfires and roasting meat, blood dripping down greedy chins.

They give me the creeps—some of the vehicles, and never mind the guys. I'm not even sure why. I'm not sure why beyond the gun racks, of course. Though maybe that's too easy. After all, I'm carrying a small arsenal myself, so it's not just the guns that bother me. Something ugly in the air that they leave behind as they tear through the forest. I have no plans on using my guns. I'm imagining that all of their plans involve them employing theirs.

So I'm standing on Arcadia Bluff and it's dusk. The sun is hitting fluffy white clouds with a purple intensity. The world is silent, but for the forest. Until it is not. One of the vehicles circles back in the purple dusk about half an hour after a convoy of them have passed. The vehicle that does the circling is dark gray with a camouflage pattern, though what is camouflaged by gray, I'm not certain. Night maybe? Is it disruptive camouflage, meant to make it difficult to see against many backgrounds? Or it might just be a fashion statement because there is no war here from which to hide.

I feel rather than see the two men watch me as they pass. The driver is heavyset. Bearded. The left-hand passenger looks like he's whip thin. He's wearing a farmer's cap.

The driver lifts one hand in my direction. A lazy salute. I don't salute back. After a while the sound of their motor disappears in the distance. I don't breathe until after they're gone and then I set about preparing for another night on the road. It looks like rain, plus I keep replaying that lazy salute in my head. It gives me a bad feeling at the pit of my stomach. I push away the feeling, but it trickles right back after a while. I contemplate packing up; heading down the road. But where am I going to go?

I opt to sleep in my car this night, rather than putting my bedding on a groundsheet under the stars as I often do, or pitching my little tent. I tell myself it isn't because I'm afraid of the dark or anything else. It's more from an abundance of caution. What can go wrong if I'm watching?

The back seat of the Volvo is not perfectly ample, but it'll do. I've slept in this car before. I put a blanket down on the front passenger seat for the dog, protecting both it and him. My bedroll is the right weight for the season—it will easily ward off the worst of the night's chill. I spread it out in back. The Bersa is in my purse as it mostly always is. It is loaded, ready for business. That seems more important tonight than other nights, though I don't let myself think about why. I tuck the purse and the gun within easy reach, right in front of the back seat, and then I try to put everything out of my head.

As I'm heading toward sleep, I think about this difficult road I'm traveling. I wonder idly about where this road is taking me, and why, when I'm so certain I have no place to go. I wonder. But Nyctophobia. And it's all so very dark.

Finally, I sleep and I'm only sure of this because of how I wake.

CHAPTER FOUR

THE SOUND THAT brings me back to consciousness is out of context. All I've been hearing is the delicate rush of wind through the trees and the occasional call of a nightbird. The chirp of insects. The gentle cacophony of sound that presents itself as absolute stillness. The desert at night is far from silent, but the desert alone doesn't make sounds like the one I've just heard.

I am perfectly still, trying to figure out what the sound might be. And then I place it. It is the faraway growl of an engine and the much nearer growl of the dog. A glance at my phone. It is 3:00 a.m.

I stay still for a moment, gauging the situation. It's possible it is nothing at all. No cause for alarm. A ranger, come to check to make sure I'm okay: *Are you out of gas?* A tourist, lost in the dark: *I am out of gas!* Anything. Nothing.

Then the sound changes. The engine stops. There are footsteps, quiet but absolute. And I hear someone try to open the door of the Volvo, though it is locked, of course, with Swedish precision.

I force myself to stillness. Wishing for it all to go away. But don't wishes mostly go unanswered? That, at least, is what I've heard.

There comes a tapping at the window, something like a knock. Not overly loud, but present. Someone is trying to either get into the car or get my attention. The dog growls again, low in his throat. I'm not certain what to do, so I don't do anything. I just maintain the stillness and the fiction that I am either not there or fast asleep. I hold my breath, waiting. Though that doesn't seem like much of a plan.

A male voice, thick with drink, breaks this impasse. I know the sound of that. I've heard it before.

"Come on, girly." The voice seems closer than it should be. Just a few feet from where I lay. "I know you're in there. Open up that door. We can have a bit of fun."

I hesitate, not answering. Hoping he'll go away. And then the car door shakes—with some force. Playing possum clearly isn't going to work in this case. Can I scare him with the truth? It's worth a try.

"Get away," I say, pleased that my voice betrays none of the shake I feel. It sounds strong and confident. More confident than I am. "I don't want company and I have a gun."

"I don't want company," he mimics, pushing the drink-laden voice into an awkward falsetto. "And I have a *gun*." And he says it in a way that makes me certain he doesn't believe me about the gun. I'm about to move, to show him the weapon, when there is a slight "tap tap" against the window, and then the glass shatters into a million tiny pieces. To my surprise, it doesn't all fall on top of me, but stays there suspended, until he pushes on it, and then the whole sheet of broken glass falls toward me in a single fractured piece; I manage to slide in the other direction just in time to avoid it hitting me.

It all happens quickly, as though I'm watching it in slow motion. I feel frozen for a heartbeat, then get my feet under me as fast as

I can, moving toward the opposite door as he reaches through to unlock the one he's broken.

The gun is in my hand as I exit the car, pushing the sheet of broken glass to one side. It occurs to me I could have just blasted him in the face, but that would have been a foolhardy move. At that range and with the car all around me, there was the chance the bullet would have gone wide and ricocheted. I value my life and I'd like to preserve it, despite occasional evidence to the contrary. And even in my near panic, I realize that's not quite right. There are times when I could allow my life to be extinguished, but it would not be due to stress. When there is danger, I am mostly all instinct. And if I fall at a time like that, it won't be because I wasn't doing everything I could have done to save my ass.

The night is fully dark. There is not even a sliver of a moon. It takes me a while to calculate the source of the light, and I realize it is coming from the camouflage gray off-road vehicle, the one I'd seen earlier that day. And this guy here now, I figure him to be the one with the rough salute, come back with the idea of giving me a hard time.

There is additional light that comes from the hand of the heavy-set bearded man. Now illuminated and outside of the car, I see he has a short bright orange tool in his hand. It looks something like a wrench but with two stubby butt edges on one end. It looks as though it could do some damage to a skull, but I suspect that it is this tool that shattered the glass of my car window. A safety hammer. The name drifts past me from some unconscious place where my biggest mission isn't merely staying alive, even though right now the name of the thing doesn't matter.

He sees me slip out the door and is just about to pull himself out of the mess of glass when the dog growls again and begins to move toward the bearded man. It is an uncharacteristically aggressive move for this beast. I figure it must be borne of the dog's own fear and desperation: for me or himself? Maybe both.

The man moves toward the dog with the safety hammer and I rely on instinct, purely. I draw myself up, the Bersa in my right hand, my left hand steadying the gun. And though he's moving and it's not fully light, I choose a spot between the man's eyes and prepare myself. I am expert. And I have done this before.

"Don't move," I say, more to draw his attention from the dog than anything else. It surprises me, sometimes, the deep affection I have for this dog. A bottomless well of affection. I don't pretend to understand it.

I see the bearded man hesitate, but not for very long. Not for long enough.

"You won't," he says into the hesitation as he thrusts the safety hammer toward the dog. The dog shrieks with pain in the same moment I feel the gun recoil in my hand. I have acted as quickly as I could. But was it quickly enough? I'm not sure and, for the space of a few beats of my heart, I am too afraid to look.

CHAPTER FIVE

THE UNSILENCED GUN is loud. Louder than I ever remembered a gun being. I realize right away it's the venue that has given this impression as much as anything. Out here, there are no walls or buildings to absorb the sound. It bounces a long distance, hits a mountain, then ricochets back in my direction.

The sound takes a while to stop reverberating off the canyon walls. Reverberating through the empty night. Before the night goes quiet again, I am on the ground, next to the dog. I am relieved to see that he is already recovering; the glancing blow maybe knocked the wind out of him and there is a break in the skin so slight, I can tell that I'll be able to tend to him with the limited first aid kit I carry in the Volvo. I am so relieved I weep, though the weeping concerns him further. He raises himself up. Licks my hand.

I pat the dog. His safety is my first concern. I am more frightened at the thought of losing him than I would have thought possible.

I give him water from the jug I carry in the car. The fact that he can raise himself up enough to lap at the water I offer gives me hope. Water. It's our most essential thing.

When I'm certain the dog is going to be okay, I turn to deal with my assailant. My late assailant. I don't actually need to check if he is dead. When pressed by urgency, I had gone straight to muscle memory. With the light from the safety hammer, I can see I've shot him neatly between the eyes. It seems likely to me that he was dead before he hit the ground. I pause and wonder: Had he told his friend he was coming back here? Might someone come looking? I shoot a glance over my shoulder, then push it out of my mind. There's only one direction to go.

It takes me a long time to leverage the man's dead weight back into his vehicle. I feel the sweat stick to my light shirt. "Horses sweat." I hear my mother's voice. "Men perspire, but women only glow." Well, I was glowing plenty now.

The going is so difficult that, at one point, I nearly give it up. So what if someone finds out where he's fallen? It seems to me his fall was inevitable, in any case. Everything about him indicates someone who would come to a bad end. Still. A single bull's-eye from a .38 dead between the eyes could arouse questions. Would it bring platoons of cops searching for an assailant? I bet that a man out here dead by violence will bring more official interest than one missing yahoo. His pals would maybe think he had taken off with some babe or gone off on an adventure in which they hadn't been included. Or maybe they'd think he was on a bender. His pals would maybe be resentful; possibly not concerned.

But a body dead by gunshot wounds is a different matter. If nothing else, it would probably cut short my magical time alone in the forest. I think about the drink-thick voice again, coming for me in the dead of night. I admit it's possible I'm wrongheaded about the whole thing, but it does not seem like a terrible loss.

By the time I am successful in getting him fully inside the gray camouflage utility task vehicle, dawn is creeping into the sky. I have to work quickly because I might not have much time. I take a few precious seconds and use the edge of my T-shirt to wipe any surface in and on the vehicle that I might have touched. As far as I know, my fingerprints aren't on record anywhere, but it seems like a good idea to take no chances.

With any potential prints wiped, I move past the big knobby tires and get into the driver's seat, popping the manual transmission vehicle into neutral and pushing it and its posthumous cargo toward the edge of the cliff. It's hard going on the rough ground, but getting it to move is not impossible. It doesn't task me beyond available strength though there are moments when it seems a close thing.

When I get the off-road vehicle near the edge of the cliff, I load the dog into the Volvo, then get behind the wheel of my car, and we take a run at pushing the UTV into the void. I am so relieved when it finally moves, I feel physically weak with relief.

The vehicle falls. In the early morning light, I see gray camouflage twist dramatically into the canyon. It catches for an instant on a rocky jutting ledge, and just as it hangs, I think again about my fingerprints. Did I remember the bumper? And then the movement begins again and, as the UTV twists, rolls, and falls, I give up this bit of regret. Life is too short for remorse at the best of times, and this isn't one of those.

When the UTV stops moving it seems also to disappear. I realize it might be visible from some other angle. Hell, it might even be visible from the sky, but all I can do is hope it stays hidden for a while and by the time it is found I'm long gone from the vicinity. And in one way, it doesn't matter. The man himself does not seem regrettable, and me? I don't exist at all: I have no identity and the little I had put together, I gave away. In some ways, that's an uncomfortable position. In other ways, it's an advantage. People can look for me, but there is no one left to find.

For a heartbeat I try to feel badly about the outcome, then I realize this is the best ending for this situation. The predator has been dealt out.

And the prey moves on.

CHAPTER SIX

TIME TAKES ON a sandlike quality. It shifts through my hands; under my feet. I forget to keep track, and I don't need to. Plus, after a while I forget about the roads that led us here; I just follow the road that I'm on. After a while I also forget about the voice in the night. I try to forget about the feeling of exposure. I try to put the feeling of violation out of my mind. I don't know if I am successful. After a bit, it feels like I have forgotten. Maybe that's enough, at least for now.

Out here the world is untouched; it is perfect. It is mostly how it has always been. It makes it difficult to believe in blemishes.

This is the road less traveled. I have a feeling that we are farther out in the world than anyone has ever been before. Farther than anyone has dared to venture. That's ridiculous. Of course. Someone paved the road; it didn't just erupt here. Someone painted the faded yellow lines that edge it, long ago enough for them to fade. But there is no other traffic, and after a while, it's been so long since I saw another car, I almost forget the shape of them or what the companionship of other humans looks like. Their voices. Their petty thoughts.

More miles fly past and the pavement ends. I keep going along Forestry Service Road 16, even though I don't know where it might come out; or even if it does. It is beautiful, though. Pristine. There are no signs of other people, and I am lulled into this feeling of alien aloneness. It's not a bad feeling, until suddenly the dog becomes anxious. Something like a ghost walking on his grave, though that's a human expression. Or is it a goose? A goose walking on your grave. Does that even make sense? Why would a goose walk on your grave? Never mind.

Here we are—truly—in the middle of nowhere and the dog is pacing on the back seat, back and forth. He is impatient. I wonder if he has to relieve himself, though he's not acted like this before, and I've known him for a while. The fact that I don't recognize the behavior doesn't matter, I realize. He is increasingly frantic. I need to stop the car; let him attend to whatever business he has in mind.

There is a widening in the road, and a definite track—not paved, but certainly wide enough for a car—leads off into a scrub forest. I pull onto the track, just off the road. Park the car. Open the door.

"Okay," I say to him calmly. "Go explore."

To my astonishment, this good boy who never leaves my side shoots out of the car and heads off down the track as though pulled by some silent call. A weatherworn wooden sign swings over what I can now see is a driveway. The sign is suspended by two huge logs. It says, OCOTILLO RANCH, and if I weren't so distraught, I'd probably guffaw.

"Argh," I cry, heading in the direction in which the dog disappeared, regretting for the first time not having a name to call the dog back with even though he looks intent enough on whatever has caught his attention that I'm not certain he would have stopped even if I'd had something to call him.

The track he's following is rocky but good. I sprint along behind him for a bit, but I'm no match for his speed. After a while, he is out of my sight. I pound along in the direction I last saw him, but as I move, my heart is sinking. This behavior is unprecedented. We have logged many miles together ever since he entered my life when he was a pup, and he's never acted this way.

After a while there is no sign of him, and I stop running, dropping to the ground on the worn track to catch my breath. The earth is scratchy, warm. That feeling of being somewhere no one has ever been increases here, and it is dead silent. A slight breeze keeps the heat from being oppressive and brings the scent of things that are growing. Those smells are exotic to me. I suspect sage and the sour tang of ocotillo. Sun on baked earth. The mild, fresh fragrance of desert pine. It's a heady, magical mixture, and I'm not certain I recognize all of the components.

The dog has disappeared so completely—without a trace— that there is a heaviness in my heart. After all we've been through together, to have lost him in this way is impossible to contemplate. I'm not going to give up that easily, but a part of me isn't hopeful. He had acted so strangely. Something must be up. Even so, I can't just leave him. It's not possible that my beautiful golden dog will survive out here alone. The wolves and coyotes; the big cats and, deadliest of all, the two-legged predators. But what are the options? I can go back for the car, but I feel the battle is lost. At the pace he was going, I'll never catch him.

I am just getting up, wiping the dirt from my pants—the heaviness from my heart—when the wind picks up a notch and I hear something that doesn't belong. The sound of fairy bells in the middle of a desert forest, but I know that can't be right: Even if fairies existed, why would they wear bells?

I move in the direction of the sound, still trying to place it. It is light and bright and lovely. Then I realize: it isn't a mystery at all, but the faintest tinkle of wind chimes. As unmistakable and unlikely as the sound is in this location, I'm sure I'm not wrong, which means some semblance of civilization is nearby. And from the volume, I judge the chimes to be not far ahead.

I pick myself up and head farther down the track, toward the sound. The bright lightness of the chimes invigorate me. Gold-on-brass. I haven't gone much farther before a homestead appears around a bend. I am looking at an oasis. I see a tidy house, a swimming pool, and some outbuildings, all surrounded by shade-giving trees, so precious in the desert. The small river that runs through the homestead appears to be the lifeblood of all that green. Shallow hills nearby provide a feeling of shelter in the little valley. It all appears as idyllic as anything could. A secret garden in the desert. It is beautiful.

As I near the house I see an old woman sitting in the shade of a breezeway attached to the house. The dog is sitting next to her, his head in her lap. My dog. And he is staring up at her in adoration.

"Hullo!" I call out as I approach. "I'm sorry to intrude."

She smiles a welcome at my approach, reaches up a hand, and beckons me forward. It's as though she is expecting me. Up close I can see that she is even older than I thought at first. She's as pale as natural silk and her skin looks so thin it is almost translucent. A blue light seems almost to shine through her. At first glance, she seems a magical figure, perched here in her hidden garden, the dog sitting quietly and adoringly at her feet.

"I suspect I know why you're here," she says, stroking the dog's head. Her voice seems creaky, like it hasn't been used for a while.

Close up, she seems to emit the faintest scent of lavender. Present but not unpleasant. It seems to radiate from her, like heat.

"I'm so sorry to disturb you," I say. "I can't imagine what got into him. He's always such a good boy."

She starts to laugh and then the laugh turns into a cough. I stand by politely, waiting for the cough to subside. When it does, she grins at me apologetically.

"Sorry," she says. "For the coughing. I never know when I'm gonna go off. Should be okay for now."

"That's all right," I say.

"So the dog," she says. "Is this the strangest thing? It was like he knew me. Though, of course, I've never met him."

"Certainly." I don't know what to say.

"What are you doing in these parts?"

"Drifting," I say honestly.

"That's interesting. I didn't know people still did that. You have nowhere you need to be?"

I shake my head.

"No one waiting for you?"

"Not anymore." I say it without emotion and am interested to see her absorb the words. It's like she is a sponge for them. And it's like she has been waiting.

"And you didn't arrive in order to find me?"

I shake my head. "Sorry," I say. "No. I don't even know who you are."

She nods her head, but she only looks half-convinced.

"No, really," I press. "Now I feel as though I should know who you are, but I don't. I'm sorry."

"I'm Imogen O'Brien," she says, and I can tell she's watching my face closely to see how I react to the name. I recognize it, of course. Who doesn't know Imogen O'Brien? She is a legend. I peek at her from under my lashes; wondering if she is pulling my leg. I can't believe it is her, and yet I don't doubt. And I don't tell her that I didn't even know for sure that she was still alive. She is such a legend that I had probably assumed she was not still among us, if I'd thought of her at all. Which I hadn't.

"Really?" is all I say, but of course I believe her. And now I recognize her, as well. She is a recluse, that much I know. She is famous for it. And she has lived "somewhere in the Arizona forests" forever. Thirty years. Forty. More. She is one of the most famous living painters in the world, and I have stumbled across her. Or my dog has. Either way. Here she is. Looking more like a beautiful and ancient gnome than an icon.

"Really." She nods back at me with a smile, and she does not seem the least bit weird or reclusive. I find myself almost waiting for her to ask me to tea.

"How is it you have a property in a national forest?"

"It's called 'in holding,'" she tells me. "It's from the time before there were national forests: the title is grandfathered in. There are lots of properties like this one."

"Lots?"

"'Lots' I guess being a relative term."

"Your relatives have them?"

She laughs out loud at that. "You know that's not it. But you're quick. I like that."

"So there are other properties 'in holding'?"

"I guess. I'm not sure how many. But they exist."

"Not many, I'd guess. That makes this place extra special, I guess."

"It does," she agrees. "I'm trying to figure out the business with the dog," she says mildly. "Obviously he and I have never met."

"Obviously," I agree. The possibility that their paths have crossed before are slim to impossible. But I don't say any of that. Instead, I shrug. "He's pretty intuitive sometimes."

"Intuitive about what?"

"Stuff. In general. He knows things. What do you need?"

It takes her a long time to answer. When she does, I have to strain to hear her because she's answered so quietly.

"Companionship," is what I hear when I strain.

I don't answer quickly, either. What can one say?

"He's good at that," is what I settle on after a while. I don't know what else to offer. But also, it's true. No one is as good at companionship as he is. I've witnessed this for myself.

She strokes his head softly. The dog's eyes roll back in bliss at the motion.

"I would imagine he is," she says. "What's his name?"

I never like the question and realize in that moment that I should make something up to tell people. Have something handy to say. But wouldn't that be naming him? I realize it somewhat would.

"He doesn't have one," I answer sheepishly.

"Have one what?"

"He never told me what it is," I say, trying for a thin joke. "His name. He never let me know."

"He has to have a name," she says, resolute. There isn't admonishment in her tone, exactly. But something certain, anyway.

I shrug.

"I'm going to call him Phil," she says after some consideration.

"*Phil?*"

"Yeah." She grins at me. "He seems so philosophical. Almost magical. Philosopher dog."

"Phil." I nod, understanding. In my mind, Phil works. And it could certainly be worse.

"Phil." She smiles, caressing the smooth dome of his head. "Suits him." Then, looking at me—"Would you care for some tea?"

CHAPTER SEVEN

I FIND IT extraordinary that I have stumbled across the legendary Imogen O'Brien. Being inside her home, close to where so much of the art created during her long career was made, leaves me momentarily speechless. It's like a dream that I never even realized I had suddenly coming true. Unexpected and beautiful. I work at not going all fangirl on her.

Inside the house it is surprisingly cool, though I don't hear any air-conditioning.

"Is the house straw bale construction? It's so cool and beautiful."

"Close, no cigar," she tells me. "It's adobe."

Of course, I think. Sometimes traditional methods are best. And yet, what do I know about it? Construction methods. Some resonance from another lifetime is what I am imagining. No real and conscious knowledge at all.

She makes us tea—*Imogen O'Brien makes us tea!* I continue to be slightly overwhelmed by the fact that it is her. One of the world's greatest artists. Making us tea. I take a chair at her kitchen table and just watch her. Her movements are sure, but somewhat jerky. Arthritis, I think. Or something else that causes pain.

The dog—Phil?!?—takes up a position near me and watches, too. Imogen measures the tea while the water is heating.

The tea is green. When the water boils, she adds some to the pot. Swishes it around, then dumps what was in there into the sink. Then she fills the pot with hot water. Loose tea is added. Large leaves. Bright green. The pot is covered and placed lovingly on the sideboard.

While the tea steeps, she takes down a plate and a tin. Arranges cookies from the latter on the former. She does all of these things with a certain practiced delicacy. A firm and loving care. There has never been a more important tea party, that's how she makes me feel.

After a while she brings tea, cups, and cookies on a tray and she takes a seat across from me.

"So tell me," she says looking straight into my eyes.

"Tell you?"

"How did you come to be here?" She looks at me expectantly. "I'm sure it's a good story."

I smile at her. Place my hand on either side of the cup as though to warm my hands because it's cold out. It's not. It's the opposite, but I suppose it is comfort that I seek rather than warmth.

"It *is* a good story," I say after a while. "I don't think I'm going to tell it though. Not today."

I take a cookie. Shortbread, I notice absently. I break off a corner of the cookie and put it in my mouth where it begins to melt. All that butter. I cherish the moment.

"Not today," she repeats. "Fair enough. I've had days like that, too."

"What about you?"

"Me?"

"The story. Of how you came to be here. Alone." I look around. "You are alone, right?"

"I am. Or close enough to it. And it's a story everyone wants to know."

"I'll bet."

"But there's not too much to it. How does a life happen? One day it's filled with things. The next day it's not."

I ponder that. Think about it. It resonates. That's how it had been for me, too. Only one day, there had been the dog. And now here we are.

"I'll bet there are good stories here though." I smile.

"I'll bet there are, too," she says with equally good humor. "I find, though, that the older I get, the less it all matters." She hesitates, and then, "You want to see what matters?" She's asked it, but she's already gotten up creakily. I follow where she leads.

A short distance from the house there is a building. It is neither large nor small. It proves to be part studio and part gallery. I try to hold the feelings back—that lurking fangirl again—but I am in awe of every aspect. Some of the work is so familiar to me—seen in books and magazines and postcards over the years. The work is iconic. That word again. And I almost don't believe what I see all around me.

"You know my work," she says, following my eyes.

"You can see that?"

She smiles again. "Yes," she says. "There is a certain recognition."

I nod my agreement. Yes. There is that.

"Would you like to see the studio?" She's asked it shyly, as though I might refuse. As though I would.

"Yes," I say. "I'd like that very much."

She leads me to the back of the structure where a door leads to a space about the size of a two-car garage. Light falls into the room from skylights above and from big windows in the garage doors and the walls. It seems to me to be a perfectly conceived studio space. Of course it is, I remind myself. This is Imogen O'Brien, after all. Why would her studio space not be perfect?

Iconic.

Through all of this the dog—now Phil?—has followed placidly along. It is my conceit that he watches us cautiously, but in reality, is it possible that all he ever does is watch?

What the studio contains exceeds my expectations. It is unexpected. I had seen O'Brien's work mostly online and in books and magazines. I had not realized how consistently large she had worked over the length of her career. The canvases dwarf the walls of the studio. It is as though the versions printed in books were cartoons of the possibility of reality. And now here they are, and in life they are almost overwhelming in their grandeur. We round the corner and come across a canvas roughly the size of a car. My breath catches. The painting is a close-up of a flower—it is instantly recognizable as such. Even so, what it paints in my mind's eye from first glance is male genitalia. She hears my gasp and shoots a sly grin in my direction.

"You saw it right away," she says, and I like her smile. "Not everyone does."

"How could they not?" My incredulity is real.

She shrugs, still smiling. "I don't know. I'm with you, kid. To me, it seems to hit you in the face."

"So to speak."

She laughs, nodding. "So to speak," she agrees.

"What's it called?"

Her smile deepens. Something secret there.

"*Mark*," she says.

"*Mark?*"

"Yeah."

"Someone you know?"

"Yeah," she says again. "Someone I knew. The trouble with being this old. Lotta people not around anymore."

"That's sad," I say, trying for empathy. But it's true for me, too, so the empathy is real.

She shrugs.

"Happens," she says and I nod. It does.

"You live out here all alone?" I ask once we're back in the house and the shock of "*Mark*" has worn off. "It seems like it could feel isolating."

"It is," she says. "That's the point."

"The point?"

"Yes. I get to be alone out here with my thoughts and my work." There is a hesitation, and then, "So many of my friends have not been lucky in that way."

"One could see it that way," I say doubtfully.

"Yes," she says.

The dog has again laid his head in her lap and he rests there, watching her adoringly.

"I can't imagine what's wrong with him," I say, meaning to apologize. Intending to pull him away. "He's never like this."

"Really?" She is clearly surprised, though I get the feeling she is not as surprised as she lets on. "Well, he's a darling. I like him very much." She strokes the soft dome of his golden head. His eyes narrow down to slits, blissfully. "You should leave him with me."

"Leave him," I say doubtfully, not sure what she's driving at. Who asks for someone's dog?

"Yes. Sure. Why not? It can't be easy. Traveling with a dog."

"It's all right," I say, even while thinking about how it's sometimes been difficult. Still. We've made out okay.

"Or maybe you should both stay."

"What?"

Her conversational twists and turns are making my head spin.

"Sure. Why not? You liven things up around here."

"You think?" And I can't imagine why she would say such a thing. I've only been here for a minute; surely not long enough to enliven anything, even if that were something I've been accused of before. Which I have not.

"Sure. You need a job? I could probably find one to give you."

"I don't need a job."

"Well, I could give you one anyway. Pay you cash. Not a hard job. Stuff you could do easy."

"Like?" I am humoring her. I have no intention of taking her up on it. Even so. I don't need a job, but where do I have to go?

"You could be my executive assistant," she says with a grand air and a grin. Waving her hand regally. "I've long thought I'd like one of those. Doesn't that sound fancy?"

"I don't know how to do that."

"You do," she says. "Everybody does. Just do what I say."

"I imagine everyone always does."

She nods with a grin. "That's true," she says.

"Anyway, I've never been particularly good at doing what people say," I tell her honestly.

She laughs at that.

"Me neither," she says. "That's probably why I sense we'll get along. But never mind any of that. Let me show you where you're staying."

"I'm staying?"

"Yeah, sure," she says. "You and Phil."

"Just for tonight," I say, because again, there's no place I have to be and maybe recent events have caused me to lose my appetite for camping.

She shows me to a small but well-equipped bungalow out back. She calls it the casita. Outside it is adobe, like the house. Inside the floors are blue and yellow tile and the walls are the color of honey. The place smells like that, too. Honey. Like someone rubbed it on the walls.

I trudge back to the road and get the car. The dog doesn't bother to come with me. It's like he's made some decision that doesn't necessarily involve me. I try not to think about that.

When I come back, I park the car in the big paved circle at the front of the house. It is thinly shaded by a brace of towering cacti. When I look back at the car, I realize the cacti seem to almost make up a fortress. Protecting what? Keeping something in, keeping something out. For just a second, I feel claustrophobic. It feels anaphylactic. I gently put my hand to my throat and just breathe until the feeling passes. No time for old demons, I tell myself. It seems possible that a new adventure is about to begin. The trouble is, the demons are so often present. They have been for a while.

I put it all out of my head. Try to gauge where I am now. Not geographically, but in my heart. There had been in me, maybe for a long while, a sort of anger. Something that felt unshakable. Now, in Imogen's presence, it feels distant. At least diffused. Almost as though all of that anger had belonged to someone else. I feel more peaceful at Ocotillo Ranch, that's what I realize as I bed down for the night. I feel like something I had been storing inside of me has been let out. The beginning of something.

I had been surprised on this night when the dog got up and came to my heel as I left for the casita. The way he'd been acting, I'd kind of expected he wouldn't want to leave Imogen's side.

She had made a simple supper for the two of us and we'd chatted a bit in the easy companionship one sometimes finds with kindred spirits, even when decades apart.

The dog, by now firmly "Phil," had spent the evening near Imogen's feet as we ate and then chatted. I didn't figure he'd bother getting up when I did, and I discover that I'm strangely pleased and even grateful when he does. The tacit approval of his company.

On the short walk to the casita I am enveloped by the desert. The bright song of the crickets, the dark musk of the desert plants at night. The sultry warmth made slightly humid by recent rain. Nothing is happening and it's dead quiet, but so much is going on.

When I'm on my own in a small but comfortable bed, I think about my future; try not to think too much about my past. I have already spent far more time in the desert than I had ever planned. I'd come to do something simple—an assignment that had gone awry and become complicated. There had been a beautiful man whom I loved for a moment; someone whom I was supposed to kill, but who is still alive now. He loved me, too, I think. But, in the end, I realized for him to have done some of the things he did meant he wasn't someone I truly could love properly. Or maybe I feared he couldn't love me. Whatever the case, it's all in the past now. Things about water and bridges. And, in any case, it all seems like a lifetime ago. So much has changed. And now? Well now I'm drifting. Or I was. Whatever else is true, I no longer feel as disconnected as I did even a few days ago. I examine that feeling. Surely that tells me something?

And where is it I imagine I still have to go, anyway? It's not like there is anyone out there who is anxious to see me. I think a brother is all the blood I have left in the world, and if anyone asked, I think he'd be hard pressed to even know that I'm still kicking. Thinking about Kenneth, I feel the shadow of him. Or maybe it's more accurate to say I feel the lack of his shadow: the lack of him in my life at all for several years. It's been a good long time since I had a real family connection. He'd been trying to reach me some time ago. I find I suddenly can't stop thinking about him and what he might have wanted. What has happened in his life, I wonder, since the last time I saw him? Is he healthy? Happy? Is he well? Is he *alive*, even? It's curious, this sudden longing I have to see him or at least to reconnect with what is left of my family. Maybe it's feeling a family-like connection with Imogen that has me thinking about it at all. That part of me has not been serviced. Not for a while.

As though he's been awakened by unsettling and unfamiliar thoughts, I hear Phil get up from the rag rug he'd positioned himself on at the foot of my bed. In the pitch dark, I hear him shuffle to my side. I put out my hand, and he sticks his muzzle deeply into my palm.

"Hey," I say.

He snuggles into my hand more deeply.

"What would I do without you?"

He doesn't answer, just breathes shallowly into my palm. It's enough. With this thin comfort I fall into something that looks like sleep.

CHAPTER EIGHT

IN THE MORNING, Phil and I move beyond the confines of the casita in search of our hostess and breakfast. Imogen has gotten up ahead of me and is sitting in her garden shielded by the shade of the house.

Her face brightens when she sees me. "Howdja sleep?" she asks.

"Terrific," I lie. My sleeplessness was not the fault of the bed, after all. Or that of the hostess. My own demons, and who wants to hear about that? And who do I want to tell? In any case, I know that the demons don't respond to comfort. Or reassurance. Failure. Or success. They simply are. And they are mine.

"Good, good," she says. And then, slightly more quietly, "I was not entirely honest with you last night."

I just blink at her. It's obvious she has more to say. I wait for her to come to it.

"About the work. My work. And about how you might fit in."

"I don't understand," I say.

"Of course," she says. "How could you?"

More blinking from me.

"For a while, I've been wanting the work to be different." She hesitates over the last word, drawing out the three syllables.

"I don't understand. What work?"

I cast about, thinking. Farm work? Yard work? She sees my confusion and supplies the answer.

"My art. The way I do it. Dream it. Think it."

"Your art," I repeat. That at least makes more sense, though not what it might have to do with me.

"The nature of it, I guess. I've been doing things the same way for so long. What if I mixed it up?"

"Mixed up doing things the same way. Like the techniques? Or the subject matter? Or . . . how?"

"Well, all of that, I guess." She hesitates, but I can see it's not because she hasn't given this a lot of thought. "I've been doing this for . . . how long? Forever, I guess. And what have I changed?"

"You'd know that better than me."

"That was rhetorical," she snaps sharply enough that I feel like pulling back.

"Of course it was," I say soothingly and she softens a bit. Either the words or the tone have mollified her. There's an edge of something on her this morning that wasn't there last night. And it seems a rare peek into a famous creative person's mind. I don't love the tone, but I'm enjoying the insight. And a funny shadow walks on my heart at the same time. There's something familiar here. Something I can't quite place. What is she putting me in mind of?

"Nothing significant, that's what I've changed. Oh, I'm working smaller these days, but that's just the vagaries of age."

"I don't understand."

"The large canvases. Everything about them is difficult for me now. Stretching them. Moving them. Reaching all of the parts, even, to paint them."

"Oh," I say. Of course. I wouldn't have thought of that aspect.

"But a difference in size: it's not enough. It's not what I want. I wish to create work that is significantly different."

"I . . . I can see that," I say. And I can. My own limited experience painting has shown me that. Once you reach a goal, you want to push through it. It sounds like maybe she has come to that conclusion late. I keep my mouth shut about that.

"Anyway, I apologize."

"No need," I mumble politely.

"Truly. I fear I am not entirely well this morning."

I look at her more closely. Note the faint purple under her eyes and a somewhat blueish tint to her skin. I'm not the only one who didn't sleep.

"I'm sorry to hear that," I say. "Can I do anything to help?"

"You can, actually," she says. "I had thought to soft boil a few eggs," she tells me. "Put on some coffee, make some toast. For your breakfast. I'm afraid . . . I'm not quite well enough to pull any of that off. Could I prevail on you . . . ?"

The change of subject takes my breath away. A moment ago, the rambling complaints of a ranking artist. And now? We're talking about toast.

"Of course," I say, wondering for a moment if it's a ploy to keep me around. But I look again at the faint bruise-like marks under her eyes, see the slight shake of her hand, and realize that her symptoms are real. Not only that, she has some distress about it. "Sure," I say. "I can do that. You can stay put, and I'll make us breakfast."

She beams at me gratefully, and I smile in return, but determine to keep an eye on her. She may be old and she may also be talented, but it seems she is capricious.

I settle in to make our breakfast. The kitchen and the stove are both old, but functional.

I put water on for coffee. A copper kettle, possibly older than I am. I find an ancient toaster and a pot to boil the water for the eggs. Cream. Sugar. Mugs. All the accoutrements for our upcoming meal. I even find a perfect tomato, its uneven sides and variegated green and orange color giving it away as the heritage kind: you just know it never saw the inside of a hot house. I search around and find egg cups, butter. A tray. Just when I'm about to carry it all out to the terrace, Imogen appears at the edge of the doorway, obviously weak, but leaning on a cane to reinforce her steps.

"I would have brought it out," I say.

"I know you would have, but it's a lot of moving bits."

"Well, your timing is terrific. I'm just finishing."

She takes a shaky seat at the table while I set out our meal.

"The eggs are perfect," she announces when she breaks into her first one. "Not everyone can manage it. I *knew* my instincts were right about you."

I feel myself warm at her praise, even though it's only breakfast. And the eggs *are* perfect. It is a trick I learned in childhood. Eggs immersed in simmering—not boiling—water and allowed to chirp away softly for six minutes, then cooled briefly before serving. The toast is marble rye and slathered in butter, the way it should be, and the coffee is bold and strong, but not overwhelming.

And it is this memory of submerging eggs that reminds me of what had been escaping me: this blend of deep interest and capricious withdrawal—go away, come here—had been the way my mother always had been with me. I try to submerge the memory with the eggs, but it stays with me. The thing that once seen can't be unseen.

"I'd say you know your way around a kitchen," she says as we dine.

"I've been in one or two," I say deadpan.

She grins, getting the joke, if not the fullness of it.

"Have you given any more thought to my offer?"

"A bit," I say. "And maybe I will think some more."

"That'd be swell," she says. "That suits me just fine. You think all you need." She waves a hand around dramatically. "As you can see, there aren't tons of candidates standing in line."

"Well," I say, "and you could advertise. People do."

"Yes," she says. "People do. But, hmmm. I don't know quite how to say this, and it may sound real odd, but I don't like people a whole bunch. And they often don't much care for me, either."

"That does surprise me," I tell her. "You seem real sweet to me." And I don't voice thoughts about come here / stay away. What, after all, would be the point?

"Me, sweet? There are a whole lotta folks—dead and alive—that would think that was real rich," she says. Then she quiets a bit. "Still," she says. "That's nice to hear. But it might be best not to opine until you know me better."

"All right," I say, going along. I change tracks. "What's wrong with you? Your health, I mean. You seemed fine when I got here. Less fine today."

She hesitates before she answers. For a minute, I fear she won't. Then, "It goes like that; my health. Fine mostly, luckily. And then sometimes not so fine. And it's my ticker," she says, thumping the cloth of her dress at a spot between her breasts with her index finger. The sound it makes is dull. It doesn't resonate at all.

"Your heart?"

She nods. "That's what I figure. I haven't been to see a doctor in near on fifteen years."

"You think that's a good idea?" I try to keep the judgment out of my voice. It's hard.

"No, seventeen years, I guess," she corrects. "I stopped going though. I didn't like what they said."

"That's not a thing," I tell her. "You don't go to a doctor to hear words you like. That's for . . . a boyfriend," I tell her.

At first she laughs, but she's also nodding agreement. And maybe there's a touch of annoyance there as well, though I choose to overlook that part.

"That's right," is what she says. "Or a dog." And she strokes the head that is once again in her lap. "Dear Phil," she says, stroking absently.

"Okay, you've got me there. Doctors are nothing like dogs. But you go to them to help you. To get help. You don't go to get them to agree with you."

"Listen, toots, if I'd kept going to that doctor, I'd have been dead ten years ago. Maybe more. It felt like he had me halfway to the grave as things were. I couldn't afford it, that's the thing."

"But there are programs. Money shouldn't stop you from getting the care you need." The words sound pious to my own ears even as they come out of my head.

"It wasn't the money," she says quickly. "That wasn't the part I couldn't afford. There's plenty money to go around." She points at the painting nearest us hanging on the wall. It is a desert canyon that—more or less—resembles labia. "This stuff has left me plenty set up. I've got problems, but money ain't it."

"Oh-kay," I say. Meaning to prompt her to go on.

"What I mean is, I couldn't afford him telling me all the stuff that was wrong with me. It made me gloomy. That and the pills he kept trying to feed me. It didn't even make any sense, all those pills. This one for this and that one to stop that one from doing that. It just seemed like taking them at all was going to end up being bad news."

"So you stopped going," I say, and she nods. "And that made sense to you?"

She nods again.

"I'm still kicking, ain't I?"

And I grin.

"Yes," I say. "Yes, you are. Very much so."

"But those busybodies from the county come around every now and again, checking on me. I avoid 'em when I can."

"So you're saying you're . . . what? A hermit?"

"Not so much a hermit. I just want to be left to my own self. I want to paint and breathe my air and swim when I'm well enough to do that. But I mostly want to do it alone."

"That's pretty much the definition of a hermit," I point out. And she laughs at that.

"I guess it is," she says, caught.

Which reminds me.

"The pool."

"Yes?"

"How do you clean it?"

"There's Chester. Did you meet him yet?"

"Not yet, no."

"Chester . . . is . . . well, he's special, I guess. Ralph, his dad, worked for me in the studio when I was first out here. Things were pretty busy then. Hopping, I guess you'd say. I was traveling a bunch.

Making appearances and such. And there were exhibitions. It was more than I could do on my own. More than I wanted to do on my own, I guess. Ralph would stretch my canvases, prepare my pigments. You know: studio stuff. When Ralph was first working for me, he told me he had a kid who was . . . well, not quite right, I guess was the way he put it. And could I give him a job around the place."

"Not quite right."

"Yeah. Not maybe so smart? Hadn't been okay with school. Didn't fit anywhere. But he liked animals, and his dad taught him to clean the pool and whatnot. It's been an okay arrangement. He's been here ever since."

"How long?"

Imogen hesitates. Maybe counts. Then, "Thirty years? More maybe."

I whistle. "That's a long time."

"Very long, yeah. But after all this, what the hell else is he going to do? I kinda feel responsible for him."

"So Chester cleans the pool?"

"Yeah. Other stuff, too. By the time Ralph knew he didn't have long to live, it was pretty clear Chester was never going to strike out on his own. We built a little house for the two of them right here on the property: a place where Ralph could live out his days and where Chester would be safe, after Ralph was gone."

"That was good of you."

"It was, sure," Imogen says. "But also it was good for me, too. I couldn't have managed to be alone for so long if I'd actually been alone."

"And now?"

"He's like me in a way, I guess. Keeps to himself. He comes over to this side a couple times a week or whenever he wants to. We don't have anything formal. Whenever I ask him and whenever he wants. He brings groceries. Cleans the pool and does whatever handy stuff needs doing."

"Chester."

"Yeah."

"And you're still painting?"

"I am. Some of what you saw last night. In the studio. And there," she says, pointing at the canyon labia again. "More I store in a couple of bedrooms here in the house. Wanna see?"

"Sure," I say, trying not to show all of my enthusiasm.

"Okay. I'm feeling a little better. From the breakfast, I'll bet. Thanks for that. Follow me."

She leads me down a hallway, stopping in front of a closed bedroom door.

"I keep it nice and dark so the pigments stay fresh."

That doesn't sound like a thing to me but what do I know? So I don't argue with her and then, when I enter the room, anything I might have said is swept away by the wonder of seeing dozens upon dozens of canvases leaned against each other on the wall, soft cloth draped over each, presumably to protect them. Her canvases. Master works that the wider world has not seen. I feel the privilege.

"But there must be hundreds."

"Certainly," she says. "At least," and I can't read her expression.

"What are they doing here?"

"Waiting," she says cryptically, or maybe it's only cryptic to me because I don't understand.

"Waiting for what?" I ask.

"Well, that's the thing, isn't it? The big question. Look at them. Tell me what you see."

I do as she asks, pulling back the shroud of perhaps half a dozen works before the fullness of what I'm viewing sinks in.

"They are undoubtedly Imogen O'Briens," I say after a pause, pleased with the connectivity I have seen. "No one would look at any of them and doubt that you had painted it."

"Goodness," she says. "You've nailed it, I think. Said it better than I would have."

"What do you mean?"

"I am looking for the extraordinary," and as she says it, she turns her back on me and on the work and begins to walk back down the hall. "And these are ordinary. They are everyday."

"But that's . . . why . . . that's ridiculous," I say, following her.

She turns around and looks at me, as though she can't believe her ears.

"What did you say?"

"You heard me perfectly, I think," I say, feeling cowed but trying hard not to let it show. "You just didn't think anyone would."

She grins at that; an expression as though she's been caught out.

"You're right. No one talks to me like that."

"Maybe that's the problem," I mutter.

"What did you say?"

"I think you heard me." And suddenly, there it is again: I'm channeling my mother. Or rather, channeling who I was with my mother. It's not a good feeling.

"I did," she says quietly.

"Look," I begin, feeling as though if I manage to back things up, I might be able to head off the repeat of history I feel coming on, "this is no kind of pissing contest. Rather than just telling me the outcome you desire, you're dancing around what you're trying to say. And I get it. You already told me you want to do a new kind of work. So do it already. What's stopping you? Nothing. At least, nothing I can see. The only thing keeping you from doing the work you want to do is you."

We are standing in the hallway, facing each other. Not a face-off, I tell myself. We don't know each other well enough for that. And yet, this stranger has brought me her problem. And with the clarity of a stranger, I can see the outcome. Or rather, I can see where it needs to go.

She doesn't say anything for what seems like a long time. And me? I feel deflated. I feel all talked out.

Finally, she speaks, and her voice is small.

"Will you help me?"

I blink at her for a few seconds. Then I blink again. What the hell else do I have to do?

"I will," is what I say.

After a while the hallway can't hold what we need to talk about and we move back to the kitchen. Without saying anything, I put the kettle back on. It feels like, however this plays out, we're going to need tea.

CHAPTER NINE

"I THINK SOME of the nuance of this is lost on me," I say.

We are sitting at Imogen's kitchen table, a pot of green tea steeping between us.

"Tell me what you mean."

"A style change. That doesn't seem like a big deal to me. You change your mind, right? Do something different."

She laughs, though the sound is not unkind.

"I think you already get this, but it's not as simple as that."

"Okay. I can see that. But what have you been waiting for?"

"I don't know," she says. "Maybe waiting for some time that isn't now."

"But you have an agent, of course. A gallery?"

"Not anymore. I had all that stuff. More. I was a big deal."

"You are still a big deal."

She shrugs that off as though I haven't even said the words.

"Maybe that was part of the problem."

"Explain."

"People know what I do. Or, at least, they did."

"They still do."

"You know what I mean," she says, and I don't. Though also, I kind of do. "They have an expectation. The fans. They want more of what they've already seen. Only new. Do you see?"

And, suddenly, I do.

"Many of your pieces have been super valuable. They want to discover the new super valuable one that's different, only just the same."

"That's it exactly."

"And yet, people do it. I mean, Picasso—"

She doesn't let me finish.

"Oh for gawd's sake. We can't all be bloody Picasso, can we? For one thing, he had a dick."

I feel my eyes widen at that.

"Oh-kay."

"Do you think it has been easy being the ranking woman artist of my generation? After a while, I just got tired of all of the sameness of it, and the life I led then became less important. It just seemed meaningless. The gallery openings. The fawning fans. The money."

"We all need money," I say, feeling a little prim at the words. And thinking also of the stacks of currency secreted in the false chamber in the trunk of my car. Under the mats. And in the engine compartment. If anyone ever knew how much cash I was carrying in my crappy old Volvo, I wouldn't last the night.

"I have enough," she says enigmatically. "Plus, every now and again I give Chester a canvas and he comes back with cash."

That didn't strike me as a particularly efficient way of managing a career, but I kept my mouth shut. Mostly.

"And the agent? The gallery?"

"After a while I didn't care for those folks much. They craved the sameness. And I found I wanted to have people around me I cared about or no people at all."

"So no people at all," I repeated, stating the obvious.

"I guess."

"Was the agent stealing from you?"

"No," she says, and I can see her considering her answer. "We just had different things in mind. He wanted more from me. I wanted to give less. Or maybe it's more true to say they wanted the same from me, and I felt like doing something different. Finally, I told them to go to hell."

"That's strong."

"It was how I felt at the time. We both felt it strongly. Suddenly, it seemed, we just parted ways."

It struck me that there was more unsaid in that sentence than what was said, though I didn't pursue it.

"So you told them to go to hell. Then did you do things differently?"

She looks stricken at the question. I'm immediately sorry I asked.

"No," she says quietly, looking at a spot on the wall. "I didn't."

"Why?" My voice is quiet.

"I'm not sure." She meets my eyes. "Maybe I was afraid."

"That's fair," I say. "Change can be hard. Is it too late now?"

"Maybe. Maybe it's too late."

I decide to let that go. For now.

"You said you wanted less people around you, yet you offered me a job practically minutes after we met."

"Things are getting more difficult for me," she admits. "Plus I could tell right away that you and I would get on."

I grin at her at that. She grins right back. She's not wrong. So I say it.

"I guess you weren't wrong about that."

And so I don't leave right away.

CHAPTER TEN

THINGS SETTLE INTO a peaceful tempo. I don't say I'll take the job, but I don't say I won't, either. I was at loose ends when I arrived. Because I control his schedule, the dog was at loose ends, too. Open for possible opportunities, both of us, though there was a time that I wouldn't have thought of it that way.

Things are comfortable at Ocotillo Ranch. I consider taking Imogen up on her offer, if it ever was even that. Are our interactions always perfect? I would not go that far. But in her imperfections there is enough of a resonance to what is behind me that it intrigues me. Also, who among us is perfect? Not me. And also not her. So I decide to play it out.

On my third night at Ocotillo Ranch, I am idly thinking about all of these things while crossing the courtyard toward the casita when the rumbling of an engine catches my attention. It is a shattering break in the perfect stillness. I feel for the Bersa at the back of my waistband, but there is no gun there. I wasn't expecting company, so I'm not locked and loaded, but my hackles go up: my instinct letting me know that trouble is ahead.

When the off-road vehicle that had been making the sound rolls into view I feel something catch at my throat. The knobby tires make an imprint in the dusty driveway. All of it feels like *déjà vu*: different place, different circumstance, but I've felt all of this before.

The driver is alone in the vehicle. He is rail thin, and I suspect the farmer's cap he wears hides a bald spot, though I know I have nothing to base this on. Of all the things I don't know, I'm sure about one: this is certainly the companion of the man who tried to assault me at Arcadia Bluff. The one that ended up going over the cliff. It's the other guy in the gray camouflage vehicle that had driven by me when I was on that forestry road, preparing to camp for the night. I identify something in his profile. Something in the jut of his chin. It is not the same vehicle, of course. I saw that one plummet. But there is a lot about him to recognize, even before he says, "Hey! Don't I know you?" and my heart drops to my knees.

"I don't think so," I reply without hesitation, heart drops notwithstanding. "How can I help you?"

"You here on your own?" And I don't like the light in his eyes as he asks.

"No. I live here with my husband," I lie. "He's just up in town. Due back any time."

"Huh," he says. "You look familiar to me."

"Lots say that," I say evenly, my hand describing the outline of my profile. "I've got that kinda face."

"Husband, you say?" And I can tell he doesn't believe me. And I wonder if I care about his belief or lack thereof, even while I also wonder if there's some reason that I need to. In the end I decide to ignore the unasked question.

"Is there something I can help you with?"

"A friend of mine went missing last week. This seems to be the only civilized place anywhere near there. Not a lot of houses here in the park. Thought I'd check if anyone here had seen anything."

"No one's been here," I say quickly. Too quickly? Because I see his head go up at my words, and he's sampling the air like a dog. And it's also possible I'm imagining it. I can't quite make the call.

"Haven't seen nothin', huh?" And I see that he is now fully alert. I curse myself for my nonexistent acting skills and realize: whatever I thought I was hearing, I wasn't making it up.

"No," I say carefully. Calmly. "Nothing."

"Like I said, you look familiar to me. You and the mutt," he says, indicating Phil who is lolling nearby, watching us carefully. I'd say Phil is on alert but, as usual, he is playing things pretty cool.

"Not possible," I say as casually as I can muster. "We never go anywhere."

I see a coldness fall on his face. Snake cold. And I see him looking at me appraisingly, though appraising me for what, I can't be certain. Suspicion or desire, though I realize it could be either one. Or both. Neither of them hit very well.

"That right?" He just says those two words, but I find that I am afraid, which is an unusual emotion for me. I'm not usually afraid.

"Yes. Maybe you'd like to talk with my husband in a while? Like I said—"

He doesn't let me finish. "Yeah. He'll be back any time. All right," he says. "I'll check back then."

Despite his words, he doesn't move back toward his truck. We stand there frozen for some moments, our eyes locked. And for just a few seconds it is as though we are one single creature with very different goals.

When the energy changes, it takes me by surprise. I sense more than see him spring into motion, a motion that is both unexpected and not. I move just before he does, sprinting in the direction of the studio, avoiding cactus and other objects in my path. I am not sure where I'm going, other than away from him and also away from Imogen, who is vulnerable due to her infirmities. I would not want to lead this in her direction.

The big studio doors are pulled open to let in the early morning cool and I dash in there without any type of plan, just wanting to get away.

He is behind me, though not right behind. It gives me the moment I need to duck into the workshop where the canvases are stretched. I grab a hammer and a box cutter as I pass the workbench because they are there. I'm not sure what I have in mind, but I feel better with the weight of them in my hands.

Still holding the tools, I hide behind the door. What if he comes this way? Or maybe worse, what if he doesn't?

I'm so focused on what I'll do when he comes this way that he manages to take me unawares. I am crouched behind the door when he rounds the corner. He grabs first one of my legs, then the other, and the grip is viselike. I try to wriggle free, but I quickly realize that I'm caught.

I scream. It is pure instinct: this distance from the house and the rest of the world, even as the sound tears through my lungs, I realize I have no hope of being heard.

He pushes me onto my back and the tools clatter uselessly nearby. My heart sinks at the loss of them.

My heart sinks.

And then he is on top of me, overpowering me easily, despite my struggles. He is close enough to me that I can smell him. Something slightly rank; the clearance rack at a substandard thrift store. And also something stale and vile. Yesterday's cheap gin.

He pins my legs with one of his. As he reaches also to pin my arms I extend them as far above me as I can until I feel one of the legs of an easel. I have no plan or hope, but my hand curls around the soft wood and I pull. As hard as I can.

I'm aware of the easel teetering above me, though I'm not sure what it'll mean. But I wish. In that split second of longing, he gets his hand on the top button of my jeans and he's focusing on getting me free of them when easel and canvas topple onto both of us and it seems as though my hopes and wishes and dreams have all been answered.

It's a big canvas, but it's not a crushing weight. It startles him and he let's go of me. That's just enough for me to wriggle free and grab the hammer and box cutter I'd dropped earlier.

With these lame little weapons in hand, I turn back to him, unsure of exactly what I intend to do, when I discover fate has gotten there first. He's bleeding from his temple and out cold, and I see from how the canvas landed that I got lucky—and he didn't—and the edge of the thirty-pound painting knocked him out.

Now I have a new dilemma, though I admit it's not huge: What should I do with him? The place where this one's buddy attacked me is maybe twelve miles from Ocotillo Ranch, and that weighs on me. It's a hike.

The "right" thing to do would be to call the police, file a report, and let the cops pick him up, take him away. But there are so many reasons I can't do that I almost don't know where to start and, anyway, it's never a real consideration.

For one thing, I'm completely disconnected from the identity I was born with, and even the one I adopted after that. There is no radar I am on. Me calling it in would ask more questions than it answered. And even if I got Imogen or Chester to be the ones reporting, their stories would be lies and there was just so much that could go wrong with that. But even if all of that went well and the police took him away, how long would it be until they let him go and he came back for me? He's already figured I did something with his buddy. At first opportunity he'll be back for me with questions I don't have answers for. Or worse. And how do I avoid that?

He stirs then. A hand reaching up to touch his temple where it connected with the easel. Barely dried blood comes away with his touch. I close my eyes. Rub my own temple. What needs to be done is inevitable, but I feel as though I don't have it in me anymore. Not right now. And what does that say about . . . well, anything? I'm not quite sure.

The hammer is heavy in my hand. The box cutter has less weight but the results would be more conclusive. I find I'm not ready for that either. I don't want to kill him. I just want him to go away.

He begins to collect himself, as though to rise, and it forces the issue. I take the third, previously unoffered choice. I grab a nearby piece of two-by-four, intended for a canvas, and see his eyes widen in surprise as I swing it back, baseball bat–style, and whack him with it gingerly. He goes back down, though in truth he hadn't gotten very far up. I check his breath. He isn't dead, but I figure he won't be getting up again any time soon.

So now I've got another yahoo out cold and only an inkling of what to do with him, and when I act, it is almost pure instinct. I grab the wheelbarrow, leverage him into it, and bump him back to his car. There I have another sense of *déjà vu* as I struggle to get him into the off-road vehicle. The best I can do is leverage him into the back of the UTV, even while I hope he stays out cold long enough for me to complete my mission. He falls into it. It's inelegant but there are no witnesses. And when his left sneaker comes off in the process, I pick it up and toss it in after him.

As I work, I realize after a while that I am in shock. And how do I know this? I have an almost impossibly sharp urge to laugh at my own bad decisions. Am I actually thinking about dragging him back to the place where I pushed his buddy off a cliff? And then I answer myself: Why, yes. Yes, I am. And why? Because I don't have a better idea, and I have to do *something*.

I check his condition—still out cold—and so I risk leaving him for a few minutes. I run to change into my trail runners. As I run, I find myself wondering where the dog is, then stop wondering when I pull open the door and he lifts his head from the rug and looks at me balefully and it comes back to me: he'd been snoozing when I'd trotted toward the house to grab a bite to eat and check out the day. And now I'm grateful: I would not have wanted him to be a part of any of this. It's funny how sometimes life takes care.

I grab a hat, sunscreen, a rag, a backpack, a flashlight, and three bottles of water. Good Girl Scout, I think while I move. I like to be prepared.

When I go to leave, Phil looks at me longingly.

"Not this time, buddy," I tell him. "No joyride. You stay here. Keep an eye on things."

He doesn't understand me, but you can't tell that from his face. I swear he looks betrayed, but also he cooperates. He settles back on his haunches and watches me reproachfully as I go out the door.

When I run back, I check on the yahoo. He's still out cold. I don't know how long that will last but, from the looks of him, he's not going anywhere soon.

In the driver's seat of my assailant's vehicle, it takes a heartbeat or two to get the gearshift pattern of the vehicle's manual transmission under control. Then I get it into gear and head out into the desert.

Arcadia Bluff isn't far as the crow flies, but it takes a bit to get there over forestry roads, at least it seems that way to me today. Am I seriously thinking about doing this thing? It's too stupid to contemplate, yet I consider it. For one thing, the parameters are perfect. More so than many of the mostly flat spots I can get to by car. Oh sure: I could probably hunt something down, but I know this place and it worked perfectly last time for this purpose. I feel like an idiot revisiting something that had been an instinctive jerk of the knee that last desperate time. And now I'm here on purpose? All of my instincts tell me I'm wrong, but I go ahead anyway.

I drive the vehicle as close to the edge as I dare, then I grab the rag I brought and give everything I touched or might have touched a quick wipe-down. I spare a glance for my passenger. His breathing is shallow, but he lives. I'm figuring that, with what I'm planning for him, he won't be that way for long.

Outside the vehicle, I drop my backpack on the ground, and with the rag wrapped around my hands, I pop the UTV into neutral and get out and push at the light but sturdy vehicle. As it goes over, there is once again a moment when the four-wheeler hangs onto some shrubs just below the cliff's edge, at a spot where it would be plainly visible to passersby, no matter how infrequent. Then it moves forward a little, and I breathe. It is pushed on now by its own weight and even picks up a bit of momentum before it plummets. I peer over the edge and feel gratified when I don't see even a trace of the rugged vehicle. I don't kid myself: those bodies, those vehicles are down there. Someone might spot them, haul them out. I decide not to dwell on that. With luck and a tailwind, by the time that happens, I'll be on the other side of the country, or at least some other place far from here.

I sling my backpack over my shoulders and head out. I have hours of walking in front of me. It will be well into the night before I get back to the ranch. But my heart is lighter than I might have thought: this wasn't a great outcome, but it could also have been worse, even if I'm not quite sure how.

And so I walk: one foot in front of the other and keeping myself company with my thoughts.

Dead men don't tell tales, isn't that what they say? Even so, the base of my stomach aches in apprehension. It's something I figure no amount of sleep or soup or even large leaf green tea will put right. I wonder if, by the time I get back to the ranch, I'll have forgiven myself for how all of this went down. After a while, though, I forget the question because I walk for a long time and my feet come to hurt more than my conscience. Maybe that's part of the process.

CHAPTER ELEVEN

NOT LONG BEFORE I met Imogen, I'd taken up plein air painting. It seems an unbearable coincidence now.

It was about a year before I met her that I'd taken it up. Maybe slightly more. Now at Ocotillo Ranch, instead of the online lessons and books that had started me off on my painting journey, I had a living, breathing mentor. A notably talented one, too. If I wanted to improve and grow as a painter, I could not have put together a better situation if I'd tried.

Hardly anyone even knew Imogen O'Brien was alive anymore. And here she was: Working with me. Helping me hone my technique. Helping me develop one. There were times around all of this that the whole thing just felt magical, even if she was sometimes demanding. Sometimes a little mean. I didn't know quite what to do with that, and so I ignored it. Putting my head down and working, not thinking too hard about why I suddenly felt like a ten-year-old kid.

With all of this, my life at Ocotillo Ranch became very full. First, there was painting. Also the cooking of nutritious meals. That was all me, and I found I enjoyed having someone to cook for again. I hadn't had that for a while. And there was the ebbing and flowing of a nonagenarian whose timeline was simply running down.

There were signs of that, for sure. But also other days, with less auspicious corners.

There comes a day when at three o'clock in the afternoon, I find Imogen in her room in darkness, the blinds drawn against the relentless sun.

The door is open, and Phil is at her side. Not on the rug, where he's always been banished by me. He is on the bed next to her, his beautiful golden head settled on her flank and he's watching her adoringly. When I come into the room, I can feel him notice, but he doesn't move. I get the idea he doesn't want to disturb her.

"Hey," I say softly. "You good?"

I ask it automatically, but I can see she isn't that.

"Hey," she says back. "I'm glad to see you. Phil has been good company, but I suspect yours will be better." She finishes the sentence, then lapses into a bout of coughing so severe, I feel sorry for her lungs.

"Can I get you anything?" And, really, it would be anything at that point. She could ask me anything at all and I'd do it, if I felt it would ease whatever she is going through.

"Tea would be lovely, actually," she says when the coughing has stopped. "That green one I like."

Once the tea is made, I find a tray and carry it and a few biscuits into her. Imogen looks up gratefully. I wait until she has sipped at her tea and nibbled a biscuit before I ask what is foremost on my mind.

"Did something happen?"

"It's been coming a while," she says, not meeting my eyes.

"Doctor?"

She shakes her head. "I told you about doctors."

"Surely you can see you are unwell."

"I know what it is," she says, and she looks gloomy about it. "I know how this ends. All of our stories end the same way."

"Imogen, please. There is no need for drama. This is not the dark ages. These days people get to extraordinary ages *because* of modern medicine. Not despite it."

"That wouldn't be me."

"Imogen. Please." And even though I've used the word again, I try to keep the pleading out of my voice. It won't help in this situation.

I let Imogen rest while I finish cleaning up and begin to scratch together some dinner. There's not much to eat in the larder so I make do, putting together beans and rice and spice with the few pathetic vegetables and the single onion I find. When I'm done preparing the food, I find it is actually quite good and I can't help but think it will be restorative because, after all, who even knows what type of stuff she was eating before I got there? She seems often to feel subpar and Chester is never around at mealtimes, either to eat or prepare. So what might she have been eating? I can't imagine.

"Full marks, chef," she says after we're done. She has managed to pull herself away from the dining table in the kitchen, though I don't know what it cost her. After we've eaten, her color and demeanor seem brighter. I reflect that it might be the difference being cared about makes.

"Thank you," I say. "I guess I'll have to go shopping tomorrow. Fill your larder."

She looks smug, but I don't say anything. She has gotten the thing that she wanted, it seems. It appears I am staying.

Or, at least, not going. But how could I leave her? There just seems to be so much at stake and—again and anyway—I have no place to go.

"Shopping is necessary, yes. There's not much left to eat, for sure. But there are other things I'd like you to give thought to."

"Other things?"

"Yes. I have a franchise. I wonder if you understand what that means?"

"Not in that context, no. I'm quite sure I don't."

"These days they call what I have built a 'brand.' I've been doing this—painting—for a long time. A *long* time. I have a loyal following. And I am among a handful of painters whose canvases can command the prices that mine do."

I nod. All of this is true.

"Yes, but . . ." I don't see the point of her talking about this now.

"If something should happen to me—say I die?—all of it. All of what I'd built will be gone."

"Well, no," I say immediately. "What you've built will live forever."

She waves my words aside.

"Yes, yes, of course. I understand. History books. Museums. Yes. That's not what I'm talking about."

I just nod. I'd sort of already gathered that. Even so, what she says surprises me.

"So all of that stuff, yes," she says. "But what about the cats?"

"The cats?"

"There is a large colony of cats here at Ocotillo."

"Phil didn't tell me," I say, hoping for levity.

She blinks at me. Blinks again.

"He was being circumspect, I guess," she says finally, and it takes me a minute to realize she is joking right back.

"But the cats . . ." I prompt.

"There are about forty of them. Perhaps more. In the old barn beyond the pond. That whole area. A few years ago, I connected with a group that was doing TNR with ferals . . ."

"TNR . . . ? " I prompt.

"Trap. Neuter. Release," she explains, as though it's the most natural thing in the world.

"Of course," I say.

"And the group was successful. There are no longer kittens being born. But the colony as it was? That's still with us and will be for many years to come. I feel responsible for them." A beat and then, "I *am* responsible for them." I am aware of her watching my face before she continues. "It's because of me that they live on. They are my responsibility."

"How old do cats get to be?"

"They can easily live fifteen and even sometimes twenty-plus years. We did this TNR just a few years ago, so some of them are still very young."

"You're saying you have another couple decades of cats to support."

"That's right. And it's like they're a family. There are grandparents, et cetera, out there. Many of them are related."

"Cat families," I repeat.

"I didn't mean it quite that way," she says and I feel admonished. "And I can see you don't understand. But you will. Go see them, please. Experience them. Leave Phil with me. His presence puts them off. Yours will, too, but it's worse with Phil." She's telling me that the cats don't like my dog. Now *that* I'll buy.

I can see there is no arguing with her, so I head toward the old barn, careful to close the door behind me when I leave, not that Phil had shown any sign of following.

I have to skirt the pond as I head to the old barn, and when I do, I come across a small band of wild horses cropping at the grass that grows in the shallows. There seems to be a stallion, two mares, both with youngsters at their sides. All five heads go up at my approach. All ten eyes watch me carefully. I get the feeling they would bolt as a single unit at my slightest wrong move, but I make a point of giving them a wide berth and they go about their business, even though I am aware that they never take their eyes off me.

These too, then, are among those who rely on Imogen for protection. She had told me early on that the pond was mostly for their benefit. "Well, and mine, of course," she had said. "I like to sit and watch them."

As I approach the old barn I see nothing at first. This is my first visit, and up close, I observe that the adobe structure is ancient. Calling it a barn might even be an overstatement. It is a hut, but on two levels and with several rooms on both.

At first, everything seems almost perilously quiet. There's not a single soul in sight, let alone the forty or more Imogen spoke about. And then something changes, though I'd never be able to say what. Suddenly it is as though the scene clarifies and I see golden eyes peering at me from the base of a clump of ocotillo. I stop as sharply as the cat who is watching me. A big striped tom, he stands as still as a garden statue, except for the slightest movement of his tail. The tip of it, slashing back and forth. And everything else is quiet.

Once I see him, I see others, equally hidden by their surroundings: almost invisible in plain sight.

I drop slowly and quietly to sit on the ground, trying to show them how harmless I am. I sit there patiently for a minute or two of inactivity. After a while, the big tom seems to accept my offer and decides I'm not a threat and moves forward, albeit cautiously. Not toward me, but back on whatever journey he'd been on before I showed up.

Once that happens, I begin to see motion all around me, as dozens of creatures, previously hidden, begin to stir. There is one in a barn window. And there, behind a watering trough. And over here, by some abandoned farm equipment, its striped ginger coat barely discernible against the rusting metal. It's as though the stillness is in motion and it enchants me. When I stand, all activity ceases and the cats I have in sight disappear like puffs of smoke, and as I stand there, I almost doubt my eyes. Had I ever seen any cats at all?

After a while, I go back to the house and report what I'd seen.

"It *is* magical," I agree. "But I still don't quite understand what they are doing here and how they came to be your responsibility. Surely you didn't adopt all those cats."

"Well, right. I did but I didn't. The colony was quite entrenched. I don't know how it started, maybe just a few individuals. It doesn't take long for a colony like that to grow. They're very successful breeders, feral cats. In the wild, a mature female might have two litters a year."

"*Two*." She sees the light dawn on my face as I think about it. "That's impossible. You'd have *hundreds* of cats in no time."

"Exactly. That's the point. And that's what I wanted to avoid. And I did. I love cats, of course. But *hundreds* of them? It was an unsavory idea. We'd be overrun. "

"I'll say."

"Now we just keep an eye on this, me and Chester. It's possible that some whole female wanders into the group. Cats are powerful at sensing a colony. It draws them. But, as you know, we're miles from anything. A female would have to have been dumped off somewhere nearby for her to show up here."

"Does that happen?"

"It does, actually. Sometimes. It has always seemed unlikely, but it does. You can tell when they're dumped, because mostly they're pretty friendly, even if they're skittish at being in a strange place. The ones who are born feral mostly don't want much to do with people. But the dumped pets are optimistic about people even though maybe they shouldn't be."

"Dumped pets," I say. "It hurts my heart just thinking about that. People are awful," I say without emotion.

"They can be," she agrees.

"So, I see. You watch them. Feed them. Provide them with shelter from the elements. And after many years, they just time out?"

"Pretty much, yeah. But that timing out is not fast in coming. Like I said, it can be twenty years. And you're responsible for them. To my mind, once you've done the TNR, you're on the hook for life."

I don't react to that. I just don't know what to say.

"And the horses?"

"You saw them?"

"A few."

"Aren't they beautiful?"

"They are."

"And they, well I guess they don't need me in the same way the cats do. Like, where would they get their water if I didn't keep that pond going?"

"I guess they'd find it someplace."

"Would they, though? In summer. In the desert. I'm not so sure."
I look at her closely to see if she's serious. She seems to be.

"They would," I say. "Of course they would." Though by the
end of saying it, I realize that I am also trying to convince myself.
And what the hell do I know? About horses? Nothing at all. And
the desert. From what I've seen, it's deadly.

"So the franchise," she says, pulling me back into a conversation
from an hour ago that I'd completely forgotten about.

"Okay," I say.

"What I have built can protect all of these beings for a long
time. More. There's no reason for all of this to die with me, I guess
is what I'm saying," she says finally.

"That's not something we have control of."

"Don't we, though?"

"No," I say with confidence. "We do not. In any case, you're not
going anywhere," saying it in the way one does.

"Oh, but I am," she says mildly. "If not now, then eventually.
It's the only thing we know for sure. And I need a plan to keep all
of this going once I'm gone."

"To look after the cats? The horses? The place?"

"Yes." Her voice is a low and quiet, but I can see she means
what she says.

"That's noble, Imogen. But that isn't how it works." I feel as
though I am speaking with some authority. After all, I have experience in this regard. What's gone is gone, that's what I've found.
If it could be done a different way, I'm certain I would have figured
it out. There was no question, but that there have been times in
my life I have been desperate enough to have changed anything
available to me. And I could not.

"It can this time though," she says. "It will." And there is a fire in her eyes that belies the weakness apparent in her body. There's no arguing with it.

"Tell me what's on your mind," I say, and it's like the world holds its breath for an instant. And then we begin.

CHAPTER TWELVE

THE PLAN IMOGEN outlines over the next several evenings is intricate and also completely absurd. I listen to her with all seriousness, but I feel as though a part of me is humoring her. It strikes me that there are many more reasons *not* to do as she suggests than there are to go ahead. It's impossible, that's what I realize the more I think about it. And yet again, it's a seductive thought as it answers all of my own challenges. It would be a new start for me. A new life. And so I think it through carefully, even while I continue to think about how unlikely and impossible Imogen's plan is.

And the plan. It is so serpentine; I get the feeling she's been sanding it for a while. Maybe years. And maybe also waiting for the right player to stumble onto the scene. And then there was me. Me and also Phil. Stumbling.

"It's at least worth a try," she says. "If I don't do anything, it'll all just go to hell. It's worth a shot."

And I understand that, for the sake of this conversation, "hell" is the authorities and whoever else might break up Ocotillo Ranch and sell it while not watering horses or feeding cats or, even worse, getting rid of all of the ranch creatures altogether. It isn't something she can contemplate. She wants things to stay as they are.

And she feels that an important piece is necessary in order for that to happen. In a word: me.

"What if I hadn't come when I did?" I ask at one point.

"Oh, I knew you were coming all along," she says, and I can tell the confidence is real. "It was just a matter of when."

So there is magic about Imogen O'Brien, but there is also madness. Or maybe in this case the two go hand in hand. She is mostly kind and in control. But there are times that she is less of both of those things. She is demanding, exacting, and even a little cruel. Then, just when you're about to shout "enough," and stomp away, it all turns back, and things are lovely again. Sometimes it hurts my head. And it reminds me enough of home that I don't just pack up my dog and go, though certainly sometimes I want to.

"See, it doesn't seem like you have a whole hell of a lot going on out there," she says at one point, and I bridle even while I recognize the truth in her words. That's eerily familiar to me, as well: words that are both true and launched to injure. It is my cradle language. "In the world, I mean. Not so many people could even set for as long a spell as you already have without being called upon by someone or to do something."

And I try not to either laugh or cry when I answer. "That's true," is all I say.

"There is a not inconsiderable fortune tied into my estate," she tells me. And, after all, she is Imogen O'Brien—she doesn't need to prove that to me.

"And you don't have kids." It's a statement, but it is also a question.

"I do not," she says, resolute.

"Or siblings. Or parents."

She guffaws at this last, and not without reason. "Sure as hell no," she says. "What? My parents would be, like, a hundred and fifty by now."

"Okay," I allow. "Dumb question. But what are you thinking? Where is all of this going?"

"When I die, and I will—" she holds up a hand as though to fend the protests she figures will come—"you just have to take over being me."

I let the words sit there between us for a heartbeat, playing them over a few times because—surely?—I must have gotten them wrong.

"That's not a thing, Imogen." It's what I can think to say. Only that.

She smirks, as though I've told a great joke.

"It's not?" She says it with a straight face. "Well then it oughta be, I reckon. Seriously, you can pull it off. And you should. Your life, such as it is: it would be made in the shade."

Shade. And it's such a precious commodity in the desert, too. And is she right? Well, maybe she is. I've been running a long time. A long, *long* time. What she's suggesting, I gather, is that I stop running. That I lean into this desert paradise, as she has done these many years. That I continue what she has built forever, or at least for as long as I can. She's suggesting I become, at some point, Imogen O'Brien, and continue her legacy—in life, if not in art—for as long as I am able.

"That's crazy, Imogen. I just can't . . . can't start being someone else."

"Why? You've done it before."

I just stand for a beat and look at her.

"How do you know that?" I ask at length.

"Just a guess," she says lightly, and I feel ghost fingers on my spine. And at the same time, I feel transparent. Am I so easy to read? I wasn't always, but maybe I am now.

"That was different," I say, hoping I don't sound defensive.

"How?" And there is a challenge in her eyes. I look away from it.

"It's complicated."

"I'll bet."

I look back at her, but I see nothing extra on her face.

"I was someone else then. I hadn't thought to do that again."

"Listen, just think about it, okay? But don't take your time about it. I don't know how long I've got."

I look her square in the eyes then. "None of us do, Imogen," I tell her. "That's part of the deal."

There is a lot for me to think about, and I wrestle with it. It's one thing to be some sort of quasi executive assistant—and even that had felt like too big of a commitment—quite another to step into someone else's life.

The impossibility of Imogen's plan for me weighs on the fact that I don't have anything else calling me right now. And it's a pretty even weight. To stay here, at Ocotillo Ranch, safe and productive, until I shuffle off my own mortal coil. It's a seductive thought. On the other hand, well, it's just pretty nuts. And certainly not legal, though it's a bit late in the day for me to start worrying about stuff like that.

In the end I decide to wait it out, figuring life, or maybe even Imogen, will provide the answer.

CHAPTER THIRTEEN

"I DON'T THINK we should waste any time," she tells me. It's been a few days since she sprung the whole thing on me.

"What do you mean?" I ask, though I figure I know.

"I think you should start being me."

"It's just pretty nutty, Imogen." I apparently have decided on honesty.

"Well, I won't argue with that. But I'm pretty sure it'll work."

It's had a bit of time to seep into me. To gel. I've sat with it. And beyond the weirdness of the very concept, the whole thing comes up aces. Except now there seems to be a time limit of some kind. All of a sudden. That concerns me.

"What do you mean?"

"I want you to start being me."

"That's what you said before. I've been thinking about it."

"Well, maybe step it up. I couldn't be bothered going into town anymore. If we decide to move forward with this, you can start going in now. As me. Kinda set yourself up while I'm kicking."

"I'm not sure the whole thing makes any sense," I say. "I mean, there are easier ways to accomplish what you want. Why wouldn't you just talk to a lawyer? Start a trust. Set up, like, a nonprofit or a foundation. Start something that will go on, even after you're gone. There are plenty of ways to do that."

"For one thing, that would all be after I'm gone, as you said. I'm wanting to do something now. Something I can be part of."

"I don't see how giving up everything you are now to me accomplishes that."

"I guess part of it is if I become someone different, maybe it'll lead the work to a different place."

"So this is all about painting?"

"No. Not all. But it's a factor, yeah."

"Okay. So a trust doesn't accomplish that," I concede.

"Also, lawyers. You haven't known me long, but you know me a bit. I hardly trust anyone. You think I'm going to trust some random lawyer to put this together correctly?"

"But me. Being you? Folks would see through that in a heartbeat."

"You'd think so, wouldn't you? But no. People are so busy with their own business, they barely take the time to notice what's going on around them. I wouldn't be surprised if no one uttered a peep."

The thing is, she doesn't know that her timing has been perfect. There would have been times that none of this would have worked for me. That time isn't now. Now there is nothing left. Less than nothing. And so even before I decide, I entertain the notion. During this time, Imogen watches me. And I can tell from the quality of the watching that she thinks just getting me to this point has me more than halfway there. She's not wrong.

"It's not as simple as all that, Imogen. There's more to me taking over your life than just a driver's license."

"Is there?" She sounds smug.

"There is. For instance, who do you then become? If I am to become you. What happens to you?"

"That's the beauty. I don't need an identity, don't you see? While I'm still on this side, you will execute all of the business things. We'll do them together. I don't need anything beyond this property."

"That's not possible," I say.

"It is," she replies. "Think about it. What more do I need beyond what is here? And I'll have you and also Chester to get me anything I require from the outside, as it were. But truly: there's nothing out there that I wish to do. My heart, my work, my *life*: all here."

"And what if you change your mind?"

"I won't."

"There'd be no going back."

"I won't change my mind. There's no back for me to go to."

"What about your will?"

"Yes. *This* is my will," she says majestically.

"Oh," I say, and I'm holding back laughter. "I'm your *will* as in, last will and testament, et cetera."

"I don't have one."

"How can you not have one?"

"Do you?"

"That's different," I say. "I don't have anything I need to give away, nor anyone to give it to."

"Maybe the way I see things, I don't have anything either."

"That's dumb," I say.

"It's not."

"So you'd risk dying intestate?"

"Now who's being dumb?"

"Explain," I say.

"I won't be 'intestate.' I'll be dead. What does it matter then who gets which painting or what scrap of sculpture? Who gets my car? No. I'm taking a much greater action than a will." She hesitates, then, "You. You will be my will. A living will."

And then we both laugh because on the one hand, what could be more absurd? And on the other, well, it starts to seem as though it all could work, after all.

*   *   *

I keep thinking about it. Posing questions to myself. Bringing some of those questions to Imogen.

We are in the studio setting up for work and it's a brand-new day. Light is careening through the skylights, rocketing from surface to surface. Dust motes swirl as gently as seagulls on delicate breezes. It is a moment filled with possibility.

"And what about if, as you have suggested, this change leads to new work? Different work. Even *monumental* work. You wouldn't be able to do anything about it."

I haven't told her what I'm talking about, but I don't need to. She knows.

"The work is the thing, dear. The work itself is the thing. And if I felt I needed to show it somehow . . . well, we could deal with that when or if it comes up. There are ways."

And, of course, she is right about that. There *are* ways. I had done them, and not only once. I could have told her that, in some ways, I am expert at all of that. We could get her a fake identity. It was only a matter of money and connection. And if she didn't need to travel, some sort of little corporation could be set up to take in the money that might be potentially generated by the work of a new artist. There were ways; she wasn't wrong.

She takes my silence for acquiescence.

"I've been thinking about it. I thought all night. We can begin tomorrow," she says. She is half-cajoling, half-excited. I can't decide which half I like best. "You can go into town for your new driver's license."

"So you're serious?"

"I am. It's perfect for both of us. Do you see that?"

I think before answering.

"Yes," I say at length. "I guess I do. But, like I said, there won't be any going back."

"Pffft," she says with a grin and a small wave of her hand, "we won't want to go back. It's all going to be wonderful. You'll see."

"I don't know—" I start to say, but she cuts me off.

"Why can you never be positive?" Her voice is low. Gravelly. I have trouble hearing her, and I want to move closer to hear, but I find I don't want to actually *be* closer.

"What?" To me this seems to have come out of left field.

"You can be such a goddamned Debby Downer."

And I have no response. I find I have no words at all. I simply stand there, watching her, holding my breath. Because it's not an expression I've heard for a long time, but I know I've heard it before and I know where, too.

My breath sticks in my chest and I look left, then right. A caged animal. No place to go. And then I do; I go. I head for the door, head for the pond. There aren't any horses there now, but that's okay. I just want to get away. I sit near the shallow water and I counsel myself to breathe, just breathe. I let the memories wash over me. After a while, I forget again.

CHAPTER FOURTEEN

THAT NIGHT EITHER I dream or, near sleep, I remember. I'm not sure which. Maybe there's not much difference, anyway.

I dream or think about my mother. And a certain blue dress.

"But it's school photos. And this dress will look so fetching on you."

And it was only a dress, right? It would have been easy for me to just shut my yap and put it on. The dress would have been stiff. It maybe would have been scratchy. But it would have made her happy. Couldn't I have just done that? Just done what it took to make her happy.

I didn't do that.

"I want to look like myself in my pictures, Ma."

"You *would* look like yourself. You're so pretty when you just take a few minutes to care about yourself. And *smile*. Most of the time in photos, you never smile."

"What do I have to smile about?"

"Heavens. Such drama. Like I said, care about yourself. Why are you always such a Debby Downer?"

"I *do* care about myself. And I want to look like myself, not your goddamn idea of what I *should* look like. But who I *am*."

And, of course, me injecting a curse right there ended the conversation, as I knew it would, with her gasping and stomping out of my room.

"Well, suit yourself, then," she threw over her shoulder, "but don't come crying to me when you're twenty-three and look at the photos of yourself and you look like a hippie."

"A *hippie*, Mom? That's not even a thing anymore."

But by then the door was slammed and I was alone in my room, contemplating my militance and my fingernails.

And, of course, even then, I could have put on that damned dress. Worn it to school. Had my photo taken. Would it really have cost me so much? It would have been easy.

Make your mother happy, my dad would have said if he were in earshot of any of this nuttiness. The dress was hanging *right there* in my room, taunting me with its structured presence, that shower of taffeta, the perfect bow. But it was just the idea of what it all meant, or maybe what it was saying to me. That I wasn't good enough as I was. That I should be someone else and act and look differently. It wasn't the worst of our interactions, not by a long shot. But it stuck with me. And here it was again.

After a while I do fall asleep. I dream of things other than stiff blue dresses and expectations that were never met. And when I wake, I wonder why all of this has come back to me now, so many miles—spiritually and physically—from where it all took place.

And I realize something else: twenty-three came and went and I never looked at that photo and thought, "Yikes!" In fact, I never looked at it at all. I've seen photos from that time, though. Seen photos that made me wish I'd been more gentle with the poor, broken kid that I was. My mother never was gentle with her—why couldn't I be? I rode her so hard. She was never enough of this or good enough for that. Echoes of my mother's admonishments? I don't like to think so, but it's hard to imagine otherwise.

Maybe we should all just be kind.

CHAPTER FIFTEEN

"TODAY'S THE DAY," Imogen says when she spots me in the morning. Her face is smooth and cheery. There is no trace of whatever it was that had passed between us the day before.

"Uh-oh," I say with a grin, matching her tone.

"Naw," she says, in a jovial mood. "Nothing like that. I think this should be the day we begin."

I just cock my head at her, like a dog trying to hear a distant sound more clearly.

"Your driver's license," she says. "My driver's license. Whatever. We got no time to waste."

"Wait. Let's think it through."

"We've done enough thinking. It's time to move!"

I am unexpectedly pulled. On the one hand, I think the plan is at least a little crazy. On the other, it solves all of my problems, long term and short term. I get a usable identity, a home, even a vocation. And maybe Imogen senses something on me, because she clinches it.

"Your painting is going well, kid," she says. "We can keep working on finding your own vision and style."

I just blink at her for a bit. I recognize a carrot when I see one. I'm a cart horse. She's looking for me to trot. I nod into the bridle. "All right," I say. "Deal."

Her arthritis prevents her from dancing or even prancing, but she makes a move that looks something like that and sallies into her bedroom. Every inch of her announces she is pleased beyond words.

After a while she comes out with a dress over her arms. I gather it is one of her old housedresses that maybe she's outgrown. I have a sense it's been chilling there, in her closet, for a long time. For one thing, the label says it's made in America and it does it in a font that looks vintage, so I figure the dress is older than me and from a time when clothes actually were made mostly in America. It makes me think that maybe she's been waiting for me for as long as she says.

From one of her closets, she produces an iron gray wig. It doesn't look exactly like her own hair, which is choppy and generally unkempt: a hairstyle determined by her work in the studio. But the wig is close enough.

"So I dress up and, what? Just waltz in and get the license?"

She nods. "Yeah. I figure it will go that easy. I'm an old broad," she tells me without rancor. "No one watches too closely what old broads do."

And so I concede. Why the hell not? I quash the part of my brain that tells me we're beginning an impossible journey. And it seems a lark, at first, when I put the wig on and take Imogen's old-but-tidy SUV and head to the nearest DMV. It's not that nearby, but in the intriguingly named town of Apache Junction, the closest place of any size to Ocotillo Ranch.

On this journey, I don't bother trying to disguise myself with makeup. I reason that if I need to use the license I'm getting, the picture should look like me. I do, however, wear Imogen's scrappy wig and her possibly fifty-year-old housedress, thinking all the while this whole thing has no chance of success.

Inside the DMV, I say I've lost my license. I show them Imogen's birth certificate. I give them her social security number. It's all so much easier than I'd feared.

There is only one brief snag.

"You're how old?" the woman at the DMV says when she goes to take my photo. There is disbelief etched on her face. But we're in Arizona, where there is more than enough Botox, fillers, and facelifts to go around. She maybe just thinks I had super good work.

"Good genes," I reply with a bashful nod of my head.

"Damn straight," she says, but she takes the picture, and if she has any questions, she keeps them to herself.

I am given a temporary paper license and told that the permanent photo ID will arrive in the mail in seven to ten days.

By the time I get back to the car—Imogen's car—my heart is pounding, though I've managed to keep my hands steady. Pure relief. And when all is said and done the most difficult step is behind me, that's what I think. Everything hinges on this one important photo ID. The license to drive. In the various identities I have had since I left being me, that's always the most important piece.

Since I'm in town anyway, I do some grocery shopping. I leave the gray wig in place and no one pays any attention to me. Being old, I discover, makes you even more invisible than just being of middle years. In the various shops I visit, other than barely looking up to take my money, I might as well not exist at all.

"It went without a hitch," Imogen says when I get back to the ranch. I realize right away that it's not a question.

"It did."

"You got the license?"

"Yes," I say. "But I don't understand how this is going to do anything..."

"It's going to do *everything*," she says. "I've been thinking this through for a while. Years. Everything hinges on the license."

"Everything," I repeat, but I'm just giving it back to her, waiting to see where all of this is going. I can tell she has more to say.

"There's more, of course. But the birth certificate you already have—from me—and the passport comes from that. But the driver's license gets you, domestically, everywhere you need to go and everything you need."

"Social security number."

"Sure. But that's easy. A simple handover."

"I still don't get why you don't just make a trust. You could accomplish all of this by putting a trust in place."

"Not all of it," she says meaningfully. "I wouldn't have you."

And I choose not to respond because the comment seems nuanced enough, there are so many things—*too* many things—it could mean.

"It's like we're planning something against the law."

She laughs at that. Uproariously. She laughs so hard I fear she'll injure herself in her present frail state. And when she stops, she finds me waiting to hear her out.

"But we are, dear. Of course we are. We're planning to outwit the system. And maybe time."

While I understand that the former is true, the latter is clearly not. No one outwits time. Time has everything on its side. I don't argue with her, though. As usual and as always with Imogen, I just go along.

CHAPTER SIXTEEN

OVER THE NEXT few weeks, I feel like I'm back in school. Like some test is coming and Imogen desperately wants me not to fail. I think sometimes she feels as though my failure is inevitable, and then I chastise myself for thinking it. Is it anything she is doing that is making me feel this way? Or whispers from my own past? I shake it off, wet dog style. There's no profit in going down those roads.

At times I feel like stopping what we're putting in motion, but I don't. At this point, I'm not even sure I could. I wonder if this is the thing that is keeping her going, this schooling of me. That if I stop it—out of reason, out of what is right—that she will simply fade away. It's complicated, this relationship we're building. After a while, I can't see the edges of it anymore.

But the schooling. That goes on.

Imogen shows me where everything is. Everything of import, plus a lot that is not. She shows me how to access the safe where she has placed her most important papers: her birth certificate, her passport, the keys to a safe deposit box she won't yet tell me the location of.

"All in good time," she says. And I wonder.

She shows me how to access her bank accounts and pay her credit cards and her taxes. I can see her racking her brain, trying to get all of the details for things that might come up if she were no longer in the picture.

"It's a lot, I know," she says at one point. "Things I just do when I do them. I'm trying to make notes all the time now."

After a few days of this, she tells me she has an idea.

"I've been thinking. For this to work," she tells me, "I need to be fully back in the circle."

"What does that mean?"

"I told you: I broke with my agent a while ago?"

I nod.

"Yeah," I say. "You said you told him to go to hell."

She smirks.

"I did," she agrees. "He's a bit of a douche. But I have to fix it," she says. Then she thinks and adds, "*We* have to fix it. I need representation so that the funds keep flowing properly. It hasn't mattered until now."

"We have to fix it?"

"Yes. If it's to be you going forward, we may as well begin as we would go on."

"That's kinda insane," I tell her. I've been going along, but, "This is all kinda insane."

She nods and grins. "Yes," she says. "I think you're right. But what the hell, eh?"

I just shake my head and grin back.

"Okay," I say after a while.

She is weak by now, but filled with excitement, as though some great adventure is spurring her on, beyond, maybe even, her own endurance. Before she retires for the evening, she gives me detailed instructions and I say goodnight, then head on my way.

In Imogen's study, I feel like an interloper. Her presence is so vast; even without her in the room, I feel her at my shoulder.

I sit at the ancient oak desk and begin to follow her instructions. First, I find the file marked "Gallery Correspondence" in her clear, fine hand. The notes are handwritten and go back many years. I'd asked her why not email, but she felt a handwritten note would be expected in this instance.

"Email is recent," she tells me, even though it's not. "This is the kind of relationship that endures."

All right.

Once I feel I've read enough of the correspondence that has led us here, I take a thick piece of velum from a scarred-but-pristine box on the desk. For a while I study samples of her handwriting, then I take up a sturdy and beautiful Montblanc pen and take practice runs at duplicating it. The pen spreads a cobalt blue ink behind as I write. My effort won't duplicate her handwriting exactly. But it should be close enough for our purposes and, after all, Imogen won't be calling me out to get it right. The handwriting I come up with is close enough for the kind of jazz we're currently playing around here.

When I feel like I have a fairly close approximation of the smooth flourishes of Imogen's handwriting, I take out a clean sheet of paper and begin to write:

Dear Beardsley,

I have been giving deep thought to our relationship these last weeks. I have decided that the best course for both of us is to mend what we have built over these many years. If it also suits you, I would like things to be restored to their previous harmony. It strikes me that this would work for you as it would seem it was mainly me who was unhappy in the relationship, unless I misread. Correct me, please, if that's the case and inform me how you'd like to go on.

Yours Sincerely,
Imogen O'Brien

I study the note. Assess it. Based on her personality and the examples of her correspondence I've seen, it strikes me that I've hit the correct balance of humility and imperiousness. It's short enough not to invite too much interpretation. And it's not an apology, though from what she'd told me, one is probably owed. There is a water-under-the-bridge tone to the note. It's what I was aiming at.

In the morning at the breakfast table, I show Imogen my handiwork. When she smiles, I feel like a schoolgirl under a favored teacher's praise. And *she* seems like a schoolgirl, too, when she reads the note. She lights up with anticipation and glee.

"Oh, that's perfect," she says. "You got it all just right."

"I still don't get why you didn't just write it yourself."

"Setting things up to go forward," she tells me, nodding sagely in a way that makes me think she's given the matter some thought. "What we're doing now doesn't necessarily reflect how things will be a year from now, and so on."

"I still don't get it," I say again.

"Doesn't matter," she says with still another wave of her hand. "Just do what I say and we'll both be fine." And she says it quickly, like she's used to people picking up what she puts down, and not too many questions asked, thank you. No arguments to be brooked. "Let it ride," she says, and then she grins. "We'll see where it all leads. Somewhere good, I'm guessing."

Me, I have my doubts, but when she plops a stamp on the envelope and asks me to trot it out to the mailbox for the mailman to pick up when he comes, I comply. Already in the habit of an obedience I don't question. Until later.

CHAPTER SEVENTEEN

BY THE TIME Phil and I get back from our walk to the mailbox, Imogen is already in the studio.

"Glad you found me," she says as I enter. She is sitting in front of an easel on a high studio chair. The painting she is working on is of a medium, usual size. That surprises me, as she has always been known to work large. "I was going to leave you a note, but I got so up into my head," she says, "I just wanted to rush here. I hoped you'd find me."

"I did," I say easily.

The piece she is working on looks intricate, almost like pointillism: tiny dots of color that together make a pattern, and in the end, together create an image. It's unlike anything I've seen from her.

"That looks interesting," I say, indicating the piece.

"It does, doesn't it? You see how you inspired all of this?"

"I did?" I am mystified by her words.

"Yes, of course. I'm not me anymore, see?" She indicates the painting. "I don't know who I am yet. It's terribly exciting. Maybe I am you."

"Oh, don't be me," I say, only half joking. "There's been a lot of darkness. I wouldn't wish that on anyone. Be someone new."

For a moment, she looks as though she might ask me more about that, but in the end, she lets it go.

"All right," is all she says. "Being someone new sounds like an altogether good plan. I guess I'll figure it out as I go. But let's leave this for now." She pushes herself out of her chair. "I may not know yet who I am, but if you're going to be me, you have some work to do."

I nod. Indicate that she should go on.

She starts us off on basics, then works her way up. The way she stretches her canvases, then sizes them. The pigments she mixes; blends. The brushes she chooses. Even the subjects. What is her thinking when she selects them? Why does she paint this and not that? I can tell that she's trying not to leave anything out.

"And I'm to paint as you?" I ask.

"Oh, no, no. That's not necessary. But it's part of our bargain, I think. Part of our deal: that I show you the ropes, as it were. There are things I know that will help you on your own journey as a painter."

"You're going to mentor me," I say, thinking that this was what I had hoped. And imagined.

"Something like that, I guess." She pauses as though thinking it through. "Sure. Why not?"

At first, it is slightly awkward, at least for me. I am self-conscious. After a while, though, I notice that, when we paint, she pays no attention to me or my progress. She tells me to ask if I have questions and then she immerses herself in her own work, leaving me to mine. I stumble a bit over her technique with the canvas. I have worked mostly in watercolor until now, no canvas involved, just various grades of paper. Once I've set myself up, I find I am at a loss, then I spy Phil happily perched on an oversize pillow in one corner of the studio. His head is drooping off one side, his back legs drip off the other end, and I think, "Why not?"

I begin to paint what I know.

At first, I feel constricted by the medium. And the company. It's hard not to feel self-conscious with someone as accomplished as Imogen working nearby. Pretty soon, beyond confirming that she is so captivated by her own work she's not paying attention to mine, I come to realize that there's no disappointing her: she has no expectations of me. Once all of that sinks in, I just let it go. I lean into the work, forget where or even who or what I am, and I fill in the shapes and follow the lines and my heart.

Time passes. A lot of it, I think. When I feel her hand on my shoulder, I become aware that the light in the studio has shifted and the gloom has deepened.

"That's very good," she says softly, looking at my work. I feel myself stop breathing.

"No it's not," I say automatically, my voice barely above a whisper.

"Don't say stuff like that," she says. Her voice is light, but I can tell she is perfectly serious.

"But—" I begin, and she cuts me off.

"We tend to be our own worst enemies, all of us. We tend to be our own worst critics. You start to change that by changing it. Send yourself reassurance, not criticism."

"Change that by changing it. Just like that?"

"Pretty much," she says. "Change your mind. Oh, it's not always easy. But you just keep at it; reinforcing yourself. And, honestly, you won't benefit from self-criticism. For one thing, your work is good."

"No."

"It is. And it certainly shows promise. Look how you've captured the light here. And here," she says pointing. "And I like the way you used purple to annunciate the profound nature of the gold in his coat."

"Annunciate," I whisper.

"Yeah. Many eyes would have kept it all umbers and yellows and whatnot, but you've captured the depth of the gold by adding the purple. That takes an eye." She meets mine. "And talent."

I feel myself shift uncomfortably under her gaze, putting my weight on one leg and then another. Did Imogen O'Brien just call me talented? She did. Or something very like it.

"Thanks," I stammer. "Thank you."

And she grins at me and at my delivery. I feel like she gets my discomfort. Understands. And so she doesn't belabor her comments, but moves us forward. But her words have meant a lot to me.

We head to the house and she sits and rests at the kitchen table while I break out the biscuits and make tea. We've both put in a full enough workday. It's showing on her. She looks done in.

When the tea is made, I join her at the table.

"You good?" I ask it, just checking in.

"I'm good," she says, smiling. "It's been a long day."

"Truth," I say. "Soup for dinner could be quick."

"That would be good," she says weakly, and I understand that she is not as strong as she's trying to appear.

What I put together for us to eat is fast and sustaining. When I serve it I understand that she is grateful for both the speed and the nutrition. I remind myself that this is my life for now. Finding nutrition for Imogen O'Brien: feeding, in some ways, body and soul. And, on the way to that, I find my own way to being a better artist. Maybe even a better person. It doesn't strike me as a bad trade.

After Imogen has retired for the night and I feel she is solidly asleep, I head back to the studio. I stand in front of my work, far enough back from it that I can take it all in. Examine it. Is it all I hoped it could be? Is it as good as I could push it? I'm not sure on either count, but my instincts are pure. Does anything else matter? I'm not yet where I intend to go, but the road, that's the thing. The road helps me rest more easily than I have for a while.

CHAPTER EIGHTEEN

THE NEXT MORNING on my way to the main house, I meet Chester for the first time. He is not as tall as I'd imagined he would be. And he has thick, medium brown hair that looks as though he hacks it off himself with kitchen scissors: short and choppy.

"You're the new pet," he sneers when I introduce myself. I am taken aback. There is something in his voice.

"Sorry?" I'm trying not to think about who the old pet might have been.

"I'm not going anywhere if that's what you're thinking."

"That is *not* what I was thinking. Why would I be thinking that?"

He pauses, as though thinking it through.

"People do," he says finally.

He continues on his way and I watch his back. I feel like, if my time at Ocotillo Ranch—whatever it looks like—is going to work, I need to soften Chester up, though at the moment I can't think how I might do that. As Imogen had suggested, there is a strangeness about him, but the insecurity hadn't been hinted at.

It seems possible to me that Imogen, who had known Chester his whole life, had never been shown that side of him.

Entering the house, I meet Imogen leaving it. There is something on her face. A fire I haven't seen before: she is keen to get to work. I wonder if this keenness is new.

By the time I get to the studio, she is immersed. I leave her to it and approach my own painting. I'm surprised to see it is closer to complete than I had imagined. I get back to where I'd left it, adding highlights here, contours there. I'm so engrossed that I fail to hear Imogen approach from behind. A hand on my shoulder startles me and we both jump.

"It's going well," she says when we both stop laughing.

"Thanks."

"Can I give you a few pointers?"

After I nod, she sets out to do just that. Her comments are insightful and I think that ultimately they will be helpful; when I have more information and can fully understand. Her caring makes me feel grateful. And I gather from her comments that it has become important for her to help me to reconnect with whatever demons she thinks are firing me.

"Are you reaching for the best that is in you?"

"I think so," I reply, not knowing for sure. Because where is the best in each of us? And what do we need to bring it home? But even the examination of it fuels my thoughts.

"Are you appreciating all that you bring?" She watches me closely while waiting for an answer.

"May-be?" I'm not even sure what she means.

She smiles.

"We'll get there."

Once we've settled back into work for the day, I turn to see what Imogen is up to. Once again, I notice that her canvases are smaller than they were in previous years. She had told me that the effort of standing on ladders to reach every inch of a giant canvas is too much for her now. That there is some arthritis in her shoulders. It gives her hell sometimes when she reaches. She tries to hide it, but I see.

Whatever pain she is in, it does not seem to impact any part of the work but the size. The vision and execution both have the same clarity that they have always had. Her vision is different than it was, I know she's working on that, but it is still brilliant.

Something comes to me.

"I could help you." I say it quietly, though I'm not sure why.

"But you are," she says. "You're helping me ever so much."

"No, I mean . . ." My voice strengthens, picks up weight as I get behind my idea. "I could help you, you know, paint." And almost before the words are in the air, I am overcome with my embarrassment at the mere suggestion. Who do I even think I am?

Despite my sudden mortification, Imogen doesn't seem critical of the idea.

"Physically assist, you mean?"

"Yes," I say.

She's nodding and thinking at the same time. "I've heard of artists doing that. Later in life. Jeff Koons uses whole fleets of assistants. Warhol and his damned factory, of course. But even some of the masters. There is precedent for that, certainly. You could assist me with the physical parts," she says. And as she speaks, I can feel her warming still more to the idea. "I would direct it."

"Of course."

"Last year I stopped wanting to go up a ladder." She says it like it's an admission: something she's afraid to say out loud. "That's why I started with the smaller canvases. But it feels so—" she waves her hand expressively—"it feels restrictive. If you were to help me, I could direct you what to put, you know, above." She makes a delicate movement of her hand.

I just nod and let her think it through. I've come up with the idea but I haven't fully contemplated the mechanics of it.

"And when I mix color." She pauses. I can almost hear her thinking. "You could do some of the physical part of that. I've been finding it increasingly difficult in the larger quantities."

I nod, easily able to imagine doing all of that.

"And stretching the canvas," I offer and Imogen agrees, smiling.

"Yes. That's a good idea."

"Though I think you said Chester does some of that. The harder stuff."

"Yes," she says, "that, too." She thinks and then goes on. "Even just moving those damned big canvases around. Yes. This can work. Your gift to me will be your physical help with the business of painting. My gift to you will be knowledge." She considers, then goes on. "That will also be a gift *to* me, honestly: someone to share these things with. So they don't die with me."

And I don't comment that this idea of no longer walking among the living seemed to be fueling a lot of Imogen's decisions of late. I just keep that thought down and try to forget it. If she's feeling vulnerable, she won't be wanting anyone to notice.

When the work begins, though, everything changes. We are painters now. Everything else falls beside this central purpose. It's not as though we are preparing for a show or there is anyone waiting to see what we produce, but it doesn't matter. The work is the thing. The excellence. The purity. The compelling *voice* of the work. It fascinates me.

I discover that, once I become Imogen's assistant and labor with her on her paintings, I don't miss working on my own. It surprises me that there is no ache where my work would have been. It is as though my personal work hasn't been abandoned, only put aside for a while, waiting to be picked up again, maybe when my skills are stronger. That would also be part of the exchange.

I fall into our shared work instantly and, in no time, it feels as though we have been doing things in just this way forever. Before long—days? weeks?—we are a well-oiled art creation machine. Imogen has a lifetime of discipline behind her, and me? I've had years filled with madness. The bright spots of both lead to a certain chemistry; even a fire at times. Imogen's art doesn't become better because of me, but the way of working we develop seems to help usher in this new era. I forget about Beardsley and the world outside. I almost forget about the dog. The two of us are consumed with Imogen's vision, the vision that, before long, becomes mine.

The only shade comes with Chester. After a while it seems to me that I don't even have to see him; I sense his presence. Lurking? Watching? In the studio as we work. It's as though when he arrives, I can feel the energy break, which is ridiculous, of course. Fanciful. But it seems true enough to be distressing.

I think about mentioning it to Imogen, but decide against it: her longtime trusty retainer. And, of course, he hasn't done anything to distress me. Being creepy isn't against the law.

When I am away from him, I can think about the whole thing rationally. The tragic life he's had: limited to this property and the small towns beyond. Who would that make you, if you were raised in that way? Especially if your education and intellect were lacking. I urge myself to compassion, not responding to what I'm reading as creepiness. He can't help what he is and my abrupt arrival might naturally make him suspicious, maybe even jealous: Imogen had been alone for so long. Alone with him. I counsel myself to kindness. And I'm successful until I see him again, and his coldness and obvious aversion to me starts it all rolling again.

Chester is the only slightly sour note in an otherwise gentle existence. Each day is similar to the last. In the morning, Imogen and I meet in the kitchen and I make us breakfast, braced with strong cups of coffee that we chase with tea. At breakfast we talk, but we don't discuss the work.

Once in the studio, we are filled with what is in front of us. When there is collaboration, it is brief and quickly sorted: it is Imogen's vision that I am helping bring to life; my ego doesn't enter the room.

We fall into a comfortable routine and life feels fruitful. For a moment—just a heartbeat—it feels as though things can go like this forever: creativity, crisp forest air, and what seems to be a growing friendship. Then the letter comes.

It's from Beardsley and I'd been so immersed in the life Imogen and I are weaving I'd almost forgotten about him and our quest. We were to make a plan, Imogen and I. We were to break his spirit. Take things back. These are the things that were unsaid between us, and then we started to paint and everything was forgotten. At least by me.

And now, with his letter in hand and his communication a reality, everything shifts. I find I'm a bit sad about that. I realize instinctively that this means things will have to change. We might still work together in this way in the future, Imogen and I, but for the moment our pattern is disrupted by distraction and possibility.

"What does he say?" I'm the one who has brought Beardsley's note back from the mailbox, a full half mile down the driveway to the road where I'd stopped on that first day to let the dog—now Phil—out of the car because of his anxiety.

Today, when I open the mailbox and pull the letter out, the first thing I notice is the gallery's logo—a stylized feather closing upon itself in a circle—and the words "Beardsley Davenport Gallery" engraved underneath. Imogen hadn't mentioned the gallery's name, but I recognize it anyway. A gallery name and a SOHO address, what else could it be?

I grab the rest of the mail, stuff it into my backpack, and then Phil and I beeline it back to the house.

"I can barely believe it," Imogen says when she's given the letter a fast read. "Here," she says, thrusting the note at me, "read it for yourself."

His letter is written on a beautifully printed note card. I recognize the image on the front. It is a well printed representation of one of Imogen's early works, *Sparrow on Snowflake*. The tiny print on the back of the card reads: "Imogen O'Brien, 1968."

The writing on the business end of the card is very clear. It is strong and in dark ink, the block printing carefully executed.

"Imogen," the strong hand writes, "so good of you to reach out. The gesture is appreciated. Let's have a conversation. It's cold in the City just now. A touch of the desert will do me good. Please expect me on the 15th. Some of your strong tea will be most welcome. You servant—Beardsley."

That "Beardsley" is capped with a flourish in an even more decisive hand. All of this old-timey correspondence has me again wondering at the wisdom of not doing this exchange in email where things are immediate and it's easy to head off surprise visits. I begin to mention this to Imogen, then just hold my tongue. What's done is done, and anyway we've got *this* to deal with now.

I feel my throat dry up. If he's showing up, it's going to be showtime soon, and I don't feel anywhere near ready.

Beardsley has presumably met Imogen before. Or has he? Even not knowing that could be disastrous. And there are so many other small things that are waiting to trip me up: pockets of knowledge it will be impossible to fill in the short amount of time we have left. And it would be one thing for me to manage a brief visit, but this is different. He's coming all this way just to see me—or, rather, Imogen—he will expect to spend the night, I read that in his message, too. In the things that are not said.

"What's it mean?" I ask.

"Well, as he says, he's coming here in a week."

"That's wonderful, isn't it? It's what you wanted."

"I'm not sure anymore what I wanted when we wrote to him. But to have him here, looking at what we've been doing. I'm not sure I can bear it."

"I don't understand."

"I guess I'm not sure I understand, either. It's instinct, in part, I think. If he is here, what all will he see?"

"The work, I guess. The cats? The horses?"

"Sure, yes. All of that. What I most fear he will see is how vulnerable I've become." She closes her eyes, as though considering on some deeper level. When she opens them again, I can see the fear she describes. "I don't want him to observe my weakness. I fear he'll use it against me."

"What else then?"

"Call him."

"Having a conversation with him is a good idea," I say nodding. "You guys can reconnect. It's been a long time, right? You can hash things out."

"It's been a long time, yeah. But I don't mean me." She's says it solemnly, and I can see her watching my face. Waiting for my reaction. "You."

"Me? How can I ever?"

"You call him," she says with more confidence, as though she's warming up to the idea. "Tell him you're me and that he shouldn't come here."

"Well, that's just silly," I say gently. "I don't even know the man. How does it even make sense for me to talk with him? And he knows your voice, Imogen. What makes you think he won't catch on in an instant and tell me to go to hell?"

"He won't," she says with confidence. "He will want this to work so badly. If he thinks he hears something in my voice, or even if my voice is different, he'll tell himself he's got it wrong. He'll sow the doubt himself *in* himself."

"How do you know?"

"I know," and then after a beat, "I know people. How they think. What they do. Why do you think I've been out here on my own for so long? And I know him. He only cares about one thing: loot."

"And you think he won't notice?"

"Oh, I think he might notice. But I don't think he'll do anything about it. It's in his best interest to believe. I want you to go there."

To me, this comment seems out of left field.

"Me? Go where?"

"To the City. To his gallery. As me."

"What?" I feel an ever-growing incredulity—it's like I'm hearing one bit of madness after another. I struggle to keep that incredulity out of my voice. Things seem to be getting more surreal by the second, and Imogen is not even that kind of painter.

"It's the only way this is going to work."

"Only way *what* is going to work?"

"I'm setting up a legacy," and she says it with a sniff, like she's holding on to some shred of dignity she feels has been challenged.

"A legacy."

"Yes. I won't always be here."

"Where will you be?" I keep my tone flat, not joking, but we both know I'm poking fun.

"Come on," she says, suddenly impatient. "You get it. I know you do. We've had these talks, you and I. And if we play all of this right, it goes on forever."

"Not forever," I say.

"Maybe. Or maybe enough of forever to be the only thing that matters."

I regard her evenly. I'd known all along she wasn't kidding, but what she is proposing seems too out to lunch to even contemplate.

"Nothing lasts forever, Imogen."

"This can be good. I have a feeling. A strong one. Trust me. I can give you everything you need."

CHAPTER NINETEEN

AND SO I trust. Like Imogen said: it's not like I've got any other gigs. Though the trust is a bit limited. I will do this thing for her, this Beardsley thing. I will, in a way, play along. There's no saying no to her anyway, plus it seems it might be a service to her. Whatever the truth is—and there are so many times I feel as though I don't get anywhere near the truth with Imogen—something is up for her around this Beardsley encounter. Whatever else she and I do together in future, I will help her get through this part. Why not?

Imogen coaches me on what to say when I call Beardsley. We do it the next afternoon.

"Keep it short and sweet," she says. "Let him to do most of the talking. He likes that, for one. But also, the less you say, the more he'll just fill in."

"That makes sense," I say. And it does. It's something I've noticed in the past. If you just shut up, whoever you're talking to will rush to fill in the space. A lot of people can't stand the empty holes.

"You know what to tell him?"

"Sure. Like you said: don't come here, I'll come there."

Imogen grins.

"Perfect. And yes. Let's head 'em off at the pass, so to speak."

"You could have avoided all of this by just emailing in the first place," I say.

"Don't start," she retorts.

The next day, before I make the call, I sit myself down in Imogen's office and I meditate. Imogen averts her eyes while I do it. It's like she thinks she's watching something secret or sacred. Maybe she's right.

And then I research a bit before I call. I pull in all of my resources. More. I pull in everything that is available to me. I think about Imogen's voice. Like the way she says "chiaroscuro," with every syllable drawn out and dripping over the consonants, almost as though you can see all of the light and shade that the word evokes. There is a strength about her voice I've noticed. Strength *and* frailty. Can I replicate those qualities enough to fool someone with whom she had spoken before? She thinks I can. Maybe that's enough.

When I'm ready, she gives me a fast test, then sits across from me while I make the call. Her face is impassive, and I work at tuning out her focus on me, refocusing instead on the work at hand.

Beardsley doesn't answer the phone. I can tell: the voice is young and dreamy. I ask for Beardsley.

"Who can I tell him is calling?"

"Imogen O'Brien." There is a hesitation, as though the youngster can't believe his ears. I think about the fact that his instincts are not wrong. "I'll get him for you right away," the young man says, and it sounds to me like he's having trouble catching his breath. I've never been a rock star before. It's an interesting feeling.

I'm on hold for all of thirty-seven seconds when Beardsley comes on the line.

"Imogen," he says, voice booming. Based on his handwriting alone, I realize I could have predicted that timbre. Hale and hearty. Not the voice of an auteur. Rather, the voice of someone who would greet you with a warm word and a slap on the back. "I'm so glad you called."

"Hullo, Beardsley," I say. I keep my tone quiet and distant, as though that might mask what is familiar to him. And not. I have no way of telling if I'm successful. I'm hoping his booming will continue, drowning out everything that isn't him. I'm hoping—and guessing—that he is that type.

"Imogen," he says again. "Your olive branch was ever so welcome. I can't tell you what it meant to me."

And was that code? Did that just mean he was relieved he would get new inventory? Maybe. But maybe, also, it didn't matter. The result was the same.

"Olive branch. That's a pretty picture, Beardsley. But I didn't really think of it that way. It just seemed like time."

"I don't disagree," he says agreeably. I get the feeling there isn't much I could say right now that he would disagree with. "And I'm so looking forward to seeing you."

"About that," I say. "I'm wondering what you're hoping to accomplish."

"Accomplish?"

"By venturing out here."

"Why, to talk, of course. To set things right between us. As you said."

"That's not exactly what I said."

"Well, to talk, then. To see how we might reconnect. Reestablish ourselves with each other."

"I can save you the trip. I have to come to the City." I'm using as few words as possible. Keeping it simple. The less I say, the less there will be to hear. Or not hear, as the case may be.

"That might work out very well."

"How so?" I say, trying to sound neutral.

"Maybe we could have a small reception."

"Small."

"Yes," he says hurriedly, though still booming. It seems to be unconscious. Like breathing. "Just a few people. Only your biggest fans."

"Fans." I try not to hear myself repeating everything he says.

"When did you say you were coming again?"

"I didn't, I don't think."

"Were you thinking around when I said I'd come out to your place? Middle of next week?"

"Something like that." I suddenly wonder what the hell I think I'm doing. I have the sensation of frying pans. And fire. Something about the heat. I look at Imogen, but she won't meet my eyes. She shoos her fingertips at me though. *Go on, go on,* she seems to say, a wisp of her silver-gray catching the light. *Go on, go on.* And so I do.

"Well, week after next would actually be ideal. Give us time to organize things. Send out a press release. Order canapes . . ."

"It's . . . it's next week," I say hurriedly. "I have . . . I have appointments."

And what is my rationale for saying that? Imogen and I have not discussed this part. *Appointments.* Is it that I'm thinking that giving him less time to prepare will make it go better for me? I know that doesn't even make sense. I sigh. Force myself to listen to what he's saying.

"Next week," he says, sounding like he's disappointed but has decided to soldier on. One of the advantages of my newly found extreme age, I am finding. People argue with you less when you get to be a certain age. It gives us all hope for the future.

"Yes."

"We can make that work," he says, sounding brighter. "Like I said—just the staff and a few important collectors. Your biggest fans." I hear the smile in his voice. He's trying to be charming. And I can tell he is used to being thought charming. It's been paying out for him, thus far. "A small group. And maybe only the top journalists."

"No press," I say quickly. Then with more composure, "Please."

"Of course, Imogen. As you wish. I'd forgotten you don't like reporters."

I don't? Thank goodness. There's backstory for my refusal, at least. I make a mental note to quiz Imogen and to research everything I can about her. There might be other tidbits I can use to my advantage. Or maybe I should google. The world might tell me more about her than she will.

"Thank you," is what I say.

"So . . ." He hesitates. I imagine him looking at a calendar. Shuffling things around. "Evening of the eighth is okay? Event to begin at 7:00 pm. But please come early. I'll take you to dinner."

"Thank you," I say, thinking quickly, "but my diet is quite restricted these days. Dinner would not be a pleasure for me." I look up and see Imogen beaming at me. She shoots me a thumbs-up as though pleased with my improvisation. I can't help but feel pleased by this pantomime of praise. "So no dinner, no. But maybe I can come to the gallery a bit early and we can chat."

"I'd like that."

As we say goodbye, I can tell from the note of excitement in his voice that he has plans to make. I'm surprised to discover that it is heady, this suddenly being a big deal. Going from nobody—less than nobody—to being an international celebrity in a heartbeat. From the start, I'm pretty sure I'm going to hate it.

When I end the call, Imogen and I regard each other without speaking for a beat. Two.

"So that's done then."

"Yes."

"You did very well."

"Thank you."

"You're going to be feted."

"Tell me how much you loved that."

She laughs. "Obviously since I've spent most of the last three decades holed up in extremely rural Arizona, I'm not a big fan of that feted-type lifestyle. It won't be awful, though." She says it as though she's trying to reassure me, or maybe she's just read the look of apprehension on my face. "Don't worry. We'll figure out all the details."

"But how can I possibly pose as you? Beardsley has met you. He won't believe it for a second."

"But he will," she insists, and she says it with such confidence she almost convinces me. "I'm an old woman. I've always been an old woman to Beardsley. If the details aren't just as he remembers them he'll scarcely notice or he'll put it off to all the time that has passed."

"He will notice," I insist.

"He won't," she says calmly. "And anyway, we'll make some of the details so grand that they will make all his people agog with splendor."

"Agog," I repeat but I let her bring me along. "Splendor."

We search together to find someone who can do my hair and makeup for this shindig in the City. The demands are so specific, we're both confident I can't do it alone.

We begin the search in SoHo, close to the gallery.

The first call I make I find myself floundering around, trying to describe what I want.

"You want to look like who?" The voice is young. Too young. I can tell from her website that she is experienced and she sounds competent but, when I think about it, theatrical makeup had not been listed on her website, and I suddenly realize that's what I need.

"An artist. A famous one."

"Are you an influencer?"

"What?"

"You know. Are you, like, a social media maven? Do people follow you?"

"Not unless they're trying to catch me," I say, pleased with my quick wit.

My quip is met with a thick silence. Then, "I'm afraid I don't understand," she says.

"I want to look like someone else."

"We all do, honey."

"Someone specific."

"And you're not an influencer."

"That's right."

A thoughtful silence and then, "I don't think we're going to be a fit."

"What?"

"And I'm pretty booked up right now. Good luck in finding what you need."

She's polite but absolute and it's only the dead silence on the line that makes me realize she has disconnected the call.

I start out my next call less hopefully than I had the first. Maybe this is going to be more difficult than I'd thought going in.

"I need to look like someone else," I say tentatively when Jennifer K. Riley answers her phone. Her website has already told me she specializes in FX makeup, and the photos she's posted make me think she can do anything. Theatrical makeup is only one of her skills.

"You want to look like someone general or someone specific?"

The question alone makes me feel like I've found the right person. And she sounds casual about it, like she's asking about the weather. I like that, too. This isn't going to be an out-of-the-ordinary gig for her.

"Specific."

"Who?"

"Who?" I repeat it, even though when I do, I feel like an owl.

"Like, someone famous, or . . . ?"

"Well, yeah. Famous. Though not a lot of people know what she looks like. Thing is, she's old. And I'm not so old. Does that sound doable?"

"It does. Is it going to take a wig?"

"Yeah. I mean, I have one. There's one here. I can bring it."

"Bring it. But it's probably going to be crappy," she says honestly. "Send me a photo of the person you're going to look like. And send one of you, too. I'll make sure we have everything we need on hand when you arrive."

She doesn't ask why I'm doing it. She doesn't ask if the person I want to look like is dead or alive or if I'm a big deal on the internet. Maybe she doesn't care, or maybe it's professional courtesy.

Confidentiality. Like talking to a lawyer or a surgeon: someone whose business requires that they keep their yaps shut.

We choose the time. She gives me the price. It has enough zeros it makes my eyes water and I put Jennifer K. Riley on hold for a second, muting my phone. I give Imogen the number and she shrugs. "If that's what it takes," she says. Then, "We can afford it." I feel like objecting to that, but I don't. I have a feeling of being in this together. In cahoots. A different feeling than those I've had before. Whatever else is true, we are partners in this. There is no help for it.

I agree to the number. Of course I agree. When I get off the phone, we search around until I find just the right photo of Imogen. And it's not that recent. She's accepting some kind of award maybe a couple of decades ago and she's looking starched and uncomfortable, like she'd rather be almost anywhere else. Even so, the hair is the same as are the basic contours of her face. The photo will do and I send it off.

"It'll be me as I was," she says approvingly after the deed is done. "I like that. You're not impersonating me now, but me then. It's kind of perfect. Okay: that's done. Now wardrobe."

I feel I don't have whatever is left in me to do this, but I go along. I get a sense of Imogen as a force of nature; a force beyond. Even with her in a somewhat weakened condition, I can't say no to her about anything. It's as though, when it comes to her, my will has ceased to exist. I ponder that distantly as we go through her clothes. Sometimes, as we sketch out all of these plans, it feels as though we are friends. At others, she can seem suddenly imperious and demanding, though I question those impressions. How can it be she is so warm and kind at one moment, then she says something sharp or stern directly after? I question myself at those times: Did

I hear what I thought I heard? Or are those sharp, stern moments a reflection of my own past?

I find myself responding to her emotionally in almost the same way I would have with my mother. It's an odd sensation. Like falling, with no hope of my feet touching down.

Even partly distracted by emotional tennis, going through Imogen's wardrobe is like taking a museum tour. A good one. Somehow Imogen has managed to keep clothing from the last four decades. I find that difficult to imagine: a life that includes forty-year-old clothes. Some older, even, than that.

In my own life—when I had such a thing—I had a policy of getting rid of anything I hadn't worn for over a year. But this vast array of clothing? It seems likely that plenty of the things she and I look over hadn't had a glance in a couple of decades. More.

In the primary suite outside of her huge walk-in closet, Imogen appraises me.

"I've grown, see? There was a time I was as teeny as you." A hesitation while she looks me over. "Maybe even teenier."

"Oh-kay," I say, noncommittal.

That primary suite moniker denotes space rather than grandeur. Even here, in Imogen's private sanctum, the decor is more homespun than high tech or old money. There is a handmade quilt on the bed, and a strong scent of cinnamon on the air. The room is large and airy; the walls whitewashed adobe with small, high windows that let in bright swaths of light. There is a warmth here. And a welcome. This is what home feels like, I muse, as I observe the golden light that spills in from above.

"We'll find you something just perfect for this shindig."

That word again.

"Okay," I say once more.

"We will. For sure. We'll find something perfect." Maybe she's sensing the end of my patience is near.

"I'm not sure perfection is quite necessary," I observe.

"Still," she says again, and then begins.

There are a couple of false starts, and then she does, indeed, find perfection. Or, at least, as close to it all as we need to be for this gig.

Imogen emerges from the closet with a red dress in her arms and a look of excitement on her face. She indicates I should try on the dress, and when I do I find it fits closely through the shoulders and midsection, but flares around my legs, falling not quite to the floor.

"It's beautiful," I say, admiring my reflection in the old mirror on the back of the door.

"It looks beautiful on you," Imogen says, nodding. "I gotta figure it looks better on you than it ever looked on me."

"I'll be the belle of the ball," I say, twirling slightly and enjoying the feeling of the soft fabric against my legs.

"That's kinda the point," she says wryly. "I'm glad we found someone pro-y for the hair and makeup. You're going to look perfect."

"Pro-y?"

"You know: professional. She's gonna have her work cut out for her, but also not, because you actually look quite a bit like me."

"I do?"

"Yeah. You probably can't see it so easily because I'm old." She must observe something on my face because she laughs and holds up her hand. "No offense taken or given. But if you'd seen me all those years ago you'd be able to spot it, I think. Well here, hang on. I'll show you a picture."

Imogen goes to her desk and pulls out an album; one I hadn't noticed before. I feel like maybe it hadn't been opened in a while either; like dust should appear in a burst when she cracks the book, though none does.

She flips through the pages quickly, clearly something in mind. She makes small noises as the pages flip. Articulations of recognition. A small chortle here. A little grunt of pleasure there. All barely discernable, but I feel as though maybe I've already schooled myself to feel the nuances of her moods.

After a while she stops flipping pages and there she is. The photo is black and white but I have a sense of a colorful kaftan draping her then-slim form elegantly.

"I could still wear it now, sure," she says. "It's loose, right? But it would look as though I need to be in a compound."

I look at her quizzically and she continues.

"You know: a tent. Or maybe a zoo."

I laugh at her poorly executed humor.

"Right," I say wryly. "I don't think so."

"But you," she says. "I think it will look well on your cute little form. I always thought that dress was sufficiently artful, you know?"

"Dramatic?" I offer.

"Yeah. Something like that. And I *knew* it would be perfect. You look every inch the painter queen."

I laugh at this description of herself, because clearly that was what it was. I was to play her, that was the thing. The Painter Queen. More than I'd signed up for at the beginning certainly, when I hadn't signed up for anything at all. But now that it was here, it was well within the bounds of what I felt I could do.

I wrap my hand around some of the smooth fabric of the dress I'm still wearing and mutter, "They'll notice." She won't think she's hearing a question, I reflect, when I weigh the sound of it. But I know that it is.

"Notice what?"

"That I'm not you."

"No, they won't," she replies. "Not once we're done with you. You look younger than I do, of course. You are! But we can do things with that, I think. Makeup, et cetera. Hair. And I haven't seen any of the people you might encounter for a long time."

"How long?" I want to know.

"Decades," she says after thinking. "At least. We'll only have to get it close."

"I'm as worried about the conversation as anything. Like, what will I say?"

"You're a painter," she says solidly. "You'll know what to say. You'll be fine."

"I'm not a painter," I reply.

"You might not think so," she said, "but you are. I've seen your work, remember? And I've seen it evolve."

"*Your* work," I say.

"Your own, too. Whatever else you think you are, you're that, as well. You can resist the idea if you like, but it won't change the fact."

I stop arguing—even if I don't fully believe it, it is clear that *she* does. Maybe that's all that matters.

"We told Beardsley we don't want the press there but, knowing him, it's possible there will be some anyway. He's kind of a bugger that way. Sneaky."

"I'll be undone if that happens." I'm trying to keep my voice calm. Trying to keep myself from panicking. "I don't know how to handle the press."

"You won't be undone," she insists. "You'll take it in stride. I'm confident of that. Painter queen, remember? Plus, it's well known how I never wanted pictures taken, of me or the work. It's not unthinkable that it will be remembered and remarked upon. That I don't like press. And hopefully that memory is respected."

"Why don't you like the press?"

"Honestly? I was just being... I don't know, uppity at the time? Doing it because I could. I thought it added mystique. I never thought it might actually come in handy."

Though in many ways life continues as it had before plans for me going to the City came up, everything is different now. I listen carefully when Imogen speaks, not just to the words but to the way she says them: her tone and her diction. I observe the way she talks about art: her own and others'. And even her opinions on everything I can glean. Can I be an authentic her? I have my doubts, but she lends me her confidence in me. Sometimes I even believe it.

"See, you won't have to go all in on the physical stuff. Truly, I was a whole lot younger when I stopped going to all of their functions."

"Twenty years, you said."

"Right." We are in the studio, late afternoon sunlight slanting in through the skylights to illuminate our painting space. "And twenty years ago, the old arthritis hadn't kicked in quite so hard as it has by now. I always had a bit of a bum knee, so if you can remember a small limp on the left, it wouldn't hurt anything."

"Left knee. Okay."

"But if you forget, it won't be a big deal. People notice so much less than we think."

"They're so busy with their own stuff," I recite.

"Yeah. They're so busy thinking about what *you* might think of them, they mostly don't pay much attention to the details about others."

"I'm not sure that's true," I say, thinking.

"Well, it is," she tells me. "Oh, they might *see* you, but they won't bother seeing the whole you. And the details? Forget it."

Somehow the thought of all of that depresses me: that people might see you, but never really look at you. That we are all so pre-occupied with our own little lives that we often find it difficult to be present in the here and now. And though I've never noticed this myself, when she says the words, they resonate. This *is* how people are. This is what they do. Sometimes even me. Maybe people *are* too busy with their own details to actually see others. Maybe we *will* be able to pull this off, after all.

On my way back to the casita, I get waylaid by a nightbird's call. It isn't calling to me, but I follow the sound anyway, finding myself at the pool where all thoughts of nightbirds disappear. It had been a hot day, but now it is a cool evening and it is dark, but there is reflected light from the moon and the buildings nearby. I want to resist the siren call of the beautiful water, but truly? I don't try very hard. I shed my shorts, my T-shirt, put my hair up in a scrunchie, but I leave on my bra and panties. It is unlikely that anyone will see, but I'd been raised a certain way, and it's not that I remember much of all of that, but swimming naked? No. I'd just as soon fly.

Once I slip into the water, though, all thoughts of any earthly restrictions are gone. The water is perfect. I don't remember what

amniotic fluid feels like, but I feel certain it is this weightless wonder of water. Floating in it, then slicing through it. I am a sea
creature. A mermaid. I am one with the water. It transports me.
In every way.

At first, I keep that scrunchie on: determined to keep my hair
dry. After a while, though, I wonder: Why? I pull off the scrunchie,
throw it in the direction of my clothes, and first push myself down,
down, down to the bottom of the pool, until my flat hand touches
the bottom and I kick, kick, kick as I move myself along.

When I realize I will soon need to breathe, I pull myself into
a crouch, then push myself off the bottom of the pool, my legs
pistoning below me, and propelling me upward with more force
than I had thought possible.

I break the surface of the pool, gasping for air, but it is a beautiful, triumphant gasp. It's not that I've accomplished anything,
but I feel as though I've won, though I don't know what. For a
while, I float on my back, watching the rise of the moon, and the
dark outlines of the clouds that I'm surprised to even be able to
see. I do a few laps for no other reason than to feel my limbs glide
through the warm water. I feel strong and well and *grateful*. I feel
lucky to even realize how lucky I am.

"If you were to arc your arm over your head when you reach,
like so?" The voice has surprised me. Imogen is standing poolside,
and she's demonstrating the move she is describing. I wonder how
long she has been there. Long enough, I bet. And my cheeks red-
den, even though I'm not sure why. "If you were to do that," she
continues, "you'd have much more power."

"Excuse me?"

And it isn't that I haven't heard. I've heard every word. It's just
that I can't believe my ears.

"Your stroke, dear. It could be stronger?"

"Why?" I say, pulling myself from the water, feeling actually naked, without a towel or a plan. I should have given the swim more thought. I'm regretting my impulse now.

"Why? Well, you want the strongest stroke, don't you?"

"For what?"

She looks at me for a moment, though it's dark enough I can't read her face. I only know I don't like her tone. And I don't like what the words say about her or about me.

"For what?" she echoes again. "Well, to be the best, of course. One must always strive to be the best." There is a piousness in her voice now. I wonder if she can hear it. A tone that belongs in a pulpit, not next to a pool.

"Maybe I don't care to be the best." I am facing her squarely now, wondering where all of this has come from and what we are talking about, because I have the feeling we're way beyond my swimming stroke.

"Don't be an idiot." Her voice feels like a lash. "Don't be a foolish little girl. What is there but to be the best? If one isn't aiming for that, why bother at all?"

The words have been delivered calmly. Too calm, I suspect. There is ice in them now, not heat, and I sense a rage so deep I can't even begin to understand it. Maybe she can't, either, because when I don't say anything, she doesn't either, just turns as nimbly as she can, and starts moving back toward the house.

After she's gone and stillness has returned to the night, I discover that I'm angry. I'm not even sure why, though in a way I do. The feeling is so familiar. Love and warmth and then an unexpected shift and everything is cold. Once again, I realize it all feels like home, but now in a completely different way.

CHAPTER TWENTY

When I wake, I find I am still hurt and angry. And, again, I'm not sure why. What did she say to me, really? She gave me a swimming tip. In one way, I suspect I am being too sensitive. In another I still feel as though I'm not quite sure what has occurred.

In the kitchen, Imogen is as bright and golden as I've ever seen her and I am perplexed.

"Good morning, sweetheart," she says with even more than her typical warmth. "How did you sleep?"

I look at her closely. Does she actually think nothing occurred between us? Or that she can just pretend it did not?

"Fine," I say, aware that my voice is flat. "I slept fine."

"Oh, that's good. Because I was hoping that, after breakfast, we could skip work for a bit and go for a walk."

"A walk," I repeat.

"Yes. You know, I'm not always so confident these days about getting around the place. And I wanted to walk out and see the cats. Maybe see the horses."

"Not so confident." I can tell my voice is too quiet. I always recognize when it does that.

"Well, you know. You've seen."

"You're saying something."

She smiles as she continues, but the smile does not reach her eyes.

"I feel as though I can *almost* grasp your meaning."

"Almost."

"Yes. But not quite."

"Ah."

"Ah?"

"Never mind. The cats, right? You said you wanted to see the cats?"

And she smiles and I can see the schoolgirl she must once have been, all eager grins and enthusiasm, and I shrug inwardly and let it go, because what does it matter, anyway?

And so we walk. And we see the cats. And whatever tension was between us disappears in a companionable half hour where I find myself asking: What had really happened, anyway? It must have been my imagination or, at least, it must have been me being more sensitive than maybe I should have been.

The following days are gentle, as well. We spend the time left to us before my trip to the City in what has become for us the most basic ways. We have meals together. Simple food I prepare. We go for short walks, see the horses and the cats when we can—her special joy—or we walk through the garden Chester tends so carefully. Sometimes we say hello to him, even bring him a sandwich or some lemonade if the day is hot. On these occasions, Chester avoids my eyes. Phil always follows us on these walks, for protection or companionship I can't be sure. Maybe for both.

Most of the time, though, we're in the studio. I wonder openly at the magic I see growing on the big canvases: she likes working on three pieces at once, allowing one to dry while moving to the next, our activities described by the rules of both nature and art.

"The work goes well," she says one day directly after we come back from our break for lunch. We stand at the center of the studio space, canvases on all three walls and with the big garage-style door open to the air. "I'm very pleased. None of this would have been possible without you."

I start to protest, but I can't: maybe anticipating my protestations, she's said it and then headed it off.

"No, no, no. It's true. You saw what I was doing before. Tiny, silly things. Half-assed things. None of the grandeur of my earlier work. But this? This is me now. I'm even getting close to some of what my heart has been telling me to move toward. And it's all because of you. I can't even tell you how grateful I am."

I continue to shoo away her words, but I recognize some truth in them, too, and am grateful that she took the time to say them. The work is larger now, sure. But also, it is richer and I felt like there was a layer that was coming just from me. Difficult to define, but present nonetheless. So I am grateful, too. And my heart warms under all of it.

My heart warms.

CHAPTER TWENTY-ONE

ON THE DAY I'm to leave for New York City, Imogen drives me to the airport. I worry about it a bit, but she insists. "I still have that much inside me. At least."

"It's dangerous, though, right? Strictly speaking, you don't have a driver's license."

"But I do," she insists. "It's right inside my purse."

"Not really," I remind her. "When I used your ID to get your license, it became mine."

"Hogwash," she says pleasantly, eyes never leaving the road. "A technicality."

"I mean . . . okay. But . . . yeah. Never mind." She had insisted I use her birth certificate to get a driver's license. I had gone along and, truthfully, I would not be able to fly without it. For domestic travel, it's pretty much the minimum required ID. None of any of it is legal, I am as clear on that as I am about anything. So why should I fuss if she insists on driving? Especially since, despite her age and apparent infirmities, she handles the car and the road just fine. I pipe down.

While we drive, I put on my crappy wig. If nothing else, it disguises me from anyone who might potentially recognize me. I don't think I look like Imogen O'Brien, but I don't quite look like me, either.

"Keep your head down," she says to me inexplicably when she drops me off. "Keep your head down and watch your back." And I think her voice sounds more stern than it needs to. There is a harsh edge to it; maybe a note I haven't heard before. Is it worry? Or something else?

"Oh-kay," I say, not quite sure what to make of her tone.

"I mean it," and she sounds more herself now as I try to listen for whatever she might be trying to tell me beyond the words. "The City is full of snakes. Beardsley Davenport has proven himself to be a champion among them. Watch your damn back and come home safe and sound." And with that she gets back into the SUV and fires off toward the freeway.

As I move through the airport, I think about her words; try to make sense of them. But between ticketing and TSA security they get knocked out of my mind as I deal with all of the indignities of modern airline travel.

The flight itself is uneventful. I sleep and read and eat my tiny bag of nuts when they're offered and soon I'm there.

As always when I am in New York City, I feel both smaller and larger at the same time. To be part of all of this teeming humanity and, alternately and at other moments, to feel alien and alone. Somehow both things are true.

I try to remember the last time I was here. I know it was a hit. I had been someone else then. Someone angrier and more determined. When I try to think back now, it seems like I'm holding someone else's memories, or at least another life. And certainly my business was different then. I put it all out of my mind, deciding that it is best left behind.

Imogen booked me into a place in midtown—not a hotel I've been to before. It is low-key elegant: boutique and bohemian with walls washed a white the color of a Grecian villa, and furniture that manages to be both stylish and easy. I can see the hotel would have suited her perfectly, back in the day. And it suits me well now, too. The new me. A painter? I'm not quite ready to accept the designation, but the more mindful, perhaps more peaceful, me could spend a few serene days at this hotel.

"It's wonderful to have you staying with us again, Miss O'Brien," the desk clerk says. My head goes up in alarm at this, but when I look at him I realize the comment was based on Imogen's long-standing relationship with the hotel, not from possibly having seen him before. The kid looks like he would have been in diapers the last time Imogen visited.

"Thank you," I say, conscious that my makeup isn't done yet and the crappy wig I am wearing doesn't fit me at all well. If the kid notices any of this, he doesn't say anything. I realize it is part of his job to barely notice things. Boutique hotels don't stay sleek and well booked when they have indiscreet staff around.

My room is spacious and airy, with a view of Central Park and a bathroom and walk-in closet each as large as most people's bedroom. I breathe the perfectly filtered air and think about my future. For the first time in maybe ever, or at least since all of my tragedy, I get a sense that I might have one.

The thought buoys me, gives me a sense of possibility, and suddenly I just want to get out and stretch and explore. Once I hit the pavement on 58th Street, I discover that it's warmer out than I'd anticipated and I'm not far into my walk before my head starts to itch. I look around and see maybe a million people but none of them appear to be looking at me at all. As Imogen had said: everyone is entirely concerned with their own thoughts, their devices, or maybe they're thinking about what everyone else is thinking about them: they're not thinking about me.

In a sea of anonymity, I peel off the wig and stuff it into my bag. Right away the air assaults my naked scalp and it feels so good I hadn't even noticed how awful the wig felt: a restriction I wasn't even aware of. And how much of life is just like that?

With a light wind playing with my hair and cooling my scalp, I march determinedly toward the park from Columbus Circle. In the park, I walk up past the zoo, without actually going near it. I travel past the boathouses and up Cedar Hill. I'm just marching happily, with all thoughts of tomorrow and the challenges I'll face pushed aside, just enjoying—for once—these amazing sights and digging the feeling of knowing that no one will have to die tomorrow, at least not by my hand.

In Arizona I had found that walking in the desert in the warm season is a challenge and even potentially dangerous. If you were to get lost and are not carrying a phone and water, you could *die*. Like, actually die. In the City, that is not the case. If you wander too far, you can always call an Uber, or spend half an hour recovering at a café or a bar. As a result, in some ways I feel more free walking in the City, even though there are so many people around. They're all doing their own things, and so I don't see them and they don't see me. Everything is perfect, and I begin to enjoy the feeling of my muscles uncoiling after a long flight, the sights and sounds and smells of the City welcoming me back.

And then, out of the blue, I feel out of sorts. As though, like they say, someone has walked on my grave. That goose again. Goose bumps. A goose has walked on my grave? That feeling again. A few minutes pass and I can't shake it.

I stop. Look around. But there's nothing to see. More people, everywhere people. But I see none of them looking at me.

I keep walking, but now I'm more circumspect. The whole goose thing. I skirt the Reservoir cautiously. Joggers pass me at lightspeed, dogs sniff at my heels and each other's butts. Kids run too fast, nannies on their heels, and sometimes the nannies are screeching. But none of it has anything to do with me.

At one point I stop so suddenly and whirl around so quickly that a jogger nearly runs into me, but that's the only view I get: I don't see anyone following me, other than someone who should have been watching where she was going. Her tight, bright red running outfit heaves faintly with embarrassment at her faux pas, and she apologizes then continues her run in a sweaty and apologetic cloud of red Spandex.

I keep going, but the goose-on-grave feeling persists. I don't feel unsafe but I *do* feel as though the time for not listening to my instincts has passed. It's one of the ways in which I've managed to stay alive and active in a field that doesn't promote great health. I have a feeling toward self-preservation, and so I go.

Looking for a place to just stop and observe, I take a path off the main one. It's not far off course, and there's even a convenient tree for me to crouch behind. From there I can see the path. I watch. And I wait. Thankfully, it doesn't take long.

"Dallyce!" I shout when I recognize him. He looks just the same. Maybe a little thicker. And maybe it's a new ballcap jammed onto thick locks, but other than that and against all odds, I'm certain it's the same guy that followed and found me a while back in impossible circumstances.

I'm surprised that part of me is happy to see the PI, but the other part—the larger one, I think—is just plain annoyed.

When he hears his name, he stops in his tracks, and for about ten seconds, he looks as though he might bolt and run. Standing in that way, he reminds me of a beefy and behatted deer that's been hemmed in. But he doesn't bolt. I see him collect himself, and perhaps his wits. When he recognizes me, he has the good grace to look sheepish and cornered, both of which I think are appropriate under the circumstances.

"Oh geez," he says, pulling off the cap and running his fingers through thick auburn hair.

I break the awkwardness with a query. "Have you been following me this whole time?"

"What whole time?"

I reformulate the prompt, even though Dallyce's intelligence is not artificial. "How long have you been following me?"

He shuffles his feet uncomfortably and I wonder—and not for the first time—how he's been as successful as he has in his line of work. Then I remind myself: He's here, isn't he? How many others have ever tracked me down? Pretty much none. And he just seems to keep doing it.

"Not so long," he says, examining his shoes. They are Air Jordans, possibly vintage or maybe a recent reproduction. Either way, I know they're expensive kicks and tailing me on several occasions has paid for at least part of them. Not from my stash, but my brother's.

"Since Phoenix Sky Harbor?" I ask, naming the airport that got me out of Arizona.

"What?" He looks bewildered, and I realize instantly that I was far off the mark. "No. I was at a café at 58th and Columbus Circle. Saw you stroll by."

"Did I have gray hair?"

"What?" If he was expecting an answer I disappoint him and he goes on. "No. It was just . . . you. Right away. I recognized you."

"So it was a coincidence?" I'm pretty sure the disbelief must be raw on my face.

"I guess. Not even that."

"What the hell are you doing here?"

"In New York?"

"Yeah."

"It's nothing to do with you."

"Are you certain?"

"Yeah," he says again.

"Then why are you following me?"

"I told you: I saw you."

"Couldn't you just shout out like a normal person?"

He cracks a grin for the first time in this exchange.

"Would you have stopped?"

"Probably not."

"There you go."

I'm about to question him further, but he pulls himself up, dives back.

"I wasn't looking for you when I saw you, but only because I didn't know where to look. The trail had gone cold."

This much, at least, I knew to be true. I'd worked hard on that cold trail.

There's a bench nearby and I lead him there.

"So you see me and start following me in the largest city in the world," I say once we're seated. I'm not sure how skeptical my voice sounds, but I feel pretty skeptical.

"Eleventh."

"What?"

"You said the largest city in the world. New York City is the eleventh largest city in the world."

"Really?"

"Yuh. Would I make up eleventh?"

"It *does* seem pretty specific. But eleventh? I mean . . . that's not even top three."

He kinda grins at that.

"You're right about that. Eleventh is not in the top three."

"That's very difficult to believe."

"What's difficult to believe? That New York is eleventh largest or that I found you in it?"

"Both of those things, actually."

"It's true. But also wild. When I saw you, I couldn't even believe it myself. I left a perfectly good pain au chocolat behind when I set off after you."

"Sorry about that," I say, even though I'm pretty sure I'm not sorry.

"No worries."

"Now what?"

He shrugs. "Your brother is looking for you," he says again. "What can I tell him?"

"I'm busy," I say. "Now. But I'll call him. Maybe in a few days."

"He needs to see you."

"He *always* needs to see me."

"Can we set a date?"

"For me to go home? No. I don't even . . . I don't even know if I want to."

"Can I at least tell him you'll call?"

"*You're* the one who told me what he'd done. You more than anyone would know why I don't want to see him."

"It wasn't conclusive that he had any bad intent. We discussed that."

"He had me declared dead."

"In the context of everything else, I can see how that would have made sense. The insurance on you, though. That was your late husband."

Dallyce saying those words—"late husband"—somehow conjures a face. A name. We'd been in love once, whatever that means. We'd shared everything until there was nothing left to share. Our marriage was dead long before my son and he followed. But maybe, Dallyce had told me a while ago, I had been the target all along.

It's a funny old life.

"I don't want to see him, okay?"

"It'll be different this time."

"Why?"

"You have nothing left to lose." Dallyce's gaze is cool and blue. He doesn't have any skin in this game, beyond finding me. And when I think about it, he's right. Whatever I'd once been protecting is gone. And he is right about something else, too: everything I was once protecting has been lost.

"I'll call you, okay? Next week. I'm busy here. Now. I'll be home in a few days. I'll call you then and we'll see if we can figure something out."

I can tell he doesn't love this suggestion; he'd like something more concrete, but it's all I'm offering, so he takes it.

"All right," he says begrudgingly. "I'll tell him I made contact." Which would mean a payday, so fair enough. "Best if you give me your phone number . . ."

"No, that's okay. But I'll take your business card again. My old phone got . . . er . . . lost. I don't have your number anymore."

He fishes a business card out of his phone case, keeping his eyes on me while he does it. It's like he thinks I might vanish if he doesn't pay attention; like he's looking at a feral cat.

"Next week, right?"

"Right. But listen: Was it really just a coincidence you saw me?"

"Good and pure," he says.

"You do always have the best luck," I say.

He nods and smiles that smile that I've seen light up a room. "It's true," he says over his shoulder as he starts to walk away. "That's why I'm pretty sure I'll hear from you next week."

CHAPTER TWENTY-TWO

In the morning I don't even risk going outside. Not on this day. I ran into Dallyce the day before—who else might be out there? Lurking. There is a whole eleventh-largest-city-in-the-world of people out there, just waiting to run into me. I decide against taking the chance. I realize that's a bit crazy, but at this point I don't care.

I order room service. A poached egg. Orange juice. Toast. Like something you only get on vacation. I feel so much like going outside, walking the City, something I've always loved, but I just don't even want to risk it. So I spend the first part of the day inside, feeling miserable and—yes—even a little afraid. When it's finally time for my big appointment, I put on the red dress and descend, asking the doorman to call me a cab.

When I arrive at Jennifer K. Riley's studio, I am pasty faced with anxiety. My palms are damp. Neither thing is a good sign.

Riley herself is a cool blonde with a perfect complexion though, considering her business, I have no idea if that perfection is natural or something she slathered on. *Two hours for the natural look.* Either way, she is stunning.

"Huh," Riley says when she sees me, contorting her face into a mindful grimace. She takes a half pace to her left, and then again to her right, never taking her eyes off me. And then again, "Huh." I'm not clear on the translation, but it's not making me feel super-confident.

"Nice to meetcha," I say, my voice toneless.

"You sent me the photo," she says. I can't tell what she's thinking. Will this be a challenge? Or a walk in the park? Is she curious? Did she recognize Imogen in the photo I sent? I don't have a clue about any of it. She's a pro, I get that. Maybe she doesn't care about who we are. Just a job to get done. I hope it's that.

"Yes," I answer, though she hasn't asked a question. "How big a challenge will it be?"

"All in a day's work," she says, cracking something that I recognize as the first smile she's sent my way. Humor. I'm not quite sure what it means. I shoot the smile back, then follow her down another hallway.

Jennifer's office is in her apartment, chic and professional.

"That's a lovely dress," she says over her shoulder as she leads me down the book-lined hallway.

"Thanks," I say, not adding any of the things that I could say that would probably interest her. That it is vintage. That the woman who wore it was one of the top artists in the world, and that she'd worn it at the height of her life and career. I don't say any of that, just keep my yap shut until we come to a large, bright room. I imagine in a previous incarnation this might have been the apartment's living room. Now it is a well-equipped salon and studio. I am surprised to see two attractive young women standing by. Assistants? Whatever the case, when I enter the room, they eye me appraisingly. The red dress. The shitty gray wig. Probably a whole bunch of other things I can't even guess at: things their expert eyes see that are invisible to mine. Whatever the case, I feel naked under their collective glances. And probably rightly so. I figure that right then they are remaking me in their minds. And I find I am ready to be remade.

The scrutiny of the trio is so close it is nearly painful. I feel a bit like meat.

As they escort me to a salon chair at the center of the studio space, I force myself to breathe while I lean into the process. I figure most of the time—people get a makeover, they're trying to look younger, not older. This was going to be a bit of a howl for everyone, whether they show it on their faces or not.

I shouldn't be surprised—though somehow I am—to see that Jennifer K. Riley is displaying the images I had sent her on a couple of monitors. Here is who I am, in person. There is who I am paying them to make me into.

"We are in luck," Jennifer K. Riley says thoughtfully, her eyes sliding from the photos on the monitor to me and back again. "You have a similar bone structure. Are you related?"

I shake my head in the negative.

"Uncanny. Well, whatever the reason, it should mean our work is not as challenging as it might have been."

And then there are no more words for a while, but there is a signal I don't see because the magicians spring to life. I lean into it. Close my eyes. Contemplate where all of this will lead.

CHAPTER TWENTY-THREE

THE CONCIERGE CALLS up. My limo has arrived. I descend in the elevator feeling like so much Cinderella heading for that much of a ball.

I don't ask where the limo came from. I don't need to. Beardsley. Imogen had warned me that was his kind of style.

"He'll do things, okay?"

"Okay."

"Little things. Big. He'll be wanting to impress you with his largesse. With his thoughtfulness. With whatever. Just keep your wits about you, girl."

"I will. I shall." I say it with a lilt. I'm making light. It's a shared joke.

"See that you do," she says, and there is no lightness in her response

The limo is an Alfa Romeo the color of lipstick. And I ponder, as we meander a short distance that I could have traveled faster on foot, without Imogen's limp or shoes, I ponder that an Alfa Romeo is a certain kind of choice. With an Alfa you are saying: "Yes, I have a ton of money. In fact, I have so much money, I don't even care if it breaks down."

In the interminable ride in the back of the lipstick red limo, I feel every inch the painter queen I have set out to imitate. And moving from the car to the gallery, I sense that the masquerade will be successful: heads turn, and then keep floating past me. To those watching on the street, I'm just a well-turned-out old broad: nothing to see here. I've accomplished exactly what I set out to do. The only thing that remains now is seeing if all of it holds with people who know her.

The Beardsley Davenport Gallery on Wooster Street proves to be exactly as I'd imagined it would be. This, in part, because I'd looked it over on Google maps before I arrive. The photos the gallery, customers, and other visitors have posted have made the space familiar to me. Seeing it, it seems like I've been here before. Only in person it's bigger than expected.

You can never go back?

It is more spacious, less intimate, and there is lots of room for the giant canvases Imogen was known for. *My* canvases, I remind myself as I look around. For tonight, at least, I have to remember that. This is my work. I shake my head at the enormity of that. I am a star. So all right. Move forward. Carry on.

For all that is unexpected, though, one thing at least is exactly as I'd thought it would be: it is a chic and carefully considered space. The concrete walls and floors give the impression of a very elegant and expensive cave. The only relief from austerity are the bright colors reflected from Imogen's huge canvases. They are everywhere. I try not to feel the delight of that but am unsuccessful. Even though they aren't actually *my* canvases I feel a surge of pride and ownership as I move through the gallery, almost wanting to strut but remembering to favor my left leg. And then I remind myself:

they *are* my canvases. All right then. I hold my head up higher and fix the idea in my heart.

"Imogen!"

I turn and know instinctively that this is Beardsley, and if it isn't, it should be. His hair is thick and silver, and it sweeps back from his forehead with a dramatic plunge. Everything about him is drama, not just his hair. From the delicate pinstripe in his perfectly cut brown suit to the shine on his oxford shoes and the crease in his pants. *Dapper.* That's the word that comes to mind.

"Imogen," he says again, "I'm so glad you made it."

I think I detect a note of relief in his voice, buried in there with the fawning. Had he been thinking all along that Imogen was never going to show up? And here preparations are in full swing for some type of event, and had he been dealing with the possibility that the guest of honor would be a no-show and maybe he'd have egg on his face? I look over at the canapes, some of them topped with caviar. *Expensive* egg on his face.

I feel some relief. There is no hesitation in his recognition. He looks at me and sees what he was expecting. For my part, though, Beardsley is not at all what I had been expecting, though I'm not sure why. He is tall and moves like someone who spends a lot of time at the gym. With all of that effort, he moves with the ease of a man much younger than the more than seventy years he's seen. I don't know quite what to make of him yet: this man who guided Imogen's career for many years but whom she had found it necessary to cut from her life. The whole picture isn't adding up. Yet. I wonder if I'll be able to connect all the dots. This meeting tonight would probably help with that.

"Yes, here I am." I pitch my voice low. That had been in my plan. I was reasoning he'd be less likely to doubt my voice if he is constantly straining to hear.

He air kisses both of my cheeks in the French style.

"Imogen! You look fantastic!"

"Thank you. You look pretty good yourself."

"Still standing," he jokes in a way that makes me understand there had never been any doubt. Keeping standing was what he is expert at. I knew I'd have to keep my eye on him.

"Everything looks very good," I say, indicating a large canvas. "I haven't seen *The Cherries* in a while. It's good to see it again."

The Cherries dominates one whole part of the gallery. I'd seen it in books: one of Imogen's more famous works. Imogen is widely associated with the image, but it is very different seeing it in person. The majesty. The exotica. Just cherries. And yet.

I could see him brighten at the mention, maybe due to the fact that I hadn't gotten right down to what had separated the artist from her agent. Maybe he is thinking we can get right back to our previous relationship, whatever that had been. And he might not be wrong. Oh, certainly: there is going to need to be some sort of reevaluation of the business end of things but, for tonight anyway, things can be business as it was before whatever break they had.

"Do you remember that summer, Imo?" he asks. "The summer of *The Cherries*?"

"Don't call me 'Imo.'" I say it sternly, but without a lot of sharp. Imogen had coached me.

"All right," he says, and I can see him eyeing me warily. "Some things don't change. But do you recall?"

"I do," I say, hoping he doesn't press further. He doesn't, switching his enthusiasm to the reason this famous painting is in his gallery now and I breathe, feeling as though I'd dodged a bullet. Because, of course, I have no idea. Fake it until you make it? Well, something like that. And also more. But fake it in any case.

"Oh, I got so lucky on that one, Imogen," he says of *The Cherries*. He straightens his already perfectly straight tie as he speaks. It is almost the same brown as his suit, a wave of tiny silver *fleur de lis* barely discernible in the background. They match the pinstriping, which speaks to me of details. Of follow-through. You don't have your shirt perfectly match your suit without some foresight. "When the owner of the piece called wanting to sell, I jumped at the chance."

"No Sotheby's? No Christie's?" I sniff, going for an imagined sleight.

"Well, certainly. They could have done. I told the owners I would be able to get them more money. Though not overnight. And now you're here." I could feel glee radiate from him and I realized this was not the first time in my life I'd come across someone in this business just like him. The first person I'd ever killed, on purpose. Long ago now. My first contract hit. He had been someone very like this. The recollection and recognition didn't make me glow. The connection said nothing positive about either of them.

"Yes, yes," I say. "Now I'm here."

I scan the gallery, hoping not to hit any questions I can't answer. Imogen had coached me in that, as well.

"I've always been a bit prickly." She had smirked while she said it. "A desert cactus. If you hit anything you can't answer, don't panic. Just sniff like you're mad, then turn and walk away." She'd made an arthritic little pirouette and turned her back on me, stalking off a few paces before turning back quickly with a grin. "No one will be shocked or call you on it." She grinned and I could see that the pleasure she was taking in all of this was real. "They're used to that sort of behavior from me. They expect me to be a bitch. I wouldn't want to let them down."

"It's good to see it again." I was back to Beardsley now. And *The Cherries*. And the statement isn't a lie. There are reasons—many of them—for Imogen being one of the ranking artists of her generation. And it had been an important generation. It seems to me, also, that Beardsley would be expecting me to do something to reconnect us. Imogen had coached me in this, as well.

"Remind me, please, how we came to fall out."

He looks at me, and I can see he is surprised at the question. Maybe that I was broaching it now, here in this space. But it strikes me that it has to be brought up. That to just let it lie there like a sleeping dog is to beg for trouble.

"You know as well as I do," he says after a hesitation, and I see his head dip a bit this way and that, and I think he's checking who is near to us—who might overhear.

"I do," I say. "From your perspective then, please. How did it come to pass?"

"I only know what you told me," he says haltingly.

"Go on." I'm careful to keep my voice low, so no one can overhear. He moves closer to me. Close enough that I get a whiff of his scent. Something like tobacco and horseradish, though that can't be right.

"You said—let me see if I can get this right—you said you'd had enough of the bullshit—forgive the word, but it's what you said—and would I please leave you the eff alone."

"I said 'eff'?"

"You did not," he says primly, and I laugh, enjoying the game. "And that was the end of it?"

"Of course not. Oh, for crying out loud, Imogen," he says again, "you know as well as I do. Why are you putting me through this?"

"I want to hear it. From you. From your perspective."

"All right then. It's a long time ago now."

"Long," I agree.

"You were always difficult," and I think he says it a little testily.

"I was," I say, not disagreeing.

"Nothing was ever quite right. People asked too many questions. Reporters wanted to take your picture. It just never ended. And the money was never enough."

"It was never about the money, though. You knew that."

"Yeah. Sure I did. It became increasingly difficult to deal with. And it got worse as time went on."

"So we ended our relationship."

"That's one way to put it."

"But how did you still have enough work for a show? I hadn't given you anything new in years."

"It is known we are connected."

"Were."

"That's right. And people would come to me to sell. And buy." He chortles then. I like him for it. "I kept you in circulation. Kept your currency high."

"Thanks. I guess."

"People are beginning to arrive," Beardsley says needlessly. I can see that the small space is beginning to fill. "It would be best, perhaps, not to make a scene? We can talk more later."

"All right. Or soon. But it's good to see you. Good to be here."

"Thank you," he says. "I feel the same." And I get the idea he means it. Does he look at me curiously? Speculatively? Part of me thinks so. But part of me is jumping at shadows, so I'm not sure. My hope is that he wants so much to believe that he doesn't question; that he just takes what he sees at face value. But sometimes, and with certain people, one can't be sure what they're thinking. I suspect he is one of those.

As soon as Beardsley leaves my side, a young woman approaches me. She has a certain cold beauty. A cloud of softly curled hair frames her face. Her eyes are blue, icelike. She is used to getting what she wants. I can tell that right away.

"Miss O'Brien, hello. I'm Heidi Reed. *New Art Times*."

"Heidi, I'm sorry. I don't speak to journalists." I say it kindly, but it is a well-known fact. No need to hammer it home.

"Sorry. I'm not greeting you in an official capacity. I'm just such a huge fan."

I doubt the words. I can't imagine her being a fan of anyone or anything—she just has that air about her. Maybe she has fans, but I'm certain that she isn't one.

"Well, ummmm . . . thanks."

"I particularly love this *Dark Rose* series." While she says it, she guides me toward that part of the gallery. "I've always felt a strong connection to the work. I think it's inspired."

"That's lovely of you to say." I've uttered the words in a cautious way. I realize I'm in a jungle and wondering if I'm prey.

"What are you working on now?" She says it casually. Butter wouldn't melt, but I've sensed something in her demeanor and in the question. I have not in my life been in a position where anyone would ever work me for advantage. Even so, I recognize it when I see it. Right away.

"Various things," I say, meeting her eyes.

"So you are still working? Some people have suggested you retired."

"I'm a painter," I say, feeling the truth of it surge up through my body, as though some electrical charge has entered through my feet. "I am a painter." I say it again, liking the way it feels vibrating through my chest. The vagal nerve? Something like that. Something indefinable, yet resolute. I feel it. "We don't retire. We die."

I smile at her. Sweet as pie. And I imagine in that moment that I am, indeed, Imogen O'Brien. I draw myself to my full height and I pirouette, just as Imogen demonstrated. I know right away I even got the scratchiness of the arthritis right. I do it so well, I wish that I could see myself. Or that Imogen could. I feel certain she'd be proud. That feels important somehow.

As I move away from Heidi Reed, I say over my shoulder, "I don't speak to journalists." And I recognize that my tone is frostier now.

Beardsley catches up with me almost instantly. I can see he's a little green around the gills.

"Is everything okay, Imogen?"

"Perfect," I say, aware that there is still some frost in my tone.

"She promised she wouldn't grill you."

"She broke her promise," I reply, wondering even while I say it if it's entirely true. Was that a grill? Whatever it was, it was not comfortable and I made it stop. No wonder Imogen had spent all those years avoiding reporters.

"I'm sorry about that. I'll have her removed."

I look at him fully then and can see he is waiting for me to protest; to tell him the removal won't be necessary.

"Thank you," I say, still looking so closely into his eyes that I can register the surprise when my words hit.

"I . . . uh . . . well, okay then. Excuse me," he says, leaving my side and heading for hers. I see some sort of low-key exchange, some of it heated, but barely. In the end she prepares to take her leave. She takes one last long glance back at me. I tip my fingertips toward my brow, a mock salute, and she turns away quickly enough that I get a whiff of rejection. I don't fight it, though. It is the perfect accompaniment.

"Happy?" Beardsley says as he rejoins me. His voice seems strained and I can't read his face.

"It's not a situation for happy," I say tersely. "She made me feel unsafe." I sound more severe than I intended, and that I'm exaggerating, but Imogen had been clear: the best way to gain and keep the upper hand was to not give in to the "energy of their bullshit," as Imogen had said. And I was feeling, like, so far, so good.

"Let me get you a glass of champagne." Beardsley is already moving away as he says it. I watch his back as he retreats, his shoulders set, his gait determined, as though facing up to something. I'll have to keep watching him closely.

It was by now a fairly full house, but I get the feeling it's maybe not going quite as Beardsley had hoped. If I was going to be curt with journalists, maybe there was some managing he needed to see to.

While I hover, waiting for the champagne to appear and pondering my next move, I spot a head of perfect hair and a familiar face across the crowd. It takes only a beat or two of my heart to identify Curtis Diamond, a West Coast newscaster I know almost as well as I know anyone in my post-hausfrau life. I can't imagine what he's doing here. Maybe covering the show. Maybe just attending an opening but, whatever the reason, I can't let him see me. I had dropped out of his life without reason and we had been better friends than that. In the time between I often thought of reaching out to him somehow, just to let him know I was okay, but I'd never been able to come up with the right words. And now here he is. The gallery is a bit of a warren, with intimate alcoves as well as open spaces. Between that and paintings suspended from the ceiling and hung back-to-back, there are plenty of routes to take if one wants to hide or get away. I push myself deep into the shadows, deep enough that I won't be easily found.

From my vantage point, basically hiding behind a couple of huge canvases, I can see that, not even an hour into the event, little red dots have already appeared on the description cards of many of the paintings: the universal symbol for a painting sold. I wonder if the evening thus far is meeting Beardsley's expectations, maybe even exceeding them. Certainly, the fact that Imogen's work still seems so much in demand must be reassuring for all concerned.

I see Beardsley reappear with my champagne; see him scan around for me, not find me; and ultimately settle into conversation with Curtis. I watch them closely and decide that, while the exchange is cordial, it is not necessarily friendly. It's clear they know each other, but they don't appear to be friends. I discover that I'm relieved, though I'm not quite sure why.

I watch them closely. In a few minutes Curtis excuses himself and I emerge from my hiding place. Almost right away, Beardsley spots me and appears directly at my elbow with my champagne. I sip it dully, lacking the palate or experience to know if it is good champagne, suspecting, despite its pink color, that it is. Beardsley doesn't seem the type to serve crap refreshments. We move through the crowd together, and I feel people register my presence, watch me. I see one tall, wiry lady poke her friend in the ribs with what appears to be a gallery catalog to get her attention. Her glance sweeps around, sees me, and her eyes widen. I nod politely, smile, and keep walking with Beardsley.

It's tough to know exactly what to do, who to be. What if someone else talks to me? And they will. I decide to go with distant and quiet. As though in answer to my thoughts, Beardsley goes right to that topic.

"There are a couple of people I'd like you to meet," Beardsley says. "Not journalists," he says, though it seems a weak joke. "Let me bring them to you," and he abandons me again. I move back, away from the throngs of people, finding another dark and quiet spot and discovering too late that the shadows I've pressed into are created by two back-to-back canvases. A couple of people are sheltered there. They are talking closely. It is dark enough in the space created that I can't make out any of the details of their features. My instinct would have pushed me back the way I'd come, but I inch closer instead, feeling an urge to listen where I shouldn't.

"But none of this is new work." The voice is masculine and filled with gravel. And I am not surprised when I don't recognize it.

"Did you hear there would be new work here?" I don't recognize the female voice, either. Not young, but polished with a boarding school accent.

"I didn't hear, but I guess I figured. I don't think Beardsley has worked with her in years."

"She's not dead, is she?"

"O'Brien? Of course not. She's not dead," the woman confirms. "You know she's supposed to come tonight?"

"To this event? No. I hadn't heard that. I'll believe it when I see it."

"So you still think she's dead? I'll tell you how you can tell she's not."

"Tell," he demands.

"If she were dead, the canvases here at the gallery would be priced three times as high."

"You think so?"

"That's always what happens when an artist at this level croaks."

"Millicent." There is admonishment in the tone, but mirth, as well. I feel myself bridle, but pull it back. They're just gossiping and guessing. They don't know anything at all. And, anyway, it isn't me they're talking about, I remind myself. And it's Imogen's fault anyway. If she hadn't wanted gossip, she shouldn't have left her fans high and dry. If you didn't want one, you had to do the other. All of this represents interest. And Imogen had not given them anything to feed it.

"I'm just telling it like it is, Skip."

"Maybe, but you don't have to sound as though you're craving it." This is Skip.

"I'm certainly not." I can tell she is trying to sound indignant, but getting nowhere near. "You know I have at least half a dozen canvases from the 1970s and '80s in my collection."

Skip lets out a low whistle and I move away, back into the main room. Practically careening into Beardsley who has an elegant young couple at his elbow. I look furtively around for Curtis and am relieved when I don't see him. Would he recognize me if he saw me? I doubt it. But I'm not taking any chances.

"Maddy and Sergai Anderson," Beardsley is saying, "I'm ever so pleased to present the artist."

"We're huge fans, Ms. O'Brien," says Sergai. Both of them are tall and handsome. Together they are the very portrait of young, affluent perfection. "*Huge.*"

"You are both so beautiful," I say almost before I can stop myself. Then I realize where it had come from: I was voicing it as Imogen, because it was certainly not something I ever would have said. I was in character now though, it seemed, and I didn't even know where it had come from. And I was surprised to discover that it felt okay.

Maddy blushed prettily at the compliment and Sergai half-bowed in delight or embarrassment, I couldn't tell which. Maybe both.

"Why, thank you, madam," Sergai says. "As my wife said, we are both very big fans of your work."

"We have two large canvases here at our home in New York," Maddy adds, "and your complete set of serigraphs from the 1980s at our place in Snowbird."

"Snowbird?"

"Utah."

"Of course," I say, not meaning it. "I should have known that."

"No, dear," Beardsley says and I wonder if he could see me bridle at that "dear." "Hardly anyone knows," and he throws a knowing look at the couple, "yet."

And in that exchange I see Beardsley's entire art. He'd managed to flatter both of us with less than six words. Not everyone can do that. Not everyone even tries.

"What we want to know is," Maddy says, a pulse jumping quietly at her delicate collarbone as though anticipating my reply. It is a heady feeling; this hanging on of my every word. You'd think it would be easy to get used to, but I'm thinking it's not going to go easy for me. "Can we expect any new work soon?"

I think quickly about how to answer. It is, after all, a fairly loaded question. And would Beardsley even want me to say if I were inclined to? Would it dampen the sale of current work if it was known there were new works coming? I scan around at all the red dots under paintings—so many red dots. By now, I'm having trouble finding a painting without an accompanying red dot. And that answers my question: it would seem that whether it was known or not wouldn't matter at all.

"There are new works, yes." I can almost feel Beardsley's intake of breath. I wonder that he hasn't asked me this himself, though we haven't yet had much time together. Or maybe he thinks this was a big enough ask: just getting me here. In a way, he isn't wrong.

"Many?" Beardsley's voice is thin. Stretched. He doesn't want to show his hand but I can see him holding his breath, waiting for my answer.

"Many is a relative term." I could have said that I could fill a warehouse with what Imogen had been up to all these years. But I didn't think anyone wanted to know that. And it wouldn't even be a tiny warehouse.

"More than ten?" he asks.

"Yes."

"Ah," Beardsley says noncommittedly.

It seems to me that Beardsley expands and then subsides. Whatever I'd hinted at, it was enough. And we both knew it.

"Another show soon, then?" This was Sergai.

"Perhaps," Beardsley says. "For now, though, can I bring you all more champagne?"

And he's offered to refill our glasses, essentially. But I have the idea that he's celebrating.

CHAPTER TWENTY-FOUR

THE REST OF the evening is more of this. A dog and pony show where maybe the pony wasn't even necessary. A nice accessory, but I am pretty sure Beardsley would have gotten it all done without me. All those red dots. After a while the people became interchangeable to me. Have I spoken with this one before? I'm sure I have, and then another wanders along and I wonder again.

Their sameness is a result of their desire, that's what I finally figure out. Whether or not they are buying, they've come for a piece of who they think I am. Imogen O'Brien, the icon, the legend. It turns out she's a rock star in the art world. I just had no idea.

I keep a steady beat on how much champagne I drink—enough but not too much—and try not to look *too* much like I just want to get the hell out of there, which I do almost from the time I arrive.

Meanwhile, through the entire rest of the evening I keep one eye out for Curtis. He's a seasoned investigative reporter. I'm pretty sure if he saw me and recognized me he wouldn't let on and he wouldn't give me away, but there would be questions, and I just don't feel like answering them. For one thing, I don't know what to say. But anyway, it seems unlikely he would recognize me. I figure

I'd barely recognize me if I saw myself. I don't feel like putting it to the test.

When I make my exit, the party is still in full swing, even though it is after the stated hour of the event's end. I walk out of the gallery into a velvety blue night and inhale the stale, cool city air. When I climb into the limo Beardsley has put at my disposal, I feel as though I've been released from some sort of trap. It was a successful evening for sure, but I don't think I've ever been happier to leave a place than that gallery on that night.

From the back of the Alfa, I look out the window, but I barely see what is passing: my mind is turned back to the hours I've just spent, to Beardsley and also to Curtis as well as several of the patrons of the art I had spoken with at the gallery. I feel the need to remember details, even though I'm not entirely sure why. And, other than Curtis, I don't feel there were any close calls. Everything, in retrospect, had gone well. If anyone had doubted Imogen's identity, they'd kept it to themselves. It went about as well as it could have, that's what I'm thinking now.

Back at the hotel, I peel off the layers of Imogen, putting the wig aside carefully for future use, even while knowing I'll never get to look exactly the way Jennifer K. Riley and her team had re-created me.

While I peel the clothes off, I run a bath, sinking into it gratefully once I've removed all of the Imogen bits: the heavier jowls, the pads of wrinkles, the beautiful red dress.

The bath gives me a few blessed moments of absolute peace while I try to integrate everything I'd absorbed throughout the evening. It's difficult. I'm not entirely sure why Imogen is making me do this, not really: preserving her legacy, she'd said. But there are other ways to do that.

After my bath I realize that, despite all of the elegant canapes around, I'd just had no appetite to eat at the gallery. And here I am in a first-class hotel with almost anything my heart could ever desire quite literally and actually at my fingertips. I call room service and order a bottle of wine and a grilled cheese sandwich—even though the menu calls it a fontina and pesto panini, I'm in the mood to call a spade a spade.

I recline on the beautiful bed, sparkles of city lights creeping into the room. I sip my wine—a nice little pinot—and just breathe. While I sip I watch some truly dumb and mindless TV. It's delightful. There is something with shopping carts and a grocery store and people running around . . . then cooking. Bizarre! Another where brides seem almost to compete to find the perfect dress for their wedding day. I can't comprehend any of it, but it feels so good and mindless. It feels like medicine, and I spend a peaceful hour—maybe two?—doing absolutely nothing of note; nothing productive.

There is so much unsettled in my life, sure. But these beautiful and simple things? Sometimes, it is just those small things that keep us moving forward. And somehow, even before I fall asleep, I feel refreshed.

The next day, I spend my last few hours in the city pushing aside my fear of being recognized. I stop looking over my shoulder, and I walk the streets and imprint what all of this feels like: visiting an important place when I had no one to kill. I'm a tourist and it feels delicious. Fresh. Without business on the horizon, I have a different relationship with everything. A freeness. I experience things in a whole new way, but I'm not sure what it means. A taste of what my life could be? A future without worry; without fear. Is that what completely embracing Imogen's idea could mean?

I start out by wandering the city aimlessly; a pleasurable meander through vaguely familiar streets. When I find myself in front of the Beardsley Davenport Gallery on Wooster Street, I am a little surprised: I didn't know I was going there, though having arrived, I imagine that some part of me knew exactly where I was headed. So much of my life has been that: pure instinct. It hasn't always served me well. Pure survival is possibly not the route to a happy life.

But here and now, outside the gallery, I am not in disguise: just me in joggers and a comfortable T-shirt, my own natural hair swept up in a ponytail, a purse over one shoulder: just any woman doing any shopping on any Friday morning ever conceived. And so I feel comfortable lingering nearby for a few minutes, enjoying being outside, looking in other shop windows while keeping one eye on a single shopfront.

Is it instinct? It might be instinct. Or maybe also pure blind luck, but after just a few minutes of watching Beardsley's gallery, I see the door open and a familiar cloud of dark hair pop out. It only takes me a second to recognize her: Heidi Reed. There are a million reasons the reporter might be at the gallery this day, or at least a half score, but my gut tells me it's something I want to know about; something I won't like.

Heidi stands outside the gallery for a few minutes, her package under her arm. She looks around like she's waiting for someone. Sneaking peeks, I can see from the way she is holding it that the package is something small and precious. Beyond that, I don't have a guess.

After a couple of minutes, I get the idea that I'll never know what's in the package because the Alfa pulls up—the same car Beardsley had me taken back to the hotel in the night before. The reporter steps into the Alfa gingerly and the limo spirits her away. And where is she going? I can't collect myself quickly enough to follow her, so there is no way I will ever find out.

CHAPTER TWENTY-FIVE

THE FOLLOWING MORNING, I head back to the desert. I fly home.

The man sitting next to me looks as though he should have bought two seats, but he only has one. He's painfully self-conscious about it though. He's in the center seat and he overflows both armrests and I feel him holding himself in and holding himself back. It's like he's a clam, and he's just gotten too big for this shell. His discomfort is so palpable it would be laughable if I weren't, also, so uncomfortable, albeit for different reasons. It makes me wish I could get him a new shell.

The trip goes by quickly. The flight crew cracks jokes over the PA like it's some kind of Vegas act and it strikes me that this is what America's airspace needs now: humor and goodwill, because so much else is just going to shit.

When we land, I take my phone out of airplane mode and the first thing that floats to me is a text from Imogen.

"Welcome home! I wasn't feeling well enough to make the drive. Sorry. I have a Turo rented for you in my name. It's in the East Economy Lot. Look for a black Camry in aisle Q across from R. The owner said there would be a lockbox on the passenger window with the key inside. Here's the code for the lockbox."

I quell the worry I feel and follow her instructions. After I retrieve my suitcase from baggage claim, I take the Phoenix Sky Train from the "friendliest airport in America" to the East Economy Lot, as instructed. The journey is easy, clean, and free, in fact the Skytrain feels like science fiction; like I'm trundling through the future, only the future is now.

Once I get there, I follow Imogen's instructions until I find the Camry with the lockbox exactly where she had been told it would be. The car is black, virtually new, and the lockbox opens as expected. I am on the road less than a half hour after I'd gotten Imogen's text. Not much longer than that and I am heading into the deep desert in the thickening twilight, a feeling that revives memories I thought had been put aside.

By the time I get back to Ocotillo Ranch, full darkness is on the world and I know Imogen will be in bed: I don't even have to check. I head straight for my little casita with expectations of falling directly to sleep.

I am just dragging my suitcase into the casita when I hear a scratching at the door. I figure out who it is and when I open the door, Phil joins me. He seems curious at first—almost like he's wondering who I am and keeping his distance—then with increasing enthusiasm when he realizes who the strange car had delivered home.

"Oh, old son," I croon, burying my hands in the dense coat at his throat while he wiggles with glee under my attention. That moment makes me realize how much I've missed everything. Home. That was how it resonated. And it surprises me to discover how much I've missed that feeling.

*   *   *

In the morning, I am making coffee and breakfast when Imogen emerges from her room. She looks wan, but good, and I am happy to clap eyes on her.

"I missed you," I say honestly.

She stops by my side and places her hand over mine.

"I missed you, as well. And not just in the kitchen. Now tell me everything."

And so I do. In sequence. From Jennifer K. Riley's jazzy atelier and my transformation—along with the photos I'd had the women take with Imogen in mind—to my behavior and misbehavior at the gallery.

"I love every inch of all of this," Imogen says, clearly enjoying herself. "You sound like you were a better me than I ever was. Have you seen *New Art Times*?"

"Of course not," I say and we both laugh.

"The article is online already. You gotta read it."

"Now?"

Imogen nods gleefully.

I do, then I laugh out loud.

"Oh dear," I say over guffaws. "She called you ill-tempered."

"She called *you* ill-tempered," Imogen says, still laughing. "Even if my name was the one mentioned, we both know who she's talking about. Oh, I can't even tell you how happy I was when I read this. It makes my week pretty much. My year. You did me proud."

"Er . . . thank you?" I say cautiously. "I hope it's not problematic."

There is a moment when I see a shift in Imogen. It's like a switch has been hit. And I can't help but think it is in response to what I'd said. Before she speaks, I figure I know what she is going to say. It turns out I'm way off base.

"Well, not problematic. No. But this is how you handled all of it. I guess I do think I would have done that part better. More . . . diplomatically, let's put it that way."

It feels like a slap and it's out of left field. It isn't just the words either. It's like she has withdrawn somewhat. She is cold, and though I can see her struggling with what she will present to me, I am sensitive enough to nuances of expression and body language that her change of mood is obvious to me. Her state of mind just seems, quite suddenly, different.

"Wait . . . what? Please. Say more." I counsel myself not to say too much. Maybe I am misunderstanding her intent.

"Well, the people. The press. The patrons of the arts. With your limited experience, you couldn't have been expected to understand the elite level at which you'd be traveling."

"Yeah, no," I say.

She smiles. I find the smile at least slightly unpleasant. This is new to me. Her teeth pull back into something that looks like a snarl—though I chastise myself for exaggerating, it still feels that way to me. But am I? I just can't be sure. I see her top lip stick to her teeth, making the smile even more like a grimace.

"Well," she says, her tone resigned, though to me it sounds forced, "I'm sure you did the best you could."

It is then that I recognize the tone. Jealousy. But why? I decide to let it go. Press, instead, into something that is known. Maybe the other will sort itself out.

We talk for a while about things that are neutral, non-controversial, then head out to the studio to work. The tone, though. And the snarl. They stay with me, even when they're not apparent.

CHAPTER TWENTY-SIX

THE NEXT DAY, things are back to normal, or what passes for normal at Ocotillo Ranch.

"Good morning, sunshine," Imogen says cheerily when I come into the main house for breakfast. "It's good to have you back."

I find myself looking at her closely, gauging her mood and authenticity. She seems warm and genuine, but I don't quite relax.

"Thanks," I say. I maybe sound a little formal, but I can't help it. I'm waiting for the other shoe to drop. But it doesn't come.

"I've been thinking," she says. "I thought maybe after breakfast, we could walk out and see the horses."

"I'd like that," I say, feeling careful, but she just beams at me, as though in gratitude, and I feel myself soften. Is it possible I had misread her the day before? I'd been tired after my trip. And after my performance in the city.

Later in the morning we trudge out there. We don't get close to the horses, we just watch from a distance as they graze and cavort in the shallow water at the edge of the pond. They keep their eyes on us, used to human presence. If we were to walk toward them, they'd bolt, almost like a single unit. As things are, they keep an eye on us, even through their activity. They are not oblivious to our presence, but experience has shown them that we pose no immediate threat.

I watch them closely, enjoying their antics. Imogen sees the joy on my face.

"You've come to love them, too," she says, and her voice holds something like wonder. Or maybe it's gratitude. It can be easy to mix those two up.

"I do," I say simply, but it feels like an admission. I'm not sure why.

When we leave the horses, we head to the studio and all thoughts of everything else are pushed aside as we immerse ourselves into the work of this day. As usual, when we're done, I sit back, physically exhausted, and track our progress as a feeling wells in my heart. I can't name it.

"Satisfaction," Imogen says, watching me watch.

"Satisfaction. You think that's what it is?"

"I do. I recognized it in myself long ago. And it's not something that is easy to come by in this world: that feeling. I don't believe we are even taught to seek it anymore."

"What do you mean?"

"Well, think about it. Think even about the terms we use to describe our culture. It is a rat race. It is dog eat dog. We strive to achieve. To accomplish. We don't look for what satisfies us. Is that even enough?"

"We are programmed to win. Is that what you're saying?"

She lifts an eyebrow at me. Maybe she hadn't thought of it quite that way herself.

"Yes. That's it exactly. We are in competition. All of us. We aim to win, culturally, I mean. Bigger house. Bigger car. More successful life/spouse/kids. But the happiness that comes from being satisfied with an accomplishment. How does that even fit in?"

"That's easy for you to say," but I say it gently. It's just what I'm thinking. "You have been very successful in your art. It's fine for you to say: this is satisfaction. But you are well rewarded."

I say it and then I brace myself for the reaction. But it doesn't come. Instead, she seems for a moment to search for the right words before she answers.

"That's true," she says. "But why do you think I've been out here and out of contact all these years? I don't do it for that. I never have. I do it for . . . well, that feeling you have right now in your bones. It's enough."

I allow myself to become aware of how my body feels. Tired. I allow myself, also, to appreciate what we've accomplished on this day. And I realize then that she is right. Satisfied, if that's what you wanted to call it. Whatever this was, it was enough.

* * *

I have been back for a few days before I get in touch with Dallyce.

"Heads up," I say. "I'm going to call him."

"You don't need to tell me that," he says. "That wasn't part of it."

"I just wanted to let you know."

"Thanks," he says, voice even. "Now call him."

But I don't right away. I find that I *can't*; I'm not sure why.

I dial Dallyce again. Star-67.

"I can't call him," I say, trying not to sound as ridiculous as I feel.

"But you said that you were."

"I changed my mind."

"Oh. Kay."

"I know. I'm just gonna go. See him."

"Can I tell him you're coming?"

I nod my head, then realize he can't see me on the phone.

"Sure," I say, going for nonchalant. "Why not?" And, really, why had I called Dallyce if not for that?

"What should I tell him?"

And that was the million-dollar question, wasn't it? What did I want my brother to hear or know?

"Just that I'm coming, I guess. Errrr . . . soon." And I realize as I say this, all by instinct, that I don't even know what I want to accomplish with a visit. I only know that, on some level, I crave connection again with my family. And he is that. There's nothing left beyond him. Suddenly that makes it seem precious.

"Soon?"

"Within the next week," I say, and the words sound like a vow. "You know the complications. More than anyone. You understand why this can't be easy."

"You gonna call him before you show up?" It's like he hasn't heard my words. The possible question in them.

I hesitate before answering. I contemplate quickly.

"I don't think so," I say finally.

"All right," Dallyce says. I think he sounds disapproving, but I realize I might be making that part up. "So now you're *not* going to call him. Okay. I'll let him know."

For some reason, it is more difficult for me to paint after that call. I realize belatedly that this is no surprise. Something about it has messed with my satisfaction, and I'm not the only one who notices.

"C'mon now," Imogen admonishes me. "Get your head in the game. Where are you, anyway?"

"A family thing has come up," I reply, not lifting my head from the corner of the canvas I'm carefully working on.

"A family thing," she repeats. "I don't think I've heard you mention family before now."

"I haven't," I say, focusing even more closely on the work. Right on the canvas, I am mixing a color near black into a burnt umber. The color alone seems to pull at my emotion. It's hard for me to leave it behind. If Imogen notices, she doesn't comment.

"Ah," she says. "One of those sorts of families. I know about it. I used to have that, too."

I wait for her to go on, explain, but she doesn't. We both just work for a while, each of us lost in our own thoughts. The burnt-umber-to-black goes to an angry, Halloweeny vibe.

"You need to take off for a spell," she says after a while. I notice it's not a question.

"I do." I would have thought I wouldn't agree with her on this. To my surprise I do.

"When?"

"Not sure. Soon. What works for you?" I've said it quietly, without lifting my head. Right into the burnt umber.

"Depends," she says. I lift my head and look at her and find she is looking right at me. Hard. I can't decipher her expression. "You leaving Phil?"

I hadn't thought around that part. "I . . . I guess," I say. "Would that be okay?"

"More than okay," she says, beaming. "I like having him around. And also, it means you plan on coming back."

"Of course I do."

"Well, there you go. I get the feeling you need to go fast."

The shift from hesitant to enthusiastic had happened so quickly I hadn't been able to track it.

"Not so fast. Maybe . . . day after tomorrow."

"Fast enough, but okay. I'll go back to working small for a while."

I tell her I'll be back in a fortnight.

"Two weeks," she says. "Is that what you imagine?"

"I do. Maybe less."

"Okay," she says, and she sounds easy with it, but that might be a stretch. "I'll hold things down for you. But don't forget us out here." And I can tell she's trying to sound jovial and not pathetic as she says it, but she's only partially successful.

"Like I'd leave Phil," I say, totally giving up any pretense of not going along with the name. By now—and it hasn't been long—I'm even sort of convinced he's answering to it. Like he'd been waiting for a moniker and is digging having one now.

"You won't forget us," she says at one point.

"Like I could," I say.

"Exactly."

And I nod.

Whatever else is true, forgetting is not an option.

When I say goodbye, she is standing in the studio, working on part of a painting we have been working on together. I have lined up several canvases for her, all of manageable size.

"Don't forget," I tell her, "Chester can help you. Just call him."

"It won't be the same," she says, and I am touched by the child-like quality in her voice. I forget, for the moment, the times there are harsh edges.

"Of course not," I agree. "How could it be?"

She beams at me at that. As though I have given her something to hope for. It tugs at my heartstrings, both right then and in the hours after I leave. I take off in the Volvo and I can still imagine that trusting smile.

CHAPTER TWENTY-SEVEN

BUT IT TAKES me a while to leave.

I am indecisive about the day and time, and then I just give myself up to it. I realize that part of it is not knowing who I am anymore. Did I ever? Probably not, but now maybe I know myself even less. I feel as though my whole life has been inching toward some sort of understanding or self-knowledge, and now even that is gone. Am I to be Imogen O'Brien? It's difficult to imagine. Also difficult: If I *do* become Imogen, what will happen to the cypher I've already become? Will she disappear entirely? And, if she did disappear, would that be such a bad thing? And though it seems maudlin to think it, I'm certain no one would care.

As I begin my journey, I realize these are philosophical questions, not meant to be answered. They are a self-exploration and a mindfuck all at once, and like the road I'm traveling, I'm not sure where those thoughts lead.

When I pass Arcadia Bluff I stop the car. The road is empty and there is no one around. I get out and feel the silence in the air. It seems to me that, right here, time has stopped. It's not a peaceful feeling.

I walk to the edge of the cliff. Peer down. I see rocks the color of rust. Scrubby pines and tenacious cactus, clinging to the steep terrain. Brave cactus, heedless of the peril they face in their everyday. Somewhere, far below, there is a body of water, but it's something I know intellectually. All I see from this position is a painterly and distant swath of blue. I don't see bodies. I don't see scraps of metal or strewn bits of debris. There is nothing but nature to see. But it haunts me a bit, this thing I have done. It isn't regret. I'm not sorry for what I did. I don't feel as though I shouldn't have done it. Exactly. Maybe only that I should have done it differently or more completely or some other way that would have left me without this tug of unease.

After a while, with nothing out there to see, I make my way back to my car. I continue my journey. I have a long way to go.

* * *

I drive. And drive. Alone. I feel the absence of the dog. Phil. Who has always given our journeys such pathos. I can't explain it. Without him, though, there is a hole where he belongs. For a moment, I consider turning back and getting him. Bringing him along. And then the sparse desert forest of Cathedral National Forest gives way to the true Arizona desert and all these thoughts of the recent past are pushed out of my mind and I focus on the journey. Here, craggy rock faces and rolling hills and all available space are covered in sparse cactus. It is as though some ancient landscape architect had designed this arid scene—carefully measuring the distance between plantings. Some of these saguaro cacti stand tall, arms akimbo, as though reaching for the sky. I sense a pattern but can't quite discern what it might be.

I drive and drive and drive before the terrain begins to change again, and the change is abrupt and startling. No longer the dry, open vistas, but we have climbed into forest regions and the world is green again. In a few hours I emerge onto a four-lane highway, still sloping upwards. I feel as though I'm headed for the top of the world and something beyond my present location is pulling me. The feeling is magical. And frightening.

Then there are trees. Rich and beautiful deciduous trees, which, to my newly desert-trained eyes, appear lush and ripe. Promises filled. I wonder at the sheer number of them. Trees of every description and around every bend. Whoever would have thought there were so many trees left in America? At a time when cities are overflowing, it seems unimaginable to me that there is still so much uninhabited land. Yet here we are.

It's a long drive. I consider stopping somewhere for the night; some fuzzy roadside motel where the rooms are identical to those you've stayed in since childhood. In the end, though, I just press on, wanting my own company more than a few hours' comfort in a lumpy bed.

CHAPTER TWENTY-EIGHT

THE ROAD STRETCHES on. It seems to me that it is longer than I had expected. Pale green hills become raw young mountains dotted with evergreen trees. At a certain point I notice that quaking aspen line the sides of this part of the small highway and I can't remember the last time I saw a saguaro. It makes me realize the elevation has changed and, certainly, the desert is now truly behind me.

And the highway climbs.

When the landscape changes again, my heart shifts. We're getting closer, for sure. What I see out the window confirms the truth of that. The countryside is speaking to something deep inside me. I'm going home. I'm not sure yet how I feel about that.

Once I get to town, I don't need directions to my brother's house. He's been living in the same place since he got married and that's a long time ago. I know he hasn't moved because there was a time that I stalked him. After I began my current occupation. After I started moving toward the light and stopped spiraling down. All before now.

Stalked is saying more than it was. I drove to the place where he lives—this very place—and sat in my car. I watched him, just for a short time. Was I getting up my courage to talk with him? Possibly. But in the end, I didn't do it. It hadn't seemed like the right time. With all that has happened since, I realize that maybe there is never a right time. That sometimes you are just meant to plunge through in the time you have on hand and hope that your own passion and intent stand up to it.

The idea that there might not actually be right time frightens me. Is it the right time now? I don't know how to find the answer, so I start the car again; drive a few blocks away and sit and contemplate.

What if—as I've always suspected—we get together and he blames me for everything that has happened to our family? Or that I can't get past the things I've come to realize about the end of my own little family. Or we blame each other, as seems more likely. The disconnection, which, since I'd fled after a while, clearly was my fault. But was it because of who I was at that time and what was I dealing with? Or because of what I was busy becoming, because the change in me was not insignificant. That sounds like an excuse. An excuse is not what I intend. Does the grasshopper forgive her own long green legs? Does the spider apologize for her need to eat flies? Does the cat beg forgiveness from the beheaded mouse? I could go on, but you see where I'm heading. It is not my nature to kill without need, but maybe nature led me here, even though I am not now sure how it all began.

It might be that this is the thing I am afraid to show my brother. That he looks at me and thinks that what was once lovely between us is gone. Or worse: he sees me as I now am.

Is it possible he fears the same thing? That I'll look at him and somehow find him wanting? And that is how we are as humans:

Always judging ourselves. Falling short, but still looking for completion in other eyes.

I arrive and park the car and, for a few minutes, sit and watch. Finally, I approach the house, then retreat at the last minute. I feel a lump develop in my stomach. More. I'm not sure if I can go through with it. But I pick up my phone anyway. Call Dallyce.

"I'm here," I say when he answers. "In my car. Any idea how this is supposed to go? Did he say?"

"He didn't," Dallyce says and to me he sounds genuinely regretful. "I can see I should have figured that part."

"No worries," I say, even though I'm worried. "I didn't do anything to make it easier on you. Wanna call and ask him?"

"Okay," he says and I can tell even from that single syllable that he's relieved to have something to do. I understand the feeling.

While I wait for Dallyce, I start the car, and pop it in drive. I take a wheel around the neighborhood, then park a few blocks from the house and walk the tree-lined streets, feeling slightly astonished that in a world where so much has changed, so very little has changed. It sets me on my heels. Everything seems just as it was. Even the air—fresh, clean, and crisp in a way I had forgotten along with the way the aggregate sidewalks feel under my feet. All so familiar. How is that even possible? Who remembers the feeling of a sidewalk? And yet, here we are.

Kenneth and I would race our bikes on these streets. We'd run with our friends and walk to school. We lived our whole childhood lives here. And it's all just the same. And everything is different.

In the present, it's a risk, this walking. What if someone recognizes me? But I feel that is unlikely. I don't look the same. I am older now. I almost can't remember how long it has been. I'd have to struggle to remember and I don't want to. Long enough, anyway, that I am mostly unrecognizable.

I'm rangier, too. I have never run to extremes, but there had perhaps been a well-deserved whiff of matron about me the last time I was properly seen in these parts. When I was a mom. When I was, in fact, a matron. Since then I have become leaner. And meaner? There's that, as well, though I lack the objectivity required for self-examination. Whatever the case, I am now fighting fit. I am stronger now than when I was in my twenties. Physically, at any rate. Emotionally I'm never sure where I am. At all.

So I prowl around the neighborhood and what I see soothes my soul and maybe eases my apprehensions a bit, as well. In a world where everything is always changing, this little slice is just the same. The neighborhood is idyllic in the way that small, smug American towns can be when all of fate has come together in the right way.

The only people I see are children, going here or there. They pay no attention to me, busy as they are on their own very important childish missions. And what am I? Just another grown-up. Not even as interesting as I'd be if I were walking a dog.

I'm still walking when Dallyce calls me back with the news I've been expecting.

"Your brother is at home. You can go by any time."

"What about you?"

A hesitation. "He didn't feel my presence was necessary." Less smile now.

I understand that. For the moment anyway, Dallyce's work is done.

Back at my brother's house fifteen minutes after Dallyce's call, I hesitate at the front door. I've been at this house often over the years. At one point in my life I was as comfortable in this house as I was in my own. Maybe it only stands to reason that I am comfortable nowhere now. Maybe that only makes sense.

But now, though. Do I just walk in? Do I knock? I never used to knock, but that was then.

As I hesitate, the door swings open and Kenneth is standing there, a remembered scent wafting out of the house with him. I feel my eyes well. All of it. It smells and feels like home. I hadn't expected that. I hadn't remembered even to miss these most basic of things. I don't even get the chance to wonder about that now.

While I hesitate, Kenneth doesn't give me the chance to get the questions out. I get only the sense of his dear-but-now-older face before I am enveloped in a full body hug.

"Little one." He mutters it quietly. "I was afraid I'd never see you again."

Considering all that has passed between us, I am mixed about this.

When the hug is completed and he has me at arm's length, I say, "You had me declared dead." There is no emotion in my voice.

He rocks back, like I've landed a small punch. I realize that he is crying. Not crying, maybe. But his eyes are damp. Or maybe it's me. Or maybe it is both of us, the tears likely simply a visual representation of DNA.

"I did," he says, meeting my eyes. There's no attempt to deny it. I am relieved at that, anyway. If he'd denied it, I might have just turned and walked away.

"Why?"

"If you think about it, you'll understand."

"Go on." I stand there in the doorway. Waiting. But it must be clear to him that I don't understand.

"You died with them, I think. Didn't you?"

"In a way." He means my little family: my husband and my child. I was still breathing. I was still on this side, but he's not wrong. A part of me—and not a small one—was no longer alive once they were gone.

"After . . . after everything happened, I thought about that. About how you'd been gone even before you were gone. It was like you simply . . . ceased to exist. Then I learned you were using a new name. You had a different life. You rejected us, in a way. But our lives still went on."

"So I was dead to you." Still no emotion.

"Not that," and he says it in a way that my heart believes. "Never that. But you could have come to us, you know." There is something like reproach in his voice, though it is slight. And it is not all of the real estate here; just a small piece. "We would have been here for you. We always would have been here for you."

"I know. I mean, I know it now. For a while, then, I didn't know anything."

"Can we stop standing here, please? Can we go inside?"

I let him lead me more deeply into the house. We stop in the living room where that forgotten smell is all around us. What is it? I can't place the disparate parts, but I feel it represents our family. Something long forgotten but instantly recognized. Kenneth, it seems, is the keeper of it now.

Chairs and a sofa are arranged around a coffee table in a pattern I remember. Nothing discernable has changed since the last time I was there, and that was a long time ago. My sister-in-law, Abigail, is nowhere to be seen. I'm glad about that, even though I've always liked her. I'm glad to be seeing my brother alone for this first meeting.

He and I each take a seat. Him on one side of the couch, me in a battered armchair directly across from him. I feel I maybe remember the chair from my own childhood. It's uncomfortable, yet comfortable somehow. I can't explain it. Something that shouldn't be, but is.

"You just disappeared." Again, there is that whisper of reproach. I understand. Had it been me, I would have felt the same way.

"I was . . . I was not in my right mind." It is unnerving looking into his eyes just now. They are just as I remember them, and yet so different. And in more ways than I remembered, they are just like mine. It's like looking into a distorting mirror. We are both older. Maybe sterner, too.

"Maybe I'm still not in my right mind," I say.

"Maybe," he says. "Losing your little one. That was . . . well, it was a lot. More than can be imagined, I guess. He was my nephew." The grief in his face is real. And it seems familiar to his face, too. It fits into the folds and new wrinkles. "He was the closest thing I will have to a child. Both me and Abigail were devastated when it happened. You weren't the only one to lose someone that day. Your loss was greater . . ."

"It's not a contest," I say softly. It's not the first time I've said it.

He goes on as though I have not spoken.

"Plus, I lost him, and then I lost you."

"I'm sorry," I say. And I am. I hadn't even considered I was hurting him, too. It hadn't been part of the equation. And it's not that I was insensitive. It was just that, for a while, everything was about hurt. "I didn't think about that," I admit. "For a while, I didn't think at all."

"Mom is gone." Three words, but they hold so much more.

"I know."

"How did you find out?"

"Dallyce told me."

"Oh," he digests. "Sorry. That was a difficult way for you to learn."

"It was sad, of course. But I guess I'd been so disconnected for so long, to me it was like I already knew somehow."

"I guess we all had been. Disconnected, I mean." And I can read the pain on his face. It is bald.

"I'm sorry, Kenneth. I was out of my head for a while."

"Yeah. I saw your house after you left. That's when I realized I hadn't known what you were going through. I'm sorry about that. When I saw the house, and what had become of it, it brought it home."

He didn't tell me he'd felt awful about that. Beyond awful. That his heart had been broken by what had happened to me and those closest to me. And that he'd felt guilty that he hadn't been able to do anything. But I can see all of that wash over his face. And, somehow, with all this time between, sensing his regret and sharing in the loss that he'd felt, it makes it better. Not a lot, but a little. It makes a difference. I take his hand, touch the back of it lightly and gently, then go back to my chair. So much unspoken in a few simple gestures.

After my family was gone, I had lived in the house alone for months. My beautiful house. My lost family. The PebbleTech pool turned green with neglect and lack of funds to maintain it. Eating the food—the ridiculous suburban amount of food we had stored—until there was nothing viable left to eat.

It took longer to get through the goofy amount of food we had on hand than you might have imagined. From frozen steaks to frozen chicken that showed small amounts of freezer burn around the edges to fish that I figured had moved in when we did. The beans, of course, went quickly and a few tins of ridiculously shaped pasta in slimy sauce that had been my son's rare treat. I ate those, too. Frozen breads, starting with fancy French loaves, ending with end bits of various ancient buns no one had wanted and so they had sunk to the bottom of the freezer. Tricolor quinoa. Long-forgotten tuna. Tinned soup. Stale crackers. Frozen peas. Chocolate found at the back of a cupboard with so much white showing its age that the brown could barely be seen. And all of it to me flavorless in my grief. It didn't much matter what it was, but it kept me alive when, truly, all I wanted was to die.

Around the time the food began to seriously run out, the power got turned off because I hadn't paid the bill. My dream house—two dishwashers and all—had turned into my nightmare. And there was nothing left to eat there anyway.

I lived there like a homeless person for a while, like a squatter, not even well enough in my mind to think about what to do. And then one day I just left. I started living in my car. After a while, things started to make sense again. A different kind of sense. By then my life—the life my brother had been a part of—was dead. It was gone. And so was I.

"That would have been horrible for you to see," I say. "I'm sorry about that, too. Look at us: sorry all over the place. But honestly, I didn't expect you to know. I was just . . . I guess I was something like an animal. For a while, just pure hurt instinct."

"I felt some of that." He surprises me by smiling then. The grin reminds me of everything. Suddenly Kenneth is ten years old again. And I am eight and all that has happened between has vanished. He's going to run to school and get into trouble. And me: I'm going to run after him. Hide for a while. Not let him see me, then explode out from behind a mailbox or a bush and try to scare the crap out of him. I don't think I ever did actually scare him, but he played along: dutiful older brother.

"None of this is why I wanted to see you. You know that, right?"

"I don't know anything," I say, and I mean it.

Instead of being upset at my words, he surprises me by grinning again. "You've changed so much and so much has happened, but in some ways, you're exactly the same."

The way he's said it, I know the words are not meant to hurt my feelings. Maybe he even means it as a compliment. But it cuts me, just the same. I think about my son. How old would he be now? It bothers me that I can't come to the answer easily. Isn't that something I should know? He'd be tall and cool, I know that. Like, chilly cool. Like the bullshit that killed me would run off his back. And he'd be popular. People would love him. All people. He would be all of the things I have not been.

More.

So much more.

But his age. The age he would be now? That I don't know. And the not knowing is a piece of sand between my toes. It bothers me in elusive ways. It's something else I should know. But I don't.

I try to cut myself slack around that. In the normal course of things, I *would* know. There would have been candles on cakes. Many cakes. An increasing number of candles. But so much has happened in the time between. Things that get in the way of sorting what is important from what is not. Especially since so much of what I do know seems just meant to pass the time between then and whatever it is that is coming next.

"But you wanted to see me," I say, trying to bring things back to now. Keep things moving ahead. One can get lost in the past. Stuck. That doesn't seem like a good way to begin again.

"Well, of course I did. How long has it been? And for part of that time, I didn't even know if you were alive."

"And you thought he tried to kill me."

"He?" I see the alarm in his eyes. The caution.

"My husband." I can't bring myself to say his name. Even now.

Kenneth's eyes open wide. Whatever he'd been expecting me to say, this wasn't it.

"I thought that. Yeah. How do you know?"

"Think on it," I say.

"Dallyce," Kenneth says, and I detect a bit of heat.

"Don't blame him," I say. "I had to squeeze it out of him."

It had been at gunpoint, and it had nearly been an end play, but it didn't seem like the right moment to say so.

"Yuh. But if that's right," Kenneth says, "he got himself killed instead."

"That would be divine justice," I say quietly.

"Maybe," Kenneth says with something like a shrug. Trying not to care.

"That's not what you wanted to see me about."

"That's why you came," he says, and the look in his eyes tells me that fact hurts him. Though I can't help but wonder, after all this time, why he would be surprised.

"Yes." I admit it. And why not? Surely, he knows I could have come home any time? And now here I am.

"Okay. Well. Right." He's gathering himself. I know what that looks like. "Whatever the reason, I'm glad it's happened. Finally.

But yes. To answer your ques... had in mind. It's the cottage." ...ere was something specific I

I feel my eyes widen in surprise. Or ... he things he might have said, this would have been at the bottom... ...my list, in part because, somehow, the cottage had fallen right out ... ...v head. In a heartbeat, though, and at this single mention, it all com... ...ack: a stone and wood cabin shaded by towering trees at the edge of a lake. There are grandparents associated with my memories, even though the grandparents themselves are now long gone.

There's a red canoe pulled into the reeds at the water's edge and tied haphazardly to a stake driven out there for that purpose. These memories are laughter-filled. Love and light is there, as well. Childish memories. Me and Kenneth are in the earliest ones; later the two of us are grown and my husband and son are present. I feel myself start to smile and nearly cry all in the same few heartbeats. Bittersweet.

Kenneth won't have seen any of this on me. I have not gotten this far without learning to hide a thing.

"What about the cottage?" is all that I say.

"I'm thinking of selling it."

I don't say anything and he presses on.

"I thought you might want a say."

"Maybe," I say after a while. "Maybe I do. How long do I have to decide?"

"There's no hurry. Just something I started thinking about." Then, as though it's an afterthought, "I haven't been there in five years. It's gotten to seem silly to keep it."

"Why?" I want to know.

"Why haven't I been there?"

"Yes."

, of course, you were gone. You . . .

"I'm not sure, exactly

and . . . everyone."

I have been fr. . . Friends and family knew that for a while. I
was very frac. . . it's like I was peanut brittle. I could shatter with a
single b. . . bite. Also, it's possible I didn't know quite how fragile I
had become. Then I was gone, and I guess whatever fragility I had
or did not have no longer mattered.

Kenneth watches me carefully. Looking for signs of that fragility, maybe. Signs of breakage. He registers I am still there with him and continues.

"Then Mom got sick, but you know all about that."

"I don't really," I say, holding everything in. "Just that she's gone."

"Okay. Well." A deep, cleansing breath. "It was horrid. And hard. I missed you more than ever through that. It would have been good to not have to deal with it alone."

And the words take on their own tone. It would be easy to read resentment into them. But I could tell he was just stating what to him was a fact. Plus, it's a sentiment I can't disagree with. It would be very hard. Mom hadn't been easy even when things were good.

"I'm sorry it had to be that way," I say.

"Me, too," he says simply. "It was Mom, though. It was never going to be anything else."

And for a heartbeat I sit there and collect ideas about how things could be different. About how I could strike a change for what is and make what tomorrow brings different, as well. And then I realize that these are silly thoughts. What has occurred has already occurred. My mother is gone. My brother is struggling with his own reality. As am I. Certainly. As maybe we all are? Whatever seems "normal" and "good" and "right" at a different end of the

spectrum might appear flawed from .
been gone so long, I lack the emotional dis. Despite having
what is right or even needed. ...ry to know

"I wish Mama was here to tell us what to do," my ⌐

I don't disagree and for a moment the thought brings he:ays.
and she is large and real between us. I can almost taste her criticisn..

CHAPTER TWENTY-NINE

THE SPECTRAL VISION that was our mother fades and we both slump, exhausted, into our chairs. We don't talk about that, and I feel fairly certain it's because it did not happen. After that, what was easy between us seems to get brittle. It's as though some barrier has been passed and we've talked enough. Kenneth motions us to our feet, and I follow him to the kitchen.

Once I see Abigail, I realize that only some prearranged plan has been holding her back from greeting me. She's older now than when I last saw her, of course, but she still possesses the barely contained enthusiasm of a well-loved puppy. She is just as I had remembered her: bright and enthusiastic. The smile she bathes me with when she sees me confirms that, in this regard anyway, nothing has changed.

I'm surprised by the emotion that Abigail's warm greeting brings up in me. It's not that I'd forgotten her. But maybe I'd forgotten what love and warmth look like: it wasn't as though either Kenny or myself were raised with that. And here you feel it, from Abigail. You walk right into it. This is what unconditional love looks like and sometimes you don't miss it until you see it again. I hug her back hard.

She has prepared something that looks very like a Sunday family dinner. I never eat like this anymore and I'm betting they don't either, but it's like we are doing something precious together—connecting after so many years. And so we share this ancient family ritual. Mama is there again, but ever so slightly—for that. It would be impossible not to feel her. There is a pot roast and tiny potatoes and there are green beans I can tell spent some time in a can. It all gets covered with a thick dark gravy, and as horrid as all of this would be if faced with it in a restaurant, somehow in this context it is perfect. Exactly right.

I am surprised at how easy it is to be with Kenneth and Abigail again. Over dinner both ask about my life. I tell them what I can. That there are times when I travel a lot. That I don't like to talk about my work, but that I've done all right. That I paint now. And cook. That I have a dog. That I'm in the process of moving to the desert. Maybe. Arizona. That it is so good to see them and that my heart has missed their faces and the shape they leave in the world.

"I can't tell you how pleased I am that you chose to look in on us after all this time." Abigail reaches out and takes my hand over the remnants of the roast. Squeezes earnestly. It is clear that she has not been told that I didn't arrive voluntarily: that a certain level of coercion and trickery had to occur. A bit of sleight of hand, though maybe it doesn't matter anyway: here I am.

"She's going to buy the cottage," Kenneth says to his wife over dessert. It's like I'm no longer there or, at least, no longer part of the conversation. It's been decided without me.

"I am?" It's all I can think to say.

"Yes," and then he shrugs. "You would have inherited part of it anyway."

"I have a different name now," responding to something that hasn't been asked. "I'm a different person."

"I know," he tells me. "Dallyce told me. Not what it was, just how it all played out. We'll make all the arrangements through him, okay?" I can feel Kenneth being gentle. And I think about Imogen's feral cats. So many of them! How she approached them, cautiously. Never getting too close. Letting them decide on the distance between them. Respecting their space. And their fear. I feel like Kenneth is like that with me now.

I just nod. By his own good tradesmanship, Dallyce knows as much of my real story as anyone. And it's apparent he hasn't told. I feel a warm shot of gratitude toward him. He has been better than he needed to be. It's more than we can ask of anyone.

By the time I head to bed late that evening, I am all in. I've spent so very much time alone over the last few years and suddenly I'm being thrust, on several fronts, into these social situations. I would not have thought it would take so much out of me, but once I get back to my room, I can barely keep my eyes open.

I glance at my phone and am disappointed to see that there are no messages, though who had I expected would call? It's late, but I call anyway and am surprised when Imogen answers on the first ring. It's like she's been waiting.

"It's so good to hear from you," she enthuses. "Phil has been getting worried about you."

"Phil has," I say, feeling warmth and a sort of longing. I realize Imogen's voice sounds like family. More, even, than the family I am now surrounded by. Maybe too much time has passed?

She laughs at my comment, as maybe I had intended her to do. She's taken my bait, but it's not trickery. She's walked into it willingly. "Well, okay. I have, too. Like I told you before, you liven up the place."

I laugh with her. "I can see how that could be. And you haven't even heard me sing."

"Oh," she says, "that's true. So I have that to look forward to as well. When do you figure you'll be back?" And she asks this last so casually, I have a hint about what it might have cost her.

"I would think my business here is nearly concluded," I say, not mentioning cottages or weepy family dinners. "I should be back in a few days."

"Oh, that's wonderful," she says. "Phil will be so pleased."

"I'll bet," I say.

We hang up not long after, and I drift to sleep feeling looked after. And loved.

CHAPTER THIRTY

IN THE MORNING Kenneth and I have a new conversation.

"I don't have the ability to buy anything right now."

Ability, I've said. And I know it implies money, but I have that. What I don't have is the persona who could legally own anything. It doesn't seem worth spelling out.

"I thought I made it plain last night," my brother says. "I'm not worried about the money." There is an edge to his voice; an impatience. "It would be a gift."

"It's not a money situation." I say it blandly. As though if I say it quietly and unobtrusively it might just pass unnoticed. "It's complicated," I say, looking toward my collar. "I don't know if I can explain."

"Maybe try me," he says, his tone even. "I've been known to pick up a thing or two."

There. Now I'm certain of it: the irritation I hear is real.

"It's not like that, Kenneth. It's not an intelligence test. It's just that . . . for various reasons . . . I can't own property right now."

Kenneth looks at me balefully then. The same kitchen table we'd spent so much time over the night before. He looks at me with those familiar pale eyes and I notice for the first time a certain wateriness in them. And I wonder what this will mean for the future. Seeing him aging is chilling. And I suddenly wonder why I came.

"So you can't buy the place. That's what I'm hearing. Not now. And I guess, all things considered, there's no reason for me to press for a sale. Do you want to take a run up there? Just for the hell of it?"

"To the cottage?"

"Yuh."

I cast a glance at Abigail. She just looks at me and smiles.

"I don't have an opinion. I mean, I don't want to actually *go* with you guys. I've got things to do here. But you two should go for it."

"What for? To remember, you mean?"

"Okay. That. Why not?"

"Yes," Kenneth says, agreeing. "Why not?"

"Why not?" I repeat it, but it seems real enough to me. A part of me doesn't feel like seeing the place again, but I see no real reason to object, and so we make a plan to go the following day, filling in *this* day with soft reminiscences and walks around the neighborhood and even the charming little town.

"How is it that so little has changed?" The wonder in my voice is genuine. I have been to and even lived in many places. Nothing stands still.

"Hmmm . . . I don't think I see what you see. A lot is different."

"Oh, small things, sure. Jefferson's Pharmacy is now Daljeet's. And maybe the Union 76 has been turned into a coffee bar. Those are details, though. But the essence of the place. That hasn't changed at all."

Kenneth shrugs at me like he doesn't actually get it, but he'll let me have the win. We have lunch at the five-and-dime, though it's a dollar store now.

Kenneth has a "hamburger delux" and I have mac and cheese and the food is delicious and real and virtually, it seems to me, unchanged since we were kids.

"I mean, what kind of dollar store even has a lunch counter?"

Kenneth laughs.

"Okay, point. It's possible the town has been more resistant than some to change."

I don't mind it, though. It is nice to know there is a pocket of the world that aligns with my memory. I find I don't want to be there, but my heart is happy to know it continues without me. Not everything always has.

*   *   *

That night, alone in Kenneth and Abigail's guest room, I try to call Imogen. The phone rings several times, but she doesn't answer. I quell the faint column of unease that floats to me. There are a million reasons she is not answering her phone. She's painting. She's walking. She's doesn't feel like talking to anyone. And, it's true: she seldom does. I shake my head at how silly I'm being. I've seen it: she often doesn't answer her phone. Why should today be different? The trill of unease persists.

CHAPTER THIRTY-ONE

IN THE MORNING, Kenneth and I get into his SUV and head for the lake. As we drive, our conversation is both comfortable and difficult: there are certain topics we avoid. Not that we won't talk about them: just not today.

The lake, when we get there, holds all of the stillness I remember. More. As a kid I wouldn't have noticed such a thing. Not on a conscious level, anyway. As a young mom, my head would have been too busy surviving to field any of it. As an adult, though, and no longer a mom, I have come to a place in my life where I can appreciate the stillness. Cherish it. Dream of holding it in my hand.

The lake is a deep blue-green. When I stand right next to it, the lake is so dark, my vision can't penetrate the surface. What is below there, I wonder? Do I remember something about leeches? Were there discussions, when I was a kid, about sea monsters? But I remember seeing none of these things. When I think about it now, I figure maybe our mother told us those stories to keep us out of the lake. Not charming tales, no. Rather, as yet another example of the fear she kept us wrapped in while we were growing up. I remember her eyes as she shared those stories. And a sort of nervous tic that saw her touching her neck at the base of her throat, then touching the other hand, then back again. And all the while the voice would drone on: possible sea monsters. Leeches. And god knows what else.

And me and Kenneth standing next to her, our eyes meeting, waiting for her to stop talking so we could swim. For some reason that memory, long forgotten, gives me a headache when I recall it. I can't look at it straight on. It makes me want to run away. Or swim, leeches and all.

In the cottage, Kenneth motions for me to go ahead and explore while he finishes a call. It doesn't take me much to agree.

I take my shoes off; my socks. Move to the end of the dock where I sit; stick my feet in. There are houses on the distant shore; little cottages like ours. I sit and ponder and discover that I miss the dog—Phil?—with a kind of physical ache.

Now that I'm here, sitting with my feet in the lake, I realize I've never brought him to a lake or any other large body of water before, and he seems the type that would appreciate it. Water dog and all. And there are miles of water here. Miles of shore. Everything here would speak to him. So vividly. I can almost feel him at my heel as I make my way to the shore alone.

My son loved it here. All seasons. And he would be the bright center of our dull little group. I'd forgotten that until now. The way one does. My mother by then choked with what would ultimately kill her, though we couldn't see it coming. Not then. My father always wreathed in dour silence, my mother's coughing fits and our chatter both greeted with indifference.

I wouldn't let her tell him about the sea monsters. Or the leeches. Though I realize now that maybe, for her, those two were the same thing. But I didn't want my son polluted with the ghost of those things. I didn't want him bothered or haunted by the things he could not see, the way it had been for me and Kenneth. Polluted and haunted. I realize now that defined our childhoods.

I'd wanted better for my son.

"Some of the details are coming back to me," I say to my brother now. He is beside me as we trudge along the lakeshore. I've pulled my shoes and socks back on. There are prickles and rocks and other things I wouldn't want to walk on—leeches?—hope not leeches.

"Stuff from our childhood?" He's asked it, but I know he knows.

"Yeah. Memories. And I don't really want them."

He smiles wryly. "Welcome to my world." And there isn't even a touch of irony in his voice as he says it.

We circle the lake, mostly in silence, each of us lost in our own thoughts. Occasionally a shared memory rushes past, and we share them quietly.

"Do you remember old man Perry's dog?"

"I do. We couldn't even walk past this spot without old Ricochet coming after us."

"Ricochet? Was that his name?"

"It was."

"Funny. I didn't remember that part."

"Dumb name."

When we get back to the cottage, Kenneth makes a fire in the fireplace, though not before he forgets to check if the flue is open and smoke pours into the room.

"Dad would be so pissed," I laugh as he opens the flue and the front door to clear smoke out of the room.

"I know, right? I can almost hear him." And he shudders.

And then, in unison, we chant the litany we'd both heard too often: "Why don't you ever think, boy? Is that a brain in your noodle or just some kind of putty?"

And then we laugh, though the laughter is tinged with some sad and darker thing.

"He wasn't a very nice man," I say after a while, reflectively.

"No," Kenneth agrees. "I guess he wasn't. I don't always know what to do with that."

I only nod because I don't actually understand what he's saying. And yet—somehow—I do.

"They were a pair," but I say it quietly, and my head is down, inspecting my shoes. It's like, now that we're back in the house, I'm afraid someone will overhear.

"They were," Kenneth agrees. And I notice that his voice is quiet, too. Maybe he has the same fear.

"I guess I'm only surprised you kept the place this long," I say after a while.

He sighs—a deep and somehow soulful sound, barely audible over the wood that is crackling merrily in the fire.

"Yeah," he says. "Me too, I guess. I didn't know what else to do."

"Except you knew you didn't want to spend any time here."

He looks at me sharply.

"Is that it?" He says it questioningly. I can tell he's testing the air for an answer. "Yeah. Yes. I guess that's true. Ghosts."

"They're all here."

He smiles then.

"They are."

"What would you think if I stayed up here for a few days? On my own."

He looks at me sharply, but I know he won't disagree.

"Well, I think that would be fine."

"Thanks," I say, though both of us know I don't have to.

"You wanna come back and get your car?"

"Naw. I'm okay without it for a few days. Still canned goods here?"

"Like always," he says. "And Henderson's Market is just a half hour walk if there's something you need."

"I remember," I say. "Come back and get me Friday?"

"I will," he says.

*   *   *

After a while I'm alone and I reach into it. It's my normal way of being—alone—and the last few weeks have been full of other people's energies, most especially my brother's and Imogen's. I notice that I am thinking of them together, almost as though both are family, and the thought does not displease me.

I am not lonely, during this time spent lakeside, but I put a lot of my energy toward thinking of these others in my life now. My brother, like the half I'd lost, now found. And Imogen as a sort of branch into the future, at least for a while. She will provide my transition back into the world. She's going to teach me to paint, and that's not an uneven trade. The idea of that energizes me. I will be learning and growing, but I will also be providing her with companionship and even fresher limbs when they are required. It's been a long time—too long—since I've been of service to anyone besides Phil. And since Phil is a dog, I'm not even totally sure he counts.

Here at lakeside, I don't only think about the future. I don't even think I could if I tried because the past is floating all around me. In case I should forget that, evidence pops up left and right. Under the verandah, in the sheltered place we always kept the small boats, I find a tiny bright red sailboat. A day sailor, I can remember my father calling it. It was a ridiculous proposition for a lake, when the still air could seldom be harnessed enough to fill a sail. It didn't when I was a kid and I remember my son also playing at it in joyful frustration.

"How can I learn to sail if there's never any wind?"

"Paddle it," I advised from experience. It's what Kenneth and I had always done when we were small. "There's plenty of time to learn to sail later. There will be plenty of wind."

I wince at the memory because, of course, it had been a lie. There hadn't been plenty of time, had there? There'd barely been any time at all.

And would he be a sailor now, had he lived? And would he stand this tall? Or that? And when I am fully immersed in maudlin thoughts that have no answer and no reason to be, I realize I've spent enough time in the past. And then it is Friday and I discover that I'm glad this time has passed: I'm ready to go home.

CHAPTER THIRTY-TWO

HOME.

While I wait for Kenneth to come and collect me, I sit on the dock, trailing my feet in the still water, and I contemplate my use of the word—"home"—even in my head. I wonder how it is I've even made that transition: that Imogen's desert home should somehow also now be mine instead of this lakeside place where I spent whole whacks of my childhood.

In any case, I think, truly home should not be something I look forward to. It's not as though my associations with home are so great. Childhood home looked idyllic on the outside, but was chaotic behind closed doors. I realize now that my first adult home was the same, just with different players, and it ended abruptly and tragically. All of the homes I have experienced have led to gloomy ends, so why does my heart still crave something that it's never had?

When Kenneth arrives, it's a joyless reunion. By now we have both had time to reflect on what the time apart has meant. You can't go back, they say. It turns out, they were right.

"Was it lonely?" We are driving and the lake is behind us now. Drifting back into the past, where it belongs.

"It was," I say. "Everything is lonely now."

There is a pause and the silence between us is fraught. There's so much in it. Things neither of us wishes to say. Or even can.

"You're thinking I should let it go," he says after a while.

"I guess I do."

"You don't want it?"

And I think before I answer.

"I guess I can't have it."

"All right," he says.

"All right."

CHAPTER THIRTY-THREE

THERE IS NOTHING poignant about my drive out of my hometown. I don't take a last look at this or a final drive past that; I just go.

And then there is the rolling back of everything. The landscape that becomes drier; the evergreens that give way to cactus; the lush grass that gives way to sand and rock. Through all the changes, I have the oddest feeling of rolling not away from home, but toward it. It's not a bad feeling.

I see that there is a commotion at Arcadia Bluff before I recognize the spot. All of the vehicles mask the peace. There are two trucks parked and, like the helicopter nearby, they are marked in the state colors and the words "Arizona Department of Public Safety" are printed on the side. No police cars, but I'm guessing they're either on their way or gone already. A woman looking official and wearing a vest in the colors of the state is at the road, waving traffic along, though, of course, there's not much traffic to see. I roll the window down when I reach her. A part of me doesn't want to, but it seems to me it might seem even more suspicious if I just rolled on.

"Hey," I say, "what's going on?"

"The boys are keeping it close to the vest," she says. I curse myself now for stopping as she looks me and the vehicle over appraisingly, maybe trying to determine how we fit into the local landscape.

"Boys will be boys," I say with a lift of my brow.

"Ain't that the truth."

"So an accident happened?"

"Well, maybe. But someone spotted a vehicle from the air a few weeks ago."

From the air, I say to myself. Of course.

"So no big deal?"

"Well, again, maybe? They found the vehicle, but no body and no ID. They were down there with fingerprint kits and whatnot a while ago. The cops. Gone now."

"But those are search and rescue vehicles, aren't they? They must figure someone is alive down there."

"No, uh-uh," she says. "They found one body when they found the vehicles. But how could there only be one?"

"I dunno," I say. "Maybe animals got him, or whatever."

"That's what I thought at first, too. But no: the science forensic whatever guys have ruled that out. Magically, I guess." She chortles at me about that, like she figures she thinks she's cracked a fabulous joke. I chortle, too, not fully sure I'm in on the joke.

"No, seriously. You said there's two vehicles? You'd figure there'd be a couple bodies down there."

"I dunno," she says cheerily. "I just direct the traffic." And we both laugh at that because, in the time we've been chatting, there have been no other cars.

* * *

By the time I reach Ocotillo Ranch, I figure my heart rate is normal, or as close to normal as it needs to be for an encounter with Imogen.

So what if the vehicles have been found? There is nothing to connect me to them and it's a big park. I put it out of my mind when I discover that I am mildly annoyed when the dog doesn't greet me. There is no canine alarm or even the slightest expression of concern from canine quarters. Maybe I'd expected some inexplicable blend of all three of those things: a loud and alarming greeting, accompanied by a frantic wagging of that golden tail. Instead, there is nothing. It's surprising and unexpected.

Aside from the lack of canine greeting, with my feet on the ground, I know right away that things are too quiet. It's not just the absence of the dog or any single thing, just a feeling. Like an absence of light. For a heartbeat I think that a pallor has fallen over the whole compound, but it's not far from that, I realize. As dramatic as that sounds.

I look around, but there's nothing to see. Not at first. Just that quiet that is almost a peace. It seems to me that even the birds have stopped singing. A foolish thought, I realize.

I'm making ever larger circles around the house when I come upon Phil. He is lying flat-sided on what I understand right away to be newly turned earth. At my approach, he doesn't lift his head, but he seems to be okay. Nothing seems to be wrong with him and all of his vitals are fine and his golden tail thumps the earth ever so slightly. He knows I'm there. "Buddy," I say, my heart full of compassion for him. For his suffering, and he does look as though he is suffering, though there are no wounds. I drop down next to him and run my hands over his smooth coat. And, quite suddenly, I *know*. I know everything. The grief-stricken dog. The freshly turned dirt. The feeling of pallor all over the compound. I have no proof—not yet—but I feel certain that Imogen is dead. But who buried her? And what happened?

Imogen had been unwell. Had she just simply passed quietly? Perhaps in the night? Or had there been some foul play? I have no way of telling, of course, and the dog isn't talking. From the looks of him, though, I suspect that, even if he could tell me, he'd be too filled with grief to be of much use.

The grave itself is crude and recent. And if she'd been planted, as it were, practically in her own yard, that would seem to indicate that the authorities have not been called. That, for me, is a good thing because otherwise I'd have to make myself scarce. As things are, I get a sense that, more than ever, I need to stick around.

When I get up to go to the house, the dog follows me. He seems torn, as if part of him would like to stay where he is and continue his vigil, but maybe he's decided that, for now, my presence is better than solitude. We are both of us grief-stricken, the dog and I. His spectral presence makes it all the more poignant.

In the house, everything is just as it was. But different. We come to a place in the kitchen where things are not as they should be, but the story is incomplete. Her favorite teapot is broken. A memory.

"My friend Hepshen made it with me in mind. I can remember his face when he gave it to me. There was this glow to him."

"When was that?"

"Sedona. 1962."

A cherished item. And perfect, after all these years. Now broken beyond repair, yet the pieces have been set back in their normal place, as though for instant use. It doesn't make sense to me.

There is an outline of spilled liquid. Did Imogen fall here? And if so, why? I think about how she seemed when I left. Wan and blue-skinned. Faint. I should not have left, I realize now. Why am I always realizing things when it is too late? That is my burden. My curse. I pull myself up. This isn't about me. Why am I making it seem that way? There are more important things right in front of me.

But why did I leave her alone?

On the other hand, I tell myself, consoling, she was old. I look at my driver's license to confirm: she was very old. If one considers their mid-nineties to be very old, and I do. Clearly, she was going to die at some point. The only sure thing in life. It was bound to happen sooner or later, of course it was. But I feel as the dog does: my heart is weighted with grief.

I take out a broom. Sweep up the broken bits of pottery. I give Phil his dinner. He turns up his nose at it and I give him the food, piece by piece. It's like he eats these small bites from my hand just to please me and my heart overflows with love for him. He's a good dog.

After a while we pad out to the casita together. I lie down on the double bed and he hops up beside me. This is new. Something his beloved Imogen perhaps allowed or even taught him. I let him stay there, comforted by the heat from his body that seeps through the light duvet.

"Good boy," I tell him. "Good, good, boy." The silky head. The deep canine sigh.

After a while we sleep. I can't imagine how.

CHAPTER THIRTY-FOUR

THE NEXT DAY, I go looking for Chester. I find him cleaning the pool, scrubbing the bottom and the sides with a long-handled blue and white brush. Why clean the pool, I wonder? Why clean it when no one is expected to swim? Maybe he doesn't know anything, after all.

"Where is Imogen?" I ask.

"She's dead." He says this matter-of-factly, confirming all my fears. Though how, with the evidence I've seen, could it have been otherwise?

"How do you know?"

"Found her."

"You found her?"

He nods. His voice betrays no emotion, but I feel a depth of loss from him, just the same.

"In the kitchen. Fallen."

"No one was around?"

He shakes his head. "No. I found her yesterday. Maybe she had been gone for a day or two by the time I got to her."

"What makes you say that?"

"She's cold when I pick her up. And purple. On her back."

He is describing lividity; where the blood pools inside the body where it falls, once the blood is no longer circulating. It strikes me that this is a detail he lacks the skills to fabricate.

"I'm sorry you had to see that," I say, but I keep my wits about me, watching him; watching the staccato movements of his fingers as he speaks and the weight that shifts from one leg to the other. Trying to judge what these things mean, failing because I don't have the read of him well enough to know if they mean one thing or another. In fact, I pretty much don't know him at all.

"I just wanted her to be okay," he says, eyes downcast. "But she wasn't."

"No. I'm sorry. It doesn't sound like it."

"Where is she now?" I say it softly.

"Buried."

I feel my heart sink at the word. Despite everything, I'd been hoping for a different answer.

"You laid her to rest?"

"Yeah. By the little grove of palo blanco trees."

I want to ask him if it looked like she had suffered or if she had gone peacefully, but I can't make myself form the words. Maybe I will come to it on a different day.

"I saw the earth there, yeah. The dog is there, too. Have you told anyone?"

He shakes his head and I wonder at this. Why not tell anyone? Is that a natural reaction? I'm not a good judge, though. What is natural anymore, and what is not?

"Is there anyone you feel you should tell?" I say, pressing even while I know there is no wrong answer. No right ones, either, but that's a different bit of philosophy.

He meets my eyes as he shakes his head. This surprises me. I would not have credited him with the depth of thought to intentionally deceive. But here he is, with his actions, letting me know he will do whatever it takes for life to continue as it has, or that's how I read his response. That's important. A part of me knows that he has become a liability; a loose end. And so I watch him carefully. At the moment it's possible he holds the key to my future. I'm just not totally sure how I feel about that.

"No one should know," is what he says at length.

"Okay. Thank you. I agree." And then a shift to the here and now. "What day do you get paid on?"

"Every second Friday."

"Okay then. Come find me on Friday. We'll keep everything just as it was."

He blinks at me but doesn't question. Emotions flit across his face, but I can't read them. Gratitude? Acceptance? Relief? Fear? I could make a case for any of those, but decide on the first. For now.

"Thank you, ma'am," he says, putting away the pool brush and heading toward his truck before I can answer anything. And that's when it hits me: something has shifted. Everything is different now. And this is what it has always been.

CHAPTER THIRTY-FIVE

NOW THE THING that focuses the cadence of life is grief. It is the bull's-eye that pulls and holds us.

Chester continues to do his chores. The cleaning of the pool. The care of all of the animals, save Phil. He waters the gardens and he's good with the hose, careful not to overwater. Careful to make sure everyone has enough. He is mindful and gentle with plants and animals alike. If grief has altered his countenance or his rhythms, I don't see it. He is stoic and solid. Ever-Chester. Everything is different. Nothing has changed.

I paint and I work and I tend to Phil. And I feel as though I am deciding something, but I'm not sure what. A few weeks ago I had told Imogen I wasn't sure I wanted to go through with her plan; now there is no choice. And I have nowhere else to go, anyway. Nothing on that front has changed.

The only thing that has really changed is the weather, and the world suddenly begins to cool. Phil and I go for long walks while I marvel that the hellishly hot landscape can be become perfect so quickly.

When I'm not walking, I'm mostly painting. Both of those things serve a single purpose: they keep me from thinking too deeply, because the thoughts I have when I stop are tedious to me. Repetitive. Thoughts I've had before.

Things are peaceful now, but I realize that it could all change very quickly. Once the world knows that Imogen is dead, our oasis will be breached. Broken. Imogen the artist was revered. Venerated. Maybe they will make this spot into a museum, though I can't quite imagine these *they* who might act. She had no children. No lovers that she has not already outlived. If she had friends whose company she enjoyed, she didn't talk about them to me. In the time I spent with her, the phone was mostly silent and the correspondence I did for her was businesslike in nature. She was alone. She would not be forgotten, but she was no longer loved in a real and intimate way. The thought makes me sad, though I realize I helm a similar boat. Except the forgotten part. Without feeling the least bit maudlin, I realize I will be completely forgotten after no time at all.

So then the question comes to me unbidden: Does the world even have to know? That had been her plan, of course: that no one would know when she passed. It had been what Imogen wanted and what she tried to talk me into participating in. Things have changed now.

When Imogen was alive, I had humored her, in a way. In my mind the dress-up, the driver's license—all of those things were little more than an elaborate game of pretend. I had figured we had years to go. But surely no one could just pretend someone hadn't died. Now I wonder. Maybe it wasn't so crazy to think about, after all.

Could we keep Imogen's demise secret in order to preserve this spot in the way she had wanted? To keep it safe for me and Phil and also for Chester who certainly has no other place to go. And what of the half score of cats who make the place their home? And the wild horses. It's like Imogen's little world is an ecosystem. The things she loved and the art she made set the tone for the whole place. The making of art. The preserving of nature. It feels like it should be a UNESCO site. But just for us: no hordes of visitors or lookie-loos. An oasis kept safe from time and the outside world. It's what she had wanted. Now I wonder if I can pull it off.

It's a tall order, that's the thing. Here we have paradise and the memory of a woman whose only wish was for the life she had built to stay just as it was: even without her in it. On the other hand, there are the things that are expected in such a situation. Even so, there isn't much I need to do. Imogen has already been planted. It's not like I'm even considering interfering with something that has already occurred. It's not like I'm killing her, that's what I mean. And maybe, to me, that feels like a refreshing change. It's like I've been asked to keep her alive in spirit rather than removing her from the earth. Full reversal.

I'm not sure where I am when I decide and I fully commit. Was I visiting the horses, or working on a new painting or walking with the dog? Maybe wisps of it came to me from all of those places, but I find that, quite suddenly, I am committed because of "why not" if for no other reason.

It seems to me that there is some business I need to take care of before I fully immerse myself in the business of being Imogen.

I get ready for a day trip, starting by pulling all of my personal things out of my car, even the stuff under the false bottom in the trunk: my second handgun, and the boxes of ammunition. The stacks of cash and even a few small mementos.

I do this transferring without emotion or even very much thought. Even while I hide the second Bersa in the meat drawer of the refrigerator in the casita and stash ammo in the vegetable crisper, the stacks of bills in a freezer bag under a loaf of bread in the freezer compartment, I try to keep my mind blank.

I can't help but laugh at myself: turning the small, apartment-size refrigerator into a bank and arsenal, but I can't think for the moment where else to put them.

This time when I leave, I don't take the dog and I don't go to Lourdes or any of the small towns within easy driving distance. Instead, I take my own car and drive right into Phoenix, though it's a couple of hours away.

Phoenix is a big city and it seems like a good bet that I won't run into anyone I know running errands from there. I will be anonymous in a crowd. No one will even care what I'm up to.

I find a wig shop and spend a couple of hours having myself fitted with the head of hair that most, to me, resembles Imogen's head of dark gray locks. The crap wig she'd had and the scraps left over from my trip to the City won't do. Not now. Things are about to get serious, I can feel that in my bones. I'd better be ready.

Next, I use my phone to search out a place that sells theatrical makeup. As I buy various pots and jars of it, I realize I don't yet know what to do with it, but I'm about to have time on my hands and I'm confident I'll be able to figure it out. It's never going to look like it did when Jennifer K. Riley and her crew applied it, but I should be able to do it well enough so that in most circumstances it will do in a pinch.

I save the most difficult of my tasks for last. I locate a car lot in a seedy part of town. Big Red's Auto Barn has a sign out front that says they offer cash for cars. On approach, the place looks right for my purposes. A nice enough little car lot out front. A big building behind a high fence out back. It has all the earmarks. I figure I've found the right place, first try.

A scruffy-looking guy with greasy blond hair offers me four hundred dollars for my fifteen-year-old Volvo. I tell him I'll sell it to them for two hundred if they take the car without paperwork.

"Is it stolen?" He asks it, but I can tell it's a form question. He doesn't really care. The way he's asked it is telling, though. I get that my answer isn't a dealbreaker.

"It is not stolen. No," I say in the same even tone.

He meets my eyes. "Let me put it to you this way: If I buy this car from you, could I put it out front for sale?"

I hesitate, thinking of just the right answer. Then, "You might not want to do that," I say carefully.

He looks at me appraisingly for a few beats. It's like he's deciding what to do.

"Okay," he says finally. "I'll give you one fifty."

"Done," I say, because it isn't the money I care about. At all. "I need one thing though: a ride out into the desert." I give him the address.

"A ride out that far, it's gonna be two fifty."

I smile as I answer. It was more or less the number I was expecting to hear.

"Done," I say. I sign a fake name to a bogus document of sale, and dirty blond hair guy pulls someone out of the shop who gets into a battered and ancient Ford Escape. He indicates I should climb into the back, and I do. Then we roll.

CHAPTER THIRTY-SIX

THE DROP-OFF IS easy. The driver who's gotten assigned with wheeling me back to the boonies has about as much interest in me as he would if I were a cat. Or someone's mom. Or the mom of someone's cat. Edwin is the perfect driver for this mission. He has two full sleeves of ink plus a tattoo on his right cheek of a heart dripping blood. He asks no questions and barely addresses me at all on the nearly two-hour drive. It's all fine by me. More than fine. I have a lot to think about.

I have him drop me near the place I first let Phil out of the car on what now seems a very long-ago day. Then I trudge the not inconsiderable distance to the house, but my load is light. I'm able to stow everything I've brought back with me in the small backpack that made the trip into town with this purpose in mind.

At the house, the dog seems happy enough to see me, but he doesn't jump and frolic like he used to. It may seem fanciful, but I feel as though he has a heavy heart. I leave it to take its course. Grief takes time and looks different on all of us—I know that as well as anyone can. I don't imagine that it's much different for animals than people. I give him the time and space to grieve.

In that space, I have a lot to do. Thoughts to think and preparations to make. It saddens me to think about my faithful old Volvo
chopped up for parts, which no doubt it will be, but the sacrifice
had to be made to go forward with these next steps. Cutting all
ties to my past and the outside world seems like the best path. And,
anyway, I'd cut all those ties before. Getting rid of the car should
be the smallest hardship. And yet. But it's just a twang.

Though it seems at least a little crazy—even to me—I'm going
to do what Imogen wanted: I'm going to step into her shoes or,
at least, try. And why not? She has no kids, no heirs. I don't even
feel the need to rationalize it: there's just no reason for me not to
do this and there are even a few that tip the balance the other way.

All things considered, it's not a big decision—it's all just planning. Execution. A matter of how to pull it off. And I reason that,
since Imogen had been a recluse for so many years it won't be that
hard. No one has even seen her in decades, and the one time they
did, it was me. Most people don't even remember what she looks
like. Those who might recognize her have something to gain from
her being alive.

The identity I'd left behind—given away—replaced. In spades.
There are other ways to do this: to create a whole identity out of
purchased parts. I've done it before. Somehow it's different this
time, though. And there's an appropriate sort of rightness to all
of this, like I'm Imogen's heir or executor and I'm going to look
after the estate and her art and all of those she cared about. And
I will. And I am.

I sit at the kitchen table with a pot of tea—her tea, though not
of course her favorite pot—while I think these thoughts. I realize
that sometime in the last few minutes, the dog has come in and

placed his head on my lap and is looking up at me soulfully, his amber eyes filled with emotion. A new and different phase.

"It'll be okay, old son," I say softly, stroking the silky head. "It won't hurt as much after a while. You'll see." Even as I say it, I wonder if it's true. Even as I say it, I wonder if it ever is.

CHAPTER THIRTY-SEVEN

ONCE I'VE DECIDED to go through with it, I settle in to work out the details—puzzle out what the future will be, beyond the initial planning she had begun. It's one thing to think about doing something like this, after all. Something entirely different to pull it all off.

Going through Imogen's stuff, I realize it isn't entirely like starting over. More like just getting a handle on what is there. For instance, there are already credit cards in place. But how do I access account information without passwords? We hadn't gotten to that part before she moved on. Ditto all of the things that make up modern life: taxes, power bills, checking accounts, safety deposit boxes. It's like a puzzle I have to unravel. In the way all of this was first conceived, I'd figured we'd have a few years to delve into the minutiae. It hadn't worked out that way. At all.

There's a lot to get through, but I take my time. Where do I need to be, anyway? I am sorting through the life of one of the most important artists of her generation. Dealing with it all demands some respect. I conjure all of that. Let it seep in and through me. It's important work I'm doing. I feel it. And it's as real as anything I've ever done. I take pains to get it right.

Imogen had said there was no will, but I look for one anyway. With all she had accumulated in her life, the lack of one doesn't make sense, but I look in all of the likely places and no will turns up. I find other salient things though. At the back of the office, in a filing cabinet that looks as though it hasn't been opened in a long time, I come across a life insurance policy that expired more than three decades earlier. I wonder at that. What had happened thirty-five years ago that had led to her letting the policy lapse? I read it fully, looking for I'm not sure what. And then I find it: the beneficiary is Rose Reed. There is something about the name that tugs at my memory, but I can't quite place it. I turn back to my search.

Digging a bit deeper, that same filing cabinet is where I also turn up Imogene's agency agreement with Beardsley as well as the deed to Ocotillo Ranch. All of these pieces make sense to me. One doesn't. And it's only by the faintest coincidence that I find it at all. Unlike the other documents, it is not in a file folder, but taped to the back of the cabinet drawer, in an effort to conceal it, I imagine, because I can't think why else anyone would secure a thing in that way.

I pull out the envelope with interest, curious. The tape is brittle. The envelope yellowed. Inside there is a single document and a photo. The document is a birth certificate. The name on the certificate is Heather Reed. Mother is listed as Rose Reed. Father unknown. And the date makes the child just a few years younger than me.

The photo is a Polaroid. The image square and thick. The subject is a younger Imogen—I've seen enough photos of her to recognize her instantly. And she is holding a small child. And the child is dressed in pink.

I stare at the photo for a while. It is on the darkish side and the background is unclear, but it seems to me that Imogen holds the child with affection, yet clearly this is not Imogen's own child: the dates tell me that Imogen would have been close to sixty when Heather was born. The other thing that tells me this is a significant find is where I found it: you don't go to the trouble of taping something inside a drawer unless you intend to hide it or at least keep it safe.

After a while, I put the photo and the certificate aside and try to put the mystery aside, as well. It's hard though. Whatever else it means, the find tells me that there was even more to Imogen than I had thought previously. The discovery does not give me ease.

CHAPTER THIRTY-EIGHT

AFTER A WHILE, Phil overcomes his grief. Not all at once.

At first, he visits the grove where Imogen was laid to rest for shorter periods. I take it to mean that the essential her that lingered for a while has gone. Whatever the case, Phil begins shadowing me again. He has always been sweet and affectionate. Now he is clingy. I wonder how long it will last.

We settle into a routine. Early morning walks to beat the heat. On days when it will be cooler for longer, I sometimes lug my plein air stuff out with us and paint pictures of various flora and of the rocky dark red hills nearby. Phil stays near me at these times, scurrying away often when some interesting bird or rodent crosses our paths. I have to smile as Phil hops after some little animal now and again. A rabbit maybe—or is it a hare? There's a difference, but I don't know what it is—or a lizard. The desert is alive with life he likes to chase. It slows him down so much, he has no hope of catching everything. But the chase is the thing. It seems to lift his spirits and you can't help but smile.

And me, I begin to settle in. There is a certain hollow comfort in knowing that tomorrow is going to look pretty much like yesterday. That wouldn't suit everyone. It wouldn't have suited me a decade ago, but it does now. I breathe deeply and put one foot in front of the other.

After a while, even though for a few weeks I walk and paint and generally immerse myself into the reality of being Imogen O'Brien, I realize there is something I'm not quite easy with. It's like you're looking at a photo and you know the focus is off, but you can't quite put your finger on it.

Look at the eyes, that's the thing. If the eyes aren't in focus, nothing works. That's always true.

Yes, Imogen had been old. But it isn't just being old that kills one. Had she been about to die when I last saw her? I certainly wouldn't have said so. And then again, what the hell do I know? But something is not correct. I feel as though I know the signs of a death that wasn't right: I've caused enough of them.

I begin with Imogen's broken teapot. For the teapot to have fallen the way that it did, it seemed to me that Imogen would have had to have been holding it near the sink. I go out and find Chester.

"You got a minute?"

He shrugs, but follows me back into the house.

"Tell me where you found her."

He indicates a spot near the bedroom door, far from the kitchen sink. Across the room.

I try a different track.

"How did she seem to you?"

"How do you mean?"

"Did she look as though she had hurt herself? Or fallen ill? Or...?"

"She was just dead," he says. I can't gauge the quality of his voice.

"How about the last time you saw her? Did she seem okay?"

"Okay enough, I guess. She hasn't been fully right for a while, I think."

"What do you mean?"

"She just didn't seem that strong is all." Does he sound a little defensive? I can't be sure. "And she couldn't do as much stuff. She was calling on me to do more and more. Not that I minded. I always like doing things for her. I just felt like she was getting weaker."

And here, yes, I see it again. A shifting of his weight from one leg to another. A glitter of sweat on the forehead that hadn't been there just a minute before.

I breathe shallowly. And I take my time, wondering what he's holding back. If he is telling the truth, he hadn't seen very much.

"Can you describe how she lay?"

For a moment he looks as though he might speak, then he shakes his head.

"No, I'm sorry, no. When I try to think of that day, there is a blank there."

I just look at him, trying to decipher his words.

"A blank?"

"Yeah. Maybe I blocked it out? I did that once. When my dog died. I know I was there, but I can't make myself remember any of it."

"Oh," I say. "I'm . . . sorry. About your dog, I mean."

"It's okay now," he says. "It was a long time ago."

"So you don't remember anything about how you found Imogen."

"Well, she was dead."

"Yeah," I say. "I got that part."

"I'm sorry she's dead," he says simply.

"Me, too," I admit. "You didn't see anyone though? When you found her, no one was around? You would have said, right?"

"I wasn't there. She was two or so days dead when I found her."

"And Phil?" I was afraid to ask it.

"Phil wasn't here."

That doesn't make sense.

"What do you mean? Of course he was here. Where else would he be?"

"He was in the casita."

"What?"

"Yeah. He started hollering I guess when he heard me." Chester's feet are moving a little more quickly now, I notice. And the sweat on his brow. There is now a trickle from his ear to his collarbone. It disappears there into his T-shirt. I watch it, fascinated.

"He must have been locked in there for two or three days." Now he's just talking, I think. Filling in gaps. Trying to make up for whatever he said that was saying too much. If I hadn't been watching him so closely, I would have felt sorry for him.

"So he was locked in there . . ." I prompt.

"Yeah," he rushes on. "And he was some thirsty when he got out. I gave him some of my sandwich, too, as I figured he'd be hungry. He'd left a mess or two in there. I cleaned it up."

For Chester, this was a long speech. Many words. I just blink at him while I take it all in. Who would have locked the dog in the casita while I was away?

"Why didn't you tell me before?" He pauses before answering. I see him give it all deep thought. Finally, he says simply: "You didn't ask."

He had me there. I hadn't.

I wonder about how much he told me is true, but I decide to wonder alone.

"Thanks, Chester. You've been very helpful. Thanks for your time."

I watch his back retreat as he crosses the yard and heads toward the pond and the barn. I feel he's walking extra fast, like he's making tracks and putting space between us, but it's possible I don't have that right.

How would Phil have gotten stuck in the casita? I look at the lay of the land and try to figure it. Could he have turned real quick and shut the door with his butt? That seemed possible. He's a big dog and he's certainly done stuff like that before. It's just that I can't remember leaving the casita's front door open and I never use the back at all. And yes: I hadn't been on the property when it happened, but then, with me gone, why would anyone have had reason to be in the casita? So that is another mystery.

I knew that some of these mysteries were going to have to stay that way. Imogen was in the ground. It might even have been natural causes. Or not. A stroke or blunt trauma or poison or even a gun. It could have been anything. Chester had buried her. It was done. Thinking that gave me pause as well. Could Chester have been responsible? I discard the thought almost as soon as I have it. Chester's concern and distress had been genuine. I am sure of it. If he had somehow caused Imogen's death, it seems more likely to me that he would have run, not buried her. And Imogen had been Chester's protector. Why would he have wanted to kill her? It just didn't add up. But she was just as dead.

Once I get to the guesthouse, I feel like I smell something slightly foul, but it's faint and I try to acknowledge that it might even be in my mind. Chester had said he cleaned up, but I grab a bucket and a mop and clean it further now, scrubbing until I am satisfied that any trace of anything is gone.

CHAPTER THIRTY-NINE

I FINISH OUT the day in the casita, trying to read, even trying to calm myself with a bit of television. Nothing works. It feels as though I have a lot on my mind and the exercise that usually helps get me past my demons has been eluding me while I puzzle all of this out. In the evening, when I once again find myself restless, I determine that tomorrow I'll at least get a walk in.

I wake to sunshine streaming in the window and onto my forehead. It is so intense I feel all of that light might penetrate my brain. I realize that when I went to bed the night before, I'd been so distracted I'd forgotten to close the curtains and the brilliance of another Arizona desert day first thing in the morning is blinding.

This was one of the things I'd quickly discovered I didn't particularly like about Arizona: almost every day you can count on it dawning clear and gorgeous. There is little variation. If you are someone whose moods depend on clear skies and sunshine, Arizona is the place to be. I'm not one of those. My heart craves the occasional gray sky.

As of this moment, there is no flow to my new life as Imogen. I don't even know where to start and I don't know quite what to do with myself, so I just begin, with no real aim in mind.

After a while, I find myself in the studio. I try to visualize myself painting, but I'm not ready yet. There are ghosts and echoes I'm not ready to tackle.

I spend a longer than usual amount of time looking at the work Imogen had in progress; regarding it critically for the first time, dissecting it mentally. It's one of the large canvases and I remember helping her with it before I left. Fully abstract, one gets a strong impression of water as well as all of the habitats around the ranch: the pond where the horses gather and the field and barn where the cats hang out. Or was that, too, part of the magic of Imogen O'Brien: that she could make even the fully abstract seem personal to every viewer? I feel an almost irresistible urge to finish the piece for her. I can imagine just how it should be. Some stippling in the variegated green, maybe. A brush of clouds through the sky. A shimmer of what I take to be the pond. I hold myself back from taking up the brush. This had been Imogen's vision. I muse that maybe it's time for me to once again service my own art. What would my own vision look like? And would the talent Imogen felt she had seen in me still be available to me without her to coach and guide it? Here in the studio, I feel her absence in a way I hadn't allowed myself until now.

And so, as with the deciphering of mysteries, I just begin.

I go out to the field right behind the studio and pick an armload of wildflowers. I find stands of what Imogen had taught me were wild fleabane and blanket flowers. In the studio, I find a vase and plop them in. I prepare a palette, choose some brushes, but before I begin, I return to Imogen's last piece and attack it with my vision. I develop the idea of lake I had imagined, complete what I felt was the steel of the sky and the hint of sunset on horizon. I don't know how much time passes. It's as though I am filled and guided, and I just fall into the feeling; let it guide my hands. It's like she's standing next to me.

Once completed, I find I am happy with the work. It feels like transition: a handing over of the reins, her to me. I can't help but think she would be pleased.

When I go back to my vase and my wildflowers, I feel ready and I dive right in. Almost right away I realize why still life paintings have been so popular for the whole history of art: the flowers just sit there, not moving or talking back. As long as I work quickly enough for them to still be relatively fresh, they would sit there unaltered until I finished the work: unlike humans or dogs or even horses or cats, who all tend to want to move around.

The blanket flower and the fleabane are similar to each other in shape, but different in texture and spirit, if that can be said of a flower. They're different sizes, as well. Those similarities and differences result in an interesting composition.

I choose to paint them in a free-form way: more impressionistic than representational. It takes everything I have to get it even close to what my mind wants. What pulls me back into the here and now is Phil, huffing gently in the space behind me.

"What is it, buddy?" I ask it quietly, turning to look at him to see why he's raising the alarm.

His response is louder than those quiet "huffs" had been. Instead he gives a solid "hoof!" that is pretty close to a bark.

I pull myself away from the work and look outside where I'm surprised to see, instead of the nothing I'd expected, a long, low dark car parked in the paved circle in front of Imogen's house. I chastise myself. It shouldn't surprise me to see a vehicle in the middle of the day, and yet it does. In the months I've been here, other than Imogen's SUV, Chester's old pickup truck, and that one ill-fated UTV, this is the first vehicle I've seen in this space.

As I pass the car on the way to the house, I get an impression of wealth. The fact that the big car has been parked across the walkway that leads to the house also conveys a sense of entitlement.

I move slowly and silently toward the house rather than walking boldly, though I'm not quite sure why. What am I expecting to see? I don't feel entirely safe and I'm certain I don't want to engage whoever this is. I tell myself that I don't need a reason to be ultra cautious. Caution is never a bad starting point.

I creep past the windows, trying to stay as invisible as possible while keeping my eyes open for sound or movement. I am aware of Phil padding silently behind me. It occurs to me I should have left him behind, locked in the studio, but possible danger to the dog hadn't popped into my mind until it was too late to do anything about it. I pray for him to keep quiet while I press ahead.

In the house, I see the outline of a figure—possibly two—in the hallway between the kitchen and Imogen's bedroom, that room still looking exactly as it did on the day she checked out. I realize in that moment that Imogen's impromptu in-house storeroom is down that same hallway and I sprint back to the casita, my mind filled with purpose.

I grab the Bersa and a clip of bullets from the refrigerator. In another fast motion, I pull on an oversized hoodie and jam the now loaded gun into the waistband of my jeans. This time, also, I am careful to lock the dog in the casita, only because I know that worrying about him will slow my progress and cloud my mind.

I am back at the main house in just a few minutes, certain the creeper is still inside because the big car continues to block the path.

Now properly armed, I enter boldly.

"Hello," I call out once I'm in the front door and then again, "Can I help you?"

"I'm looking for Miss O'Brien." I feel shocked and also somehow not surprised to see Beardsley appear from down the hallway. Somehow, I *am* surprised to see the reporter Heidi at his elbow, her cloud of hair gently curled into a dark halo by the heat and lack of humidity.

"Why are you in the house?" I say it warily, but I have one hand on the gun under my hoodie.

"I have some . . . some business to discuss with Imogen." And then a sharp look. "Is she here?" And he watches me expectantly, like I might tell him something he needs to look surprised about. Or maybe I'm imagining that. I give the idea a second to take root before I answer. I let it take hold and spread.

For her part, Heidi looks uncomfortable, like she's been caught at something. I see her glance from Beardsley to me and back again and I notice her long fingers nervously trace the delicate bones at the base of her neck. I can't tell what any of it means.

"She's in Peoria," I say, not knowing how the name of the Phoenix suburb got into my head. I'm not even sure exactly where it is or how I'd even heard of it.

"Peoria," he repeats. Does he look skeptical? Does he look as though he does not believe me? Both of those things are possible and, then again, maybe I'm paranoid; imagining things. But I don't think so.

"What is she doing there?"

"In Peoria? Visiting a friend." I spit it out, remembering suddenly to pack in a bit of outrage. Who the hell is he, questioning me? Who does he imagine he is, having broken into Imogen's house? "More importantly," I say, "who are you and what are you doing here?" And then I lay on more outrage, and under my hoodie my hand doesn't leave the pistol's grip, just in case—though I'm fairly certain the art dealer won't be a danger to me, there is something about the situation that requests caution. "Why did you break in?" My eyes include Heidi.

His eyes grow wide at this. Alarmed. For her part, Heidi looks as though she'd prefer to be almost anywhere else.

"Break in? No, no," he says. "The door wasn't locked." This part I knew to be true. Imogen never locked the door and I hadn't been locking it either. "So I'm not breaking in. Plus, Imogen had . . . had invited me to visit when I saw her a few weeks ago."

I blink at him.

"She did?" It's all I can think to say. It's a lie, of course, what he's said to me. I was there. That was me. I know what was said. But how can I tell him that without giving too much away?

"Yes," he says, and his face is straight. "She said come any time."

"That doesn't sound like her," I say cautiously.

"It doesn't. I know. I know her well," he says. "But, in any case, it was at her behest that I came." And he sounds more confident with his lies now. "And so here I am. With that in mind, where can I pitch my tent? So to speak."

And it's pretty clear he doesn't mean he's planning on camping.

"Sorry, no," I say. "There'll be no pitching of tents."

"No, Beardsley." I realize it's the first time Heidi has spoken. "She's right: no pitching of tents. I think I saw a little inn back at Tortilla Flat. We should have checked in there in the first place."

"But that's at least an hour away," Beardsley says, protesting.

"No," I add. "It's more. Maybe an hour and a half."

"Nevertheless," Heidi says, directing herself to Beardsley, ignoring me for the moment. "I insist, Beardsley. Imogen isn't here. We can't just expect to be put up. I'm sorry for the intrusion," she says, turning to me. "I didn't catch your name."

"I didn't say it," I reply. "I'm Imogen's niece."

"I can see the resemblance," Heidi says.

"I didn't know Imogen had a niece," Beardsley sniffs.

"Well, apparently she does," Heidi says. "C'mon, Beardsley. I told you we had no business barging in here." And then to me, "I'm sorry. Please tell Imogen we were here."

"We'll check in with her later," Beardsley says, and he sounds curt.

I listen for engine noises, and when the big car purrs away, I allow myself to breathe again. I realize from the first that it is no victory. It's a stall, at best. For whatever reason, the agent knows something is amiss and he's back on the scene. And Heidi? Maybe she's just along for the ride, maybe even snooping for a story. And what a story she will have if she snoops deeply enough. My head spins a bit just thinking about it; I have to back away.

The whole snooping for stories thing gives me an idea, though I'm not sure it's a good one. I head back to the casita to breathe, release the dog, and grab my phone.

CHAPTER FORTY

I'M A LITTLE surprised when Curtis Diamond recognizes my voice right away.

"Gawd, lady," he says and the warmth I hear reminds me what a good friend he's been to me. And that I've missed him. "I wondered where the hell you got to. Gave me a scare when I tried to call you last month and your number didn't work anymore. It's good to hear your voice."

"Sorry to disappear on you, Curtis. But yeah. It's a long story."

"I'll bet," he says. "But you know me: I live for that shit."

I laugh.

"Yeah. I know. I know you do. But I'm not going there right now, okay?"

Curtis is a news reporter. He's a television newscaster, which I always kind of think of as kind of less-than when it comes to journalism. Whatever the case, he gets out there and digs for the stories he wants. Though that's not why I'm calling him now.

"And here I thought maybe we were going for dinner or something," he says.

"So you're in LA?"

"I guess that means you're not," he says.

"You're right."

"Where are you then?"

"Arizona."

"That's crazy," he says. "I'm headed to Phoenix in the morning."

He says the words without emphasis. He's talking about work now, I can tell. Even so I get a funny feeling in the pit of my stomach. Like something is happening, but it's just out of my sight and grasp.

"Tell me," I say.

"You ever heard of Imogen O'Brien?"

"I have," I say, schooling my mind to blank and my voice to calm.

"Well, she turned up after a long time gone a few weeks ago. In fact I happened to be at a show at a gallery in New York recently and she was there, or so I'm told. I didn't see her myself."

"She turned up? Was she missing?"

"Not missing exactly, no. She's like ninety-something. And no one had seen her for years and years. And suddenly, she's at her old gallery and the work is flying out of there like hotcakes. There's a story there. I smell it. Not quite sure what it is, though."

"I still don't know why you're coming to Arizona, though," I say.

"Well, again, I didn't see her but people who did said she looked fabulous. Like, better than she did twenty years ago."

"That's weird," I say, still calm, even though I now have my head pressed to the cool wood of the desk in the casita and Phil is watching me quizzically.

"Right? So I figure, I'm gonna head out into the desert, find her, and discover her fountain of youth or whatever. Or else maybe I'll see if something funny is up with her sudden reappearance or whatever. It's a story. I just know it."

"Spidey sense?"

"Check. I feel something in my bones."

"But I think she hates the press," I say weakly.

"How do you know that?"

"Oh, you know. You hear things."

"Do you? I guess. Well, anyway, I'll head out there. See what I can see. Say, maybe we can get together for lunch or something. You want to pick me up at the airport? Are you in Phoenix or someplace else?"

"I'm in . . . I'm in Sedona," I say, not even sure why, but knowing I can't tell him where I actually am. At least, not without some thought. "So maybe next time?"

"Sedona. That sounds fun. But I guess too far for a lunch run. Sorry: I've been blabbing my head off. What did you call about anyway?"

"Just . . . you know. Just to say hi. Have a great trip. Maybe we'll get that lunch some other time."

CHAPTER FORTY-ONE

AFTER I HANG up the phone I don't move for a while, just let all the thoughts and emotions run over me, hoping somehow they'll wash through and make everything okay again. I wait a while, though, and it doesn't happen.

In my mind, I run through what it looks like to go through with the plan Imogen and I had concocted. What we didn't dial in: the possibility of reporters converging once she resurfaced. The additional possibility that I was good friends with one of those who would be reporting. It occurs to me to kill Curtis to preserve what I've set my sights on. I discard the idea as quickly as it comes to me. There are people I could do that to, but Curtis isn't one of them. He has been special to me in so many ways.

No: killing Curtis is not an option. In any case, Curtis isn't the only problem. Based on what I've seen already, there are people—perhaps many—who feel that Imogen's fame and their own proximity gives them license. I am surprised someone like Beardsley would just barge into Imogen's home unannounced. At his heels, Heidi: herself looking for a story. And somehow it didn't seem to occur to either of them to just sit outside after they knocked and no one let them in. It meant that disguising myself wouldn't always be an option. Just this morning I had worked on a painting set to bear Imogen's signature. What if someone had seen me? And suddenly that seems all too possible.

No: the situation Imogen and I had conceived of seemed less plausible by the moment. If only Imogen had lived. Maybe then, combining our skills, we could have pulled it off. But with Imogen gone? I am rapidly seeing that the possibility for success of the original plan is unlikely. I am surprised at myself for not having spotted it before. In fact, it all seems somewhat foolish now. I'd allowed myself to be talked into the idea of this idyllic reality, at least for a while. Wonderful art. A secret and welcoming home in the desert. Wild horses and feral cats. The saving of a dynamic legacy.

The dream had been so complete; so detailed: Imogen and I, out here painting. Her producing work with me helping her, and me maybe attending the occasional gala; her growing and changing as an artist, despite her advanced age, trading on the franchise she'd spent a lifetime building while moving on to newer adventures in art that intrigued her more.

Looking back at that vision, it seems ridiculous I'd ever even entertained that things could happen in that way. I feel as though I am now seeing things much more clearly. Of *course* the press would be interested when the iconic Imogen O'Brien returned to public life. She had been a rock-star painter in years gone by. Now, after decades of silence, a gallery appearance, and a sold-out show? That has all the earmarks of a great story, and here's my old friend Curtis: headed this way, just in case I need it all underlined. That seems an impossible coincidence and would certainly hasten the demise of the enterprise: What are the chances that it would be Curtis, of all people, coming to put a story together on Imogen? But the fact that it is Curtis merely hastens what I can see now looks fairly inevitable. The walls are closing in; I have to be proactive.

What had I been thinking?

And still, I keep rolling it all around in my head.

After a while I get an idea and I call him back.

"I don't know why I said Sedona. Jerk of the knee?"

"You're not in Sedona?"

"No. Like I said: I'm not sure why I told you that. I panicked or something."

"I get that. Like giving someone a fake number. You've always been pretty private."

"I never gave you a fake number."

"Whatever. It's happened to me before."

"It has?" I'm honestly astonished. Who would give a handsome television reporter attached to a Los Angeles station but with a national following a fake number?

"I can't imagine."

"Never mind. I'm not telling that story. Not now. Why are you calling me back?"

I hesitate. And then I plunge right in.

"I'm in the middle of something. And nothing is quite what it seems."

"So, business as usual," he says, and I sort of blanch, because he's never known quite what business I'm in. Curtis thinks I'm CIA or something, but he's never asked, and I've never volunteered.

"It was you mentioning Imogen O'Brien. That's what threw me off."

"Oh-kay." I can hear the question, but I don't answer it. Not right away.

"This is off the record, all right?"

"With you that's automatic." He says it jokily, but I can also tell he's paying attention. Friendly banter on the outside, all business on the inside. That's always Curtis. With a touch of the flirt. It's a pretty much irresistible combination.

"Just say yes. I want it to be said aloud between us."

"Okay," he says. "Yes. I agree: off the record."

"I'm not in Sedona, I'm in the Cathedral National Forest."

"From the small world department: that's where I'm heading. It's where Imogen O'Brien lives."

"I know. I'm at her house. And . . . and she's not here."

"Where is she?"

"I don't know. Exactly. For sure. She's not where she's supposed to be."

There is a long beat. I hear him considering. In that time, I also think about what I'm doing: giving up the game this early makes no sense at all. Except, it makes all the sense. I can see now that the game is flawed. It was never meant to be. Waiting until he got here and saw me would just make matters worse. And me taking off makes no sense, either. I think about my Volvo longingly and I just want to cry.

"Do you have any idea where she is?"

"No. Not really." I flash on the newly turned earth and the bereft dog. So, yeah. I have a pretty good idea, but I'm not willing to go there quite yet.

"So now that we have established that you're not actually in Sedona, you want to pick me up at the airport?"

I surprise myself by discovering that I do.

CHAPTER FORTY-TWO

THE NEXT DAY, it also surprises me to see how happy I am to see his face.

"I've missed you," I say when he's thrown his bag onto the back seat of Imogen's car and settled in next to me. I'm startled that I've said it out loud. More startled still to feel it at all. It's been a long time since I missed anyone, except for the ones I miss all the time and with every breath. I put that out of my head.

"Ditto here," he says, settling in. "You remain the one that got away." And we both laugh uproariously at this because it's kind of true and also a fiction between us. He has been making delicate plays for me since we first met, and I've always resisted effortlessly. I see him as a comrade, a partner, in a way. It seems possible he sees me differently, but I've never allowed things to go in that direction. I mean, I could of course. I mean, I like him—he's kind and not at all hard on the eyes. But the thought of emotional connection still frightens me. Maybe it always will.

"Really, though?" This easy chemistry has always come to us without effort. It makes humor possible between us, as well as understanding. "The only one? I find that hard to believe."

"I told you the other day: I get fake phone numbers. I'm a lot less hot than I look."

"Ohmigawd," I say. And in this way we laugh our way from Phoenix Sky Harbor until the Superstition Mountains begin to rise in front of us.

"It's lovely," he says as we drive. "How did you end up out here?"

"Long story," I say, eyes firmly on the road.

"Well, of course it is. Give me the short version."

"Imogen is . . . well, she's my relative." I've already decided not to give him the whole account. At least not yet.

"Okay," he says.

"I've been working with her. Kind of assisting? I left on a short trip recently. When I came back, she was gone."

"Did she maybe just take a short trip herself?"

I shoot a look at him, trying to determine if he's kidding. I can see he's not.

"She's in her nineties, Curtis. She's not gonna run off with the mailman or something."

"I was thinking more like the FedEx guy," Curtis says.

"Amazon?"

"No. Definitely not that."

That chemistry again. Not to mention bad jokes. I feel myself breathing more clearly than I have in weeks.

"Okay. So she's gone. No trace?"

"Right."

"Where have you checked?"

"Well, there's not much *to* check, you know? There had been no talk of a trip. Her favorite teapot was broken."

"Hmmm," Curtis says.

"Right? But that might be nothing but a cat or something."

"She have a cat?"

"She kinda has a lot of cats."

"A lot of cats. Okay. She take a suitcase?"

"I can't tell. She has clothes in her closet going back to the 1960s. And I wouldn't know how many suitcases she owns. It's impossible for me to tell that just from looking at her stuff."

"And her car is missing?"

"No." I indicate the SUV we're riding in. "This is it. But she could have been picked up. Or called an Uber or something."

"Expensive ride."

"She wouldn't care. Money is not a problem."

We are now in the mountains, on the forest service road that leads to Ocotillo Ranch. As we approach Arcadia Bluff, I find myself holding my breath, but when we round the corner and there it is in front of us, there's nothing but beauty: no emergency vehicles, no flag person, no nothing. Curtis catches my look and follows my glance.

"Gosh," he says. "It's beautiful, isn't it?"

The high cliffs, the faraway water, the endless cacti.

"It is," I agree. "There's no place quite like it."

"You were saying: She's not short on beans, I guess is what you were getting at. Imogen."

"Right. There are problems, but that isn't one of them as far as I know. For instance, her agent showed up here yesterday. Unannounced. I thought it was weird."

"Is that Beardsley Davenport?"

"It is."

"I know him slightly."

"I didn't even know you ever covered the arts beat."

"Yeah. It's where I came from. Crime is just what gets you the best stories."

"The most recognition."

"Something like that. But I started out as a painter. I've always covered some of the stories from that world."

"Geez, Curt: You're a regular renaissance guy, aren't you?" This because it always seemed like he knew at least a little something about everything I ever asked him. And if he didn't have the answer, he always knew who did.

"It's true. I am. But why would you think it was weird that her agent showed up? Isn't that pretty natural?"

"Until the show last month, they hadn't spoken in something like fifteen years."

"Imogen and Beardsley? I had no idea. They seemed cool enough with each other at the event."

"You saw her?"

"No, but from what I heard, I guess. There were no whispers of strife or anything."

"Okay, but yeah: they hadn't seen each other for a long time. They had some kind of falling-out back in the day."

"You thinking he abducted her?"

"No. I mean, I hadn't thought of that. I just thought it odd: They don't speak for that whole time. Then she goes to New York and they meet up. She disappears and he shows up. It's just an interesting sequence, is all."

"It is," Curtis agrees.

"So you're a painter, huh?"

"Was."

"You any good?"

"Not really," he says, and I look at him sharply to see if he's kidding. He doesn't seem to be. "Put it this way," he goes on. "Me giving it up was a hardship for nobody."

And then we arrive, and as we roll onto Ocotillo Ranch, I am relieved not to see any unexpected vehicles as I park.

"Here's home," I say.

"Nice. And there's an old pal." He indicates the dog. "He have a name yet?"

"Yeah. Imogen named him. He's Phil now."

"Phil?"

"Yeah. She says he's a philosopher. Phil for short." And my heart pangs at the memory of her pronouncement. It seems so recently she said it. And it seems like a lifetime ago.

"Hey, Phil," Curtis says as he swings out of the car. He bends over and gives the dog a good head scratch. "Good to see you, pal."

I can tell from the dog's response that the feeling is mutual.

Now that I had Curtis here, I wasn't sure what to do with him. I'd wanted to see him, wanted the comfort of his presence. Also, if I were very honest, I'd wanted to control the situation. If he was just running around looking for Imogen on his own, it was going to end badly for me if she was found. And with Imogen out of the picture, there seemed no sense to that at all.

Since what might have been guest rooms were full of paintings, and since I was in the casita, I decided to make up the primary bedroom for Curtis. I had been reluctant to invade Imogen's space. I wasn't sure why—it just seemed sacred somehow. But Curtis was here to help and was a friend and I had to put him someplace. I stripped the bed, found new sheets and generally cleared Imogen's special stuff out of the way so Curtis could have a place to put his own. It both amused and saddened me to be playing hostess in this way.

For his part, Curtis is as entranced by his surroundings as I had been when I first arrived. He could scarcely believe that he was actually in Imogen's home, surrounded by her art and the mementos from the many years she had lived and painted.

"This place is incredible. How did you say you were related again?"

"I didn't. And . . . It's complicated. Let's just leave it at that, okay?"

Curtis looks at me sharply but holds his tongue. I can see the questions he wants to ask on his face.

"Okay," he says, "you've seen that back bedroom, right? It's crazy. There must be two hundred canvases in there."

"I know."

"And is she? Crazy, I mean. The behaviors you're describing seem pretty eccentric."

I think before answering. Had she been crazy? Probably. And maybe I was crazy to have been willing to go along with her plan. And none of that matters now anyway.

As it's getting to be evening, I start thinking about dinner while Curtis settles in after traveling. I open a bottle of wine, and set about making a simple pasta dish when Imogen's landline rings. I consider not answering, then think better of it. For one thing, picking up the phone might head off unwanted visits. Answering the call seems worth the possible price.

When I hear Beardsley's voice, I am unsurprised. Hardly anyone ever calls.

"No, sorry," I tell him when he asks. "No word yet. I'll let you know when I hear from her though."

"I'm going to head back out there tomorrow, regardless." When he says it, it sounds like a threat. That thought frightens me. He sounds too aggressive. What does he think he knows?

"That sounds like it might be a waste of time," I say. "I told you: she hasn't checked in yet."

"Well, for one thing, I'm all the way out here in Arizona and I obviously can't stay indefinitely while her ladyship thinks about whether she wants to see me or not."

"It's not personal," I say. "I told you I haven't spoken with her. She doesn't even know you're here."

"Maybe you should change that." Beardsley sounds like someone who is on his last nerve.

"I can't. I'm sorry. She didn't leave a phone number, and I don't know exactly how to get hold of her."

"What is this? The 1980s? Are you telling me she doesn't have a mobile phone?"

He had a point. I don't take the bait though. I can't. Instead, I choose the most obvious response: I go on the offensive.

"Sir, I don't think I care for your tone."

"That may be, but I'll be out there tomorrow early afternoon. Regardless. If you know what's good for you, you'll find her before I get there." And when he disconnects the call, it has a sort of dull finality about it.

While I was on the phone, Curtis entered the room. I'd indicated the glass of wine I'd poured for him, and he'd picked it up and sipped, but I knew he'd heard every word, at least on my side.

"Beardsley?"

"Yuh," I say. "How did you know?"

"Just all the cheeriness I heard in your voice," he says, gently sarcastic. And then with more seriousness, "Why didn't you tell him Imogen is missing?"

"If I'm honest—should I be honest?"

"Please do."

"Okay then, if I'm honest, I'm not sure. There's just something about him . . ."

"Beardsley? Oh, he's all right. Bit of a stuffed shirt, sure. A bit pompous, you know? But I don't think he has any real harm in him."

"I wish I could be sure of that."

"No, I get it. And why take my word for it? There's lots of reasons for you to trust your own instincts. But he's been at this game for a long time. You don't get to be as successful as he's been by taking less than great care of your artists."

"Obviously, Imogen didn't always think so."

"Why obviously?"

"Well, the fact they hadn't spoken in years, for one."

"Yeah," Curtis says with a grin. "There's that. Do you know anything about why they were on the outs?"

"From what I observed, she just had a general distrust around him."

Curtis looks at me thoughtfully for a moment.

"You said 'had,'" Curtis says. "Why would that be?"

"What?" I know I'd said it. I could still feel it reverberate, but I know what he'd heard and internally curse myself. How could I have let something like that slip, especially with a reporter?

"Had," he repeats, lifting one eyebrow.

"I did say that, didn't I? I guess I don't have a good feeling about this whole thing, Curtis. Where is she? She should be here. I guess, on the inside, I'm a bit frantic."

I can see him weigh my words, consider. Whatever he thinks, though, he lets it pass. I caution myself to be more careful.

We sip the wine. I make us a simple pasta with a portobello mushroom bathed in olive oil and garlic. After a while, we aren't thinking of Imogen anymore. At least, we stop talking about her. Instead, we skate ever closer to something that has always been brewing between us and that, for whatever reasons—and there have been a bunch of them—had never been approached.

Things are different tonight, that's how it seems. The moon is closer or maybe the world is farther away and altogether, the possibilities seem more accessible. Life seems more precious.

I'm not sure how it happens.

Whatever the case, after a while I am in his arms, and then beyond, and the fit is good; right. Like together we are finding something that was never in question.

In the end, he doesn't sleep in Imogen's bed, after all.

CHAPTER FORTY-THREE

I WAKE TO full sunlight once again, cursing myself instantly for forgetting to close the blinds. I turn over, as though to rise and quench the sun, only to remember as I find him: Curtis in my bed. It's not alarming. Instead, there is the feeling of something that was inevitable coming to its natural conclusion.

I watch him for a bit before I stir. He is beautiful. The light captures the gold in his hair and on his skin, and my heart turns over just looking at him, even while our toes touch far beneath the covers and I can feel his thigh on mine. I don't know what this is, this tenderness in my heart while I watch him sleep, but I find I savor and fear it all at once, and all before I fully wake and before he wakes at all. I watch him and wish and maybe a little bit I even dream, here in the early morning light. I think about things that are impossible and let them carry me away.

"Hey." When he opens his eyes and looks straight into mine, I feel a bit startled. Silly. Somehow, I hadn't been expecting it. Like he would sleep and I would watch and dream forever.

"Hey," I reply, my voice showing none of what I feel.

"How long have you been watching me?"

"All night."

"Seriously?"

"No. I just woke up a minute ago."

"I went right out. Slept so soundly."

"It's the air out here. So clear. No toxins. It's like medicine for sleep."

He pushes himself up on one arm and leers at me.

"Is *that* what it was?"

I grin back.

"Could be."

"No word, right?"

"Sorry?"

"Have you heard from Imogen?"

"I have not. But I've been with you the whole time."

"Fair enough. But I feel like I have to do something," Curtis says, getting out of bed in what seems like a single movement. "I'm going to do what I do."

"All right," I say, not knowing exactly what he means but getting the general idea.

He grins again and both of us know and don't have to say that staying in bed and making a day of it would have been no hardship at all.

"I'm going to make some calls."

"You have a lead?"

"Not yet," he says. "But I'm going to work on it. Okay to use the shower?"

"Duh," I say and then enjoy watching the play of the muscles on his ass as he crosses the room, thinking of the horses playing in the water and wondering at this new voyeuristic part of me. Was this always in me; waiting? Or has this deepening of our connection ignited something I wasn't aware of? Something I've never quite

CHAPTER FORTY-FOUR

By NOON I have managed to drag both Curtis and myself out of bed and both of us over to the main house.

"Beardsley is coming," I tell him as I drag.

"I recall you said something like that," he says with a smirk, "but I don't think I was paying attention."

"It's true. You were not."

"I wonder if he'll have that reporter with him again," I ask idly.

"What reporter?" Curtis asks.

"Heidi somebody. Imogen mentioned meeting her in New York."

"Heidi Reed," Curtis says. I note it's not a question. And now I know I'm right: he is the opposite of elated at the prospect of Heidi's inclusion in Beardsley's excursion.

"You know her," I say.

"I do," he responds and then doesn't elaborate, so obviously he's not volunteering anything, and I wonder if it's going to be like pulling teeth to get it all out of him.

"I sense a story."

"No," he says. "Not exactly. Remember I told you someone had given me a fake number?"

"Heidi?" I can't believe the coincidence.

"It's not like that," he says, maybe reading something in my face. "We've been colleagues. Competitive."

"But a fake number?"

"It was a misunderstanding."

I look at him but don't press. This time it is me who changes the subject.

"I wonder why she's here," I ask. "Maybe the same reason you are."

He arches an eyebrow at me, melts me with a grin.

"Not the same reason."

"I'm pretty sure that's not the reason you came here."

"It's why I'm here now." He's taking me into his arms and is breathing into my hair and even though it feels so very good, both of us know it's not true even if we'd like it to be. We're here for something else.

We try not to wear an aspect of waiting, but it's hard. In the meantime, I show him the studio, enjoying the genuine surprise and delight I read on his face while he looks over the work Imogen has been doing all of these years.

"It's like a miracle," he says, "finding all of these here." And from his reaction I can see he is a true fan. Then I chide myself: of course he is. Why else drag himself to the desert to find the legend if he was not spurred on by some admiration or affection for his subject?

While we look at the work together, he snakes his hand through mine. It is sweet, this touch. As though we both feel the need for physical connection. We delight in what has been growing between us, both aware that a deadline is looming. As a result, this gentle time together does not last nearly long enough. Before long, Phil's low warning bark and the sound of tires crunching on gravel alerts us to the fact that we're no longer alone. I feel the disappointment of it to my toes. Something unexpected and tenuous has happened and it has changed everything. I would have liked a moment to savor it because the premonition of loss that wells up in me is frightening.

"Good heavens," Heidi says as they enter, her voice high and clear. It shoots through the room like an arrow. "Look what the cat dragged in."

"If we're talking about being dragged in by cats," Curtis says, "that would more likely be you guys. As I understand it, you're here uninvited."

"What the hell are you doing here, Diamond?" Beardsley sounds genuinely taken aback.

"I was about to ask you the same thing." I note that Curtis's tone is even. Measured. Whatever he's thinking, he's not letting anyone see.

"It's a story, Beardsley," Heidi says, sounding pleased with herself, even a little excited. "If Curtis Diamond is here, there's a story. I told you there was a story."

"I don't so much care about any story you or this one might have, Heidi. I just want to see Imogen." Beardsley seems to look beyond and around everyone else. His eyes sear into mine. "You know something," he says looking at me, his voice like quiet thunder. "You know and you aren't telling. Give it up. We've come all this way. You tell me what you've done with Imogen O'Brien, or else."

This is close enough to the truth that I feel my throat close up. Curtis isn't buying it though. He bashes right back with the brazen arrogance of the ignorant.

"What the hell, Beardsley. What are you implying?"

"It didn't feel like an implication to me, Diamond. That wasn't my intention. I was accusing her." He points one bony finger in my direction. "And possibly you."

"That's far enough, Beardsley," Heidi says. "Curtis is a newsman. He's here looking for a story, just like me. He won't be one."

While I know Heidi means what she says, I've seen Curtis be part of a story before. It hadn't been pretty and the outcome had been deadly.

"He said, she said. I don't give a fuck," Beardsley explodes. "I want to know where Imogen is—and I want to know now—or I will go to the police."

Phil has risen at the tone. He's not one to fly off the handle, but I can see he's keeping an eye on this suddenly shouting man.

"Do the police even know she's missing?" says Curtis.

"They do not," I say.

"Why not?" Beardsley demands.

And I feel everyone's eyes on me, waiting for an answer. I feel caught. I *am* caught. It strikes me that, since Beardsley is threatening to call the police in order to find Imogen, he had nothing to do with what had happened. He believes in the possibility of a positive outcome. I find I am disappointed about that. I wish it could have been an easy answer.

I realize that telling them puts me at a terrible risk. But what is the alternative? I could keep lying, but it seems like not telling the truth is just going to dig me further and further into a hole. In this case, too, lying leaves the memory of Imogen O'Brien without a proper conclusion and she doesn't deserve that. She deserves so much more.

And so I tell them. I explain how it all happened. About coming home, finding Imogen gone, the melancholy that gripped the dog.

I recount how Chester had told me he found her lifeless form and carried her out to the little grove of palo blancos, laying her to rest. I don't tell them about the scheme Imogen and I had hatched, because I fear it would strain their belief and cloud the issue. And, anyway, what does it even matter now? I tell them, instead, about my grief and how, for a while, I couldn't even imagine going on without her.

"You told us she was in Peoria," Beardsley says.

Curtis nods at this, not with enthusiasm, but with woe. He looks at me like he's hoping for a good explanation. I don't have one.

"I didn't know how to say it. I didn't . . . I guess, at a certain level, I didn't want it to be true." And I discover, much to my surprise, that this last is also not a lie and that everything I've been saying and feeling has been in denial of the reality of Imogen's death.

"We have to call the police," says Beardsley.

"Can you stop already with the police?" Curtis just sounds annoyed. "Let's figure this out first, okay? We don't even know if a crime has been committed until we see her."

"You don't believe me?" I say.

"Maybe we don't want to," Curtis says without meeting my eyes. "I mean, it sounds like no one has actually seen the body."

"Except Chester," I say.

"Except Chester," he repeats. "You want to show us the spot where you say he buried her?"

We make a sad little procession out to the place under the palo blancos. It is beautiful here. Chester had chosen well: and honored her with the very best he could think of.

Under the palo blanco trees, the earth is not quite as raw as it was a few weeks ago, but if you're looking for it, it's hard to miss.

"That looks like a grave all right," Curtis says.

"What now?" Heidi says. I'd been wondering the same thing.

"We dig," Beardsley says.

"I'll get a shovel," I say, taking off for the studio where we keep a lot of everything. I'm back in just a few minutes to deliver the shovel, then decide I want no part of anything. Let them dig and report what they find—the very thought of pulling Imogen out of the ground braces me for nightmares.

I head back to the house, intending to put a kettle on for tea I realize I'll probably never drink, when I run into Chester, repairing a downspout on the overhang that shades the main patio.

"Lots of people," Chester says as I pass. There is a faint whiff of disapproval in his voice. "Imogen wouldn't like that."

"Sorry, Chester. They're digging her up."

I would never have thought he could move so quickly, but he's at my elbow in seconds.

"What?"

"I'm sorry," I say again. "They wanted to see for themselves."

"Oh no, no!" he says. I'm astonished to see he's in a near panic. "This won't do. This won't ever do." He runs for his truck, and I imagine he will head toward where the mourners are digging. Instead, he drives off in the other direction, and I'm left standing there wondering if I imagined the whole thing.

Inside, I don't make tea, but head instead for Imogen's office. I sit in her big chair and I think. I'm missing something. I know I am. There is something I have overlooked.

I had found the birth certificate stuck to the side of the filing drawer. Where would the mind who did that hide something else? I empty everything out of the big oak desk and stack it on the top. Once the desk is empty, I run my hands over the inside of the sheaths that normally hold the drawers. When I feel an envelope stuck to the top of the second sheath I try, I feel something like gratitude or maybe relief wash through me. I had a hunch, and the hunch has played out.

The nine-by-twelve envelope I pull out is manila. It is old enough to appear worn, though there are no signs of wear. There are wrinkles in the thick paper from nothing more than being, but for a long time.

The first envelope had held a birth certificate. This one holds a death certificate, but it only takes me thirty seconds or a minute to figure out that everything is connected.

The person who is dead is Rose Reed. According to the document, she is the daughter of Imogen O'Brien and Frank Reed. I make a fast calculation of the dates and realize that Rose, had she lived, would now be around seventy years old, but she died many years ago. I look to the original document and deduce that Rose either died in childbirth or very close to the time Heather was born.

I sit heavily into the desk chair, hold my head in my hands, and try to think. Something about all of this is scratching at my brain. Something just out of my grasp.

Curtis enters then, pulling my attention. He has a piece of cloth in his hands.

"That was quick," I say.

"I went down at the center," he says. "No reason to dig the whole thing up. Turns out she's not there."

CHAPTER FORTY-FIVE

I HAVE A sensation of disassociation. Like it isn't me sitting there, wondering what Curtis is talking about, that it's someone else who has more information than I do. I feel like I'm missing pieces, and they are all the pieces that would help any of this make sense.

"What do you mean she's not there?" The world is reeling. It strikes me now that I maybe should have questioned Chester more closely. But I hadn't. Imogen's death had seemed so inevitable. Losing her had been sad, but not at all implausible.

"Just what I said. That's not a grave. No occupants. I just found this."

He hands over the cloth. It takes me a moment to recognize Imogen's favorite pashmina, covered in dirt now, but worn fine at various spots where it had been loved to near extinction.

"It wasn't very far down," Curtis explains. "I'm guessing it was put there for the dog to pick up the scent."

"But that's wacky," I say, incredulous beyond real words. It also explained why someone would have locked Phil in the casita while all of this was going on. They were probably hoping for exactly the reaction the loss of Imogen had produced in the dog.

"It is," Curtis agrees.

"Where are the others?"

"I left them milling around out there. I just wanted to touch bases with you. Tell you what we'd discovered."

"I found these," I say, handing over all of the hidden documents I'd unearthed.

He looks them over for a while, but doesn't say anything.

"Heather Reed?" is all he says at length. "That's a bit of a coincidence, isn't it?"

I shake my head.

"Sorry. I don't get it." And then with a smile, "That shouldn't be a surprise to me. I keep feeling like I'm missing something."

"Heidi Reed." He says it without emphasis.

I feel something go small and tight inside myself.

"Reed is not a rare name," I say quietly.

"I told you I've met Heidi before, ya?"

I nod.

"Well, I happen to know her birth name is Heather."

"It's not," I say, but I think my voice is so quiet, even I can barely hear it.

"Yeah. Heidi is diminutive for Heather."

"I have not heard that before." Somehow, I am resistant to what Curtis has said.

"No, for real," he says. "In German, the plant we know as heather is Heidekraut."

I laugh out loud at that.

"*Heidekraut?* Seriously. That would not be a terrific name."

For some reason, I'm relieved when Curtis laughs with me.

"You've got me there. But, no: Heidi can be an affectionate version of Heather, that's all. But let's think it through: That does seem like too much of a coincidence, doesn't it?"

I think about the question seriously before I answer. What even is coincidence, anyway? There was a time I would have answered one way, but I've had so many absurdly coincidental things happen to me over the years that, at this point, I feel like anything is possible. Anyway, Curtis seems confident in what he's positing, and the dates all seem to line up. The question, then, is what is she doing here and does she even know all of these connections, or even if they exist?

"I think I'm getting a headache."

Curtis laughs. "Yeah, I hear you. It's a lot."

"Where'd they all go?"

"Beardsley and Heidi? Like I said, I left them out there, near the 'grave.' I just wanted to tell you what we'd found."

"Thanks," I say, "but we'd better go find them before they do something stupid."

CHAPTER FORTY-SIX

We encounter the two of them in the studio. I know that it is foolish for me to feel protective of the space and of the work, but I find I can't help myself. It seems to me that no one else should be here.

When I enter, Beardsley looks at me in wonder.

"She wasn't kidding when she said she had done a lot of work." He seems breathless. "*A lot* might even be an understatement."

Despite everything, I smile. You could say what you liked about Imogen, she had discipline and talent. In my limited experience, I've observed you need ample supplies of both of them to make a mark in the creative world.

I don't say any of that.

"That's right. Even more than a lot would about cover it."

Standing in front of the painting Imogen had begun and I had completed, he looks from it to me, his eyes wide and emotion plain on his face.

"This," he says. And then again, "This. It's stunning."

I don't comment. I can't. What could I say?

"Curtis told me she wasn't there," is what I do say. "But if she isn't," I ask, "where is she?"

"It seems like you were telling the truth all along," Beardsley says. "You just didn't know it: she's missing, after all." It's possible that seeing Imogen's recent work has softened him. Or maybe there is just no arguing with the truth when it's laid out like this.

"I don't know what to do," I say, for once at a loss for either words or actions.

"I'm not sure there's anything *to* do," Curtis says. "I don't think she's a missing person. It feels like she's maybe just gone off somewhere."

"Someone wanted us to think she was dead," Heidi says. I look at her closely: Her features. Her profile. And I see it now: her resemblance to Imogen and, in a not-too-distant way, she looks also like me.

"Someone wanted *me* to think she was dead," I say. "Else why try to fool the dog? And why bury the scarf anyway? I was the only one here . . ."

"You and Chester."

"Right. Except I wasn't even here when it happened. I came home to discover she was dead and had been buried."

"Where's Chester now?"

"Oh." At the mention of his name, I remember. It's like a light going on. "He took off in a hurry when I said digging was happening. Maybe he knows more than he's letting on."

"I'd bet on it," Curtis says.

Heidi asks where Chester lives.

"I know he lives on the property," I say. "I'm just not sure where."

"Didn't you tell me there was a barn with cats living in it?" Curtis asks.

"I did."

"Could it be around there somewhere?"

"It must be," I say. "I can't think where else."

"Do we need a four-wheel drive to get there?" Curtis asks.

"Well, we would if we drove. But it's not that far. We can walk."

We move beyond the main structures on Ocotillo Ranch, past the pool and then past the pond—no horses there just now—and then the barn is in sight. It seems to me that we are an odd tribunal. Heidi is negotiating in stacked heels, but I pull my mind away from that and leave her to it: she was the one who decided to wear inappropriate shoes to a national park.

Curtis and Beardsley merely trudge. They seem to have tacitly negotiated some kind of truce. For my part, as I walk, I feel my gut bind itself into a tight knot and my throat freeze in apprehension. Something is about to happen, I can feel it, and it scares the hell out of me. Is that foreboding? Or, after all that has happened, just plain old common sense.

At the barn, there is a rare stillness. I figure it has to do with the nature of our little group: the cats would have heard us coming and gone into hypervigilant hiding mode. I can almost feel their eyes on us as we pass them, but I don't see even a hair or a whisker. So it's that, but maybe something else, as well.

"Someone's here," Heidi says, pointing to a pickup truck I recognize as Chester's. The truck's presence at this time of day and after our exchange puts my back up. What is in store for us here?

"That's Chester's truck," I say, confirming. "He has no reason to be at this location right now." I figure we're not far off.

It's broad daylight and it's too late for us to begin with stealth: anyone who is here would likely have heard us by now. I don't know what I was expecting to happen, but I do know that what I was least anticipating was for the door to open as the four of us approach and Imogen herself to briskly step out, almost as though she has been waiting for us.

Maybe she has.

"What a motley crew," she says.

And there, ranged in front of the semi-abandoned barn with hiding cats nearby, I can see she is not wrong: the four of us don't fit together. We could not be more different if we tried. Motley, indeed.

From the first, though, I can see that there is something different about her. I can't place it.

"Imogen," Beardsley says. "I can't tell you how relieved I am to see you."

"I'll bet you are," she says without hesitation and with sarcasm heavy in her voice. "I'll just bet you are. And you"—her eyes turn to me—"you just couldn't wait for me to be out of the way before you took every bit of advantage of me."

The words are unexpected. It's like she's punched me in the face.

"Imogen," I say, my voice rough from being stuck in my throat, "it wasn't like that at all. I thought you were dead. I've been filled with grief."

"Ha," she says, "'filled with grief.'" Her voice is falsetto and mimicking and it is somewhere in here that I place the difference in her: the sweetness that seemed almost always to lay on her is gone now. She seems filled with venom and, for the moment anyway, a lot of it appears to be aimed at me.

Along with the sweetness, her weakness seems gone, as well. Had all of that been an act? If so, why?

"You couldn't wait to get rid of that old piece of crap car of yours. Looking to get yourself a new one, I bet. And you finished my painting! How you must have waited for me to be out of the way so you could claim my work as your own."

I see Beardsley look from me to Imogen and back again. Confused but catching up quickly.

"That painting in the studio. The one I commented on . . ."

I nod, only, then turn my attention back to Imogen.

"No," I say, but sounding weak even to my own ears. "I wasn't trying to claim it. I was trying to fulfill your wishes. I thought . . . I thought you were gone." At the same time, I wonder about the painting. How could she have possibly known about that or my car unless she'd been lurking around when she thought no one was observing?

Beardsley looks from me to Imogen, then back again. Heidi's reaction is similar.

"My god," Beardsley says. "It was *you* we met in New York, not Imogen. Jesus Christ, you two. What have you done?"

"What have *we* done? What has *she* done," Imogen says. "She was obviously trying to take over my life."

"You *begged* me to, Imogen. Your legacy, you said."

"And who does such a thing, huh? What kind of person puts aside their own life to become someone else?"

That was the question, wasn't it? What she had done was awful. I didn't understand the fullness of it yet, but she'd used me for an end I didn't understand. And who allows themselves to be used in that way? How broken did I need to have been to even consider such madness? And it wasn't possible that she was sitting there on the day I arrived waiting for me. She hadn't known I was coming. There had to have been an element of coincidence in there. Or maybe, rather, of waiting. The plan had been spun. She just needed the right sucker. And then there I was.

"And your granddaughter," I say, taking a fairly confident step into the dark. "How does she fit in?" Because I feel certain that, somehow, she does.

I see Imogen's eyes flash toward Heidi, then back to me; my suspicions confirmed.

"How did you know?"

Her voice is quiet. I have to strain to hear.

"Does it matter?" I ask.

A hesitation and then, "No. I guess not."

"Does she know?"

Her eyes shift there and back again, and I already have my answer. In another half minute, it is confirmed.

"No," Imogen says. "She does not."

Heidi looks confused at this exchange, not Beardsley though.

"It was going to come out sooner or later," he says.

"Was it, though?" Imogen's tone is quieter now. "You brought her on purpose, didn't you?"

"Maybe," Beardsley admits. "Maybe I gave her something after your show that offered her a hint."

"Yeah, no. The photo you gave me only hinted at a story. Wait: the photo of the child with Imogen. You're saying that was *me*?"

Beardsley doesn't answer, and I can't, but I flash back on the package I saw her with the day after the show. Beardsley had perhaps been trying to tell her something, but she hadn't gotten the message.

"But, Imogen: Why all of this?" I'm not sure she hears me at first, my voice barely above a whisper.

"*You* know why. You of all people." The energy Imogen directs at me is so fierce and venom-filled, I take a step backwards. The other three had taken their own steps backwards, but maybe for a different reason: sensing something coming and giving us the space to have out whatever this would be.

"But I don't, Imogen. I don't know at all."

"Look what you saw when you came to me. When you viewed my work. You had expectations. I met them."

"I don't understand."

"And then you *helped* me. You *aided* me. You *forced* me to do the work I had always done, even though I couldn't anymore."

"I forced you? That's ridiculous, Imogen. You could have done anything you wanted. At any time. You were clearly in charge. In any case, you practically begged me to stay. Where is all of this coming from? And what does any of it have to do with Heidi?"

"But it can't possibly have anything to do with me. I'm the outsider here," Heidi says, and there is a desperation in her voice, like she's trying hard to hold onto that belief.

"You're my daughter, Heidi," Beardsley says.

Heidi turns to Imogen. "You're my *mother*?"

But Imogen shakes her head.

"You're her granddaughter," I say, finally putting the pieces together. "Your mother, Rose, was her daughter."

"The *Dark Rose* series," Heidi says, and it's like a light dawning. I feel compassion for her. This can't be an easy moment. "You did that for my mother."

"Her father is listed as Frank Reed," I say, remembering.

Imogen points a finger at Beardsley. "Him," she says with distaste.

"I don't get it," I say.

"Would you buy art from someone named *Frank Reed*?" Beardsley sniffs.

"Seriously?" I ask it, but it seems to me that the conversation is getting more surreal by the second. "You figured Beardsley Davenport is better?"

"Frank Reed is . . . well, a butcher. Or a clerk, at best." Beardsley seems to be quoting from some internal script. There's an awful tone deafness to the whole thing. "But Beardsley Davenport? *That's* an art dealer."

I can't think what to say. No one can. Curtis ignores him altogether and addresses Imogen.

"So that's why you stopped talking to each other," Curtis says. "Because your daughter had an affair with your agent?"

"It killed her," Imogen says. And then to Beardsley, "You killed my daughter."

"We're back there again? Come on, Imogen. You know I did nothing of the sort. It happened. It probably would never happen again. What happened to Rose was awful, but you know I didn't have anything to do with it."

"She died in childbirth," I say. "That's no one's fault."

Imogen looks disgusted. Turns away.

"Curtis is right: this was the reason for the rift," I say. "But there's more." I look from Beardsley to Imogen's back. "Isn't there?"

"In order to do innovative new work, I needed to reinvent myself. In order to reinvent myself, I needed to be dead."

"I don't think that's quite it, is it?" I'm struggling to understand. "You could just do new work any time you wanted. You had stature."

"Imogen," Beardsley says, moving toward her, sounding calm. It's as though he is talking to one of the wild horses at the pond. "I think you've been under a lot of stress. A lot. Can we let all of that go now? What can we do to alleviate whatever it is you're feeling?"

"And *you*: all you ever wanted was for me to keep churning work out. Like a machine."

"You didn't need me to do that, Imo. You've been out here all this time. Churning. I've seen the work now." He hesitates, as though considering. "It's fantastic. It *is* new and different. Your new work is spectacular. Evolved. The best you've done."

I can see Imogen sort of collapse into herself at that. She keeps her feet, but I can almost see a weight fall off her. It is as though she had been both craving and dreading the words Beardsley had spoken. And now here they were.

"But there's more than that, isn't there?" I'm surprised to hear Curtis' voice. I'd forgotten he was here.

"What do you mean?" Imogen sounds small.

"Heather." I say the names quietly. "Rose. That's where the sadness came from."

"Sadness," she says. "Pish-posh. I have only ambition."

"Who raised her?" I ask. And then to Heidi, "Who raised you?"

"Did you just say pish-posh?" Beardsley says. Three people shush him.

"I was adopted," Heidi says faintly. She looks pale. I don't blame her. Maybe all of the revelations we've had today will affect her the most acutely. "Nice people raised me. Journalists, in fact. I was told my birth parents were dead." And then to Beardsley, "You're my *father*?"

"Wait," I say. Suddenly everything is beginning to make sense to me. "Is that why you two stopped talking? Because of what happened to Rose?"

"It was a difficult time. I think she knew it wasn't my fault . . ."

"But I never forgave him. I still haven't." She looks at Heidi. "I never forgave you either."

I look at Heidi quickly, imagining maybe she will be stricken by this, but she's not.

"You're a bitter old woman." She says this calmly and without heat. "All of this has nothing to do with me." She gets closer to Imogen. "You're not even a good story anymore. You're not well. Get some help." And she turns and heads back toward the house.

"You see? I have nothing left. Nothing. You have taken everything from me." This is directed at Beardsley. "And you"; a finger leveled at me.

"Imogen. Please," I say, surprised at how calm I sound. "You practically begged me to stay. And you are right: I should not have taken you up on that invitation. It might have saved us both some grief."

"It's all right," Beardsley surprises me by interjecting. His voice is soothing and calm. "I'm so sorry, old friend"—this to Imogen. "I'm so sorry it's come to this." And to me. "I didn't know." He addresses me. "I'll take care of her from here. I don't think she should be alone anymore."

"I'm not alone," Imogen says defensively.

"No, dear. No. You're not," he says, as he leads her toward the house.

CHAPTER FORTY-SEVEN

CURTIS AND I stand there for a minute, dumbstruck.

"What just happened?" Curtis sounds confused.

"Yeah, I'm not totally sure. But I think it's okay now?"

Of all the questions I had—the questions I imagined would stay unanswered forever—I only know one thing for sure: Imogen is a genius and genius makes great demands.

Additionally, a rational person would not have listened to her pleas or ideas. And I guess I'd known for a while that I was no longer a rational person, but maybe I hadn't realized how far from center I had fallen. Until now. It wasn't something I wanted to acknowledge, but faced with it as I was, how could I not?

I head back toward the house and the casita and . . . what? I don't even have a car anymore. I have no idea what I'm going to do.

"Wait. Wait for me!"

"I'm not waiting, Curt."

He catches up to me, even though I know that the last thing I want right now is his company, no matter how sweet it has been at times. "Go on. Get your story. I just need to get out of here."

We reach the casita and Phil, who is locked inside, greets us with enthusiasm. I'm careful to close the door behind me as I enter. The last thing I want is for the dog to go running to Imogen now.

"Forget the story," Curtis says. His legs are longer than mine. He beats me here. "At least for now. It's going to take me days just to process what happened out there. What just happened." A pause, and then, "I don't think it's a story I want, anyway."

If I'd been listening, I would have seen his point. An ancient drama. A tragedy. And the loss of one of the great artists of her generation. She had been alone too long, that was my takeaway. And I hadn't seen the signs, just believed all of the things I wanted to believe. And what did that say about me? And about my mental health? It wasn't a mirror I wanted to look in, yet there it was.

"Listen," he says, "we should talk." He comes toward me, and I let him take me into his arms. I sort of melt there, into the place where my neck meets his shoulder. He smells good. Like citrus and pipe tobacco. He feels so good, too. So strong. As though to reinforce that feeling, he squeezes me with that arm, so tightly it almost hurts, and it's just what I need. *He* is just what I need. I know that now. But right this minute, I don't have space in my heart. I just have to sort things out. I have to get back in motion to sort out what all of this means.

"We can't talk now. Maybe soon, okay?" I grab my duffle bag and start throwing everything that is important into it. Everything that is mine and that I might need. "Right now, I just need to get out of here. I need . . . well, I need some space from all of this. From here. I'm sorry, but maybe even from you."

Curtis doesn't budge so I keep packing around him. His eyes widen as he sees me transferring stacks of cash and a couple of guns and some ammunition from the refrigerator into the duffle. He doesn't say anything, and I feel that, after all we've been through together, I have reason to believe he won't say anything and, hopefully, he won't follow me either. Not right now.

I grab one of the Bersas and stuff it into the waistband of my jeans.

"I'll give you that space, but tell me you'll get in touch soon, all right? There are things you and I need to say to each other. I . . . I love you. Do you feel the same? I think you do."

I don't have time to answer, though, and what might I have said? But Phil's growl lets us know that someone is at the door, and they're not knocking. I look at Curtis, and Curtis looks at me. We're both thinking the same thing: that somehow Imogen and/or Beardsley have followed us back here, probably to pursue other lines of conversation we don't want to take part in, but nothing prepares us for what we see when I open the door.

I recognize the man right away even though there is a scar across his face that wasn't there the last time I saw him. Another on his arm and he walks with a limp that's also new. He looks just as he did when I first saw him, yet different. There is a waxen look to his pale skin and I get the feeling that, under his ballcap, there is still more damage.

"You look surprised to see me. I'm guessing you didn't expect I'd be reappearing at your door."

Time stops. It slows down. I see myself hoisting his comatose form into his vehicle. See that vehicle spiraling down the canyon. I don't say any of that. I just answer him.

"Surprised. Yes," is what I say.

Curtis doesn't say anything. He just stands there, shifting his weight lightly from one leg to the other like he's trying to think what he can do or say and coming up short.

He ignores Curtis; focusing everything on me.

"I thought you might," the man says.

"Why did you come back?" I ask it, but I know the answer.

"You killed Rex. And you thought you'd killed me, too. Now it's your turn: yours and your husband's. And when it's done, I won't feel a thing, just like you didn't when you pushed me off that cliff. Garbage to get rid of. Two can play that game."

I feel rather than see him lift a handgun, level it at Curtis. Curtis extends his hand toward the man like he's got some words that are going to diffuse this situation; that are going to make everything okay.

The gun, when it goes off, is deafening and at this close range it nearly rips Curtis in two. My reaction is automatic, but also from a place of great distance. Even as he's leveling the gun in Curtis' direction, I am reaching behind me, pulling the Bersa from my waistband, flipping off the safety as I raise the gun toward him. I fire almost at the same time he does.

And then you wonder—do you spend a lifetime wondering?— but you wonder: What if I'd been just a second faster? Would I have stopped it? Or what if it had been me, instead? Would it have been easier? Would my own death have released all this damn suffering? All this pain that I seem to drag around?

In any case, there are two dead bodies in the casita. Sadly, one of them is not mine. I collect my gear, call my dog, and head outside. As I leave the casita, I'm thinking I will take Imogen's SUV, but then when I get outside, I see the dead man's sport utility vehicle: not the one I shoved off the cliff, obviously. But another, just as mottled and ugly, like my heart. It suits this moment perfectly.

Once I'm packed up, and the dog is locked and loaded, I just drive.

* * *

This time, when I drive under the sign that says "Ocotillo Ranch," I know it is for the last time. I muse a bit on the name and on the flower, considering what both mean to me.

Ocotillo are impossible plants. Impossible. There is hardly anywhere on earth that they grow. Such a small area, you wonder why they bother at all.

You wonder more when you see them. Looking at them doesn't clear things up.

Three-quarters of the year—more—they are butt ugly. Butt! Dead-looking sticks that seem to stand against all odds. Prickly sticks. Not only are they ugly, they look like they could hurt you. And you look at them, and you wonder: What could be the possible point?

Then the rains come. The inevitable rains. Green shoots appear on the barren branches. After a bit of this, bright orange flowers join the green leaves that have filled out the plant, seemingly overnight. The flowers are sour, but nutritious. High in vitamin C.

That's when you get it. And the magic sinks in. The ocotillo plant is a metaphor for the desert. And nature does love her metaphors. The plant bides its time. It waits. And just when you would write it off, it shows itself to be one of the most beautiful living creatures you've ever seen. And then you wonder again: If this is possible, what is not?

* * *

At first, I drive without reason. I have no destination in mind. I need dog food and gas and I need to put distance between myself and any of the UTV driver's possible pals. Other than that, I don't know where to go.

After a while, though, it's not that I make a decision, it's that I suddenly know some decision has been made, and I drive and drive and drive without questioning the goal. There are no other answers, so it doesn't matter anyway.

* * *

When Kenny answers the door, his eyes go wide at the sight of me. I know I must look like hell: there is blood on my face and tears on my soul and god knows what other signs he can see that I'm not bothering to look for.

"You okay?"

I shake my head.

"No. Not okay."

"All right." He says it soothingly, like one might to a wild animal, but he doesn't move toward me. Maybe I look as wild as that animal. Maybe I look like I might bite. "All right now," he says again. "You're safe. You *are* safe, right?"

"I think so."

"Okay," he says. His voice as smooth as porcelain. Calm. The sound of it nearly makes me cry.

I want to hug him, but I don't. I just stand there on the stoop, close to shaking.

"You still have the cottage?"

"Of course."

"I'd like it, please."

"What?"

"I don't want to buy it."

"Okay."

"I just want to live there, for now."

"All right."

"Me and the dog."

"That's fine, too."

"I don't know what else to do."

"You don't need anything else," he says. "You're home."

AUTHOR'S NOTE

There is a sort of sadness that runs through *Insensible Loss*. Even now, with the actual writing of the book behind me, I feel shadows of that sadness on my heart. *Insensible Loss* is the fourth book in the series. If you've been following her adventures since the first book, *Endings*, you know that by now she has gone through a lot. Too much. Certainly, more than one person can be asked to endure, yet she goes on. But is she unscathed? I don't think so. She would not be someone we believe as human if she could witness all that she has seen without being touched on some pretty extreme levels. And so maybe *Insensible Loss* is a reckoning, or part of one. And still, she just puts one foot in front of the other and soldiers through.

Everything about this book has brought me wonder. Disparate pieces came together in ways that, for me, made a kind of chemical magic. Early readers have described *Insensible Loss* as the most cerebral of the Endings series thus far. To be honest, I don't know if that's true, and if it is, I'm not certain that it's relevant, but I'll tell you this: I did more research on the workings of the human brain for this book than I have for previous works. I delved into attachment theory in particular. If you're new to the term, do some poking around on your own. This is fascinating stuff and it touches all of us—if you believe in all that stuff, and I guess I kinda do.

Another piece of wonder: the title. One summer's day, not long after I started working on *Insensible Loss*, I was playing tennis in Phoenix and one of my friends, a doctor who is a specialist in her field, said, "Come on, ladies: we need a water break. We have to look out for our *insensible losses.*"

As we stood beside the court, quaffing water, I asked her if it was a medical term. She told me it was. That it describes the physical losses we are unaware of. As I understand it, the term is specific to fluid losses, but that wasn't where my mind went.

Right then, I told her it was going to be the title of the book I was working on. "Well, you'd better mention me then," she said. And so here we are: thanks to Dr. Khai Ling Tan both for helping keep me hydrated on the court and for the gift of the book title with the very best story.

I remain so grateful to the team at Oceanview Publishing for their generous shepherding of the books in this series. It is extraordinary to get to work with people so committed to making good books. The whole team is involved with almost every aspect. That makes for a lot of love that gets poured into every one of the titles they publish every year. Bob and Pat Gussin, Lee Randall and Faith Matson work diligently at all the details that, in the end, make special books. I can't thank them enough.

My agent, Kimberley Cameron, continues to champion all of my projects and has brought so much that is golden into my life. She is laughter, warmth, grace, and perseverance. I am proud to be on her roster. Thanks, also, to my film and television agents,

Mary Alice Kier and Anna Cottle of Cine/Lit Representation, who have brought their own magic.

I feel grateful to have an incredible team of first readers. The books are better through their participation. My husband, Anthony J. Parkinson, and my dear friends Will Bass and Sarah Entz Bass are beyond generous with their time and opinions—and boy: do all three of them have a lot of opinions! Love you, guys!

Grateful to the friends, family, and colleagues who, in various ways, help make the books better. My brothers, Peter Huber and Roger Chow; my son, Michael Karl Richards, and his wonderful bride, Kristen Hauser Richards; my friends Stephanie Parkinson Briguglio, Michéle Denis, Sheena Kamal, Laura-Jean Kelly, Jeannie Lee, Chris Newell, Jo Perry, Diana Welvaert, and Carrie Wheeler, thank you all for all the things, always.

And then there's you, dear reader. The most important piece. We're nowhere without what you bring to this party. Thank you so much for continuing to care about the connection.

PUBLISHER'S NOTE

We trust that you enjoyed *Insensible Loss*, the fourth book in Linda L. Richards' Endings Series.

While the other three novels stand on their own and can be read in any order, the publication sequence is as follows:

ENDINGS (BOOK 1)

Redemption from the darkest of situations—an exploration of the costs of reinvention, questioning motivation, and if ever the ends justify the means.

"Provocative and powerful, *Endings* by Linda L. Richards sweeps the reader from leafy suburbia into the strangely seductive underworld of a woman who teaches herself to kill for a living. Page after page, Richards ratchets up the tension, weaving tradecraft, disguises, and psychology into a riveting tale that peels back the layers of the soul."

—Gayle Lynds,
New York Times best-selling author

EXIT STRATEGY (BOOK 2)

A shattered life. A killer for hire. Can she stop? Does she want to? Her assignments were always to kill someone. That's what a hitman—or hitwoman—is paid to do, and that is what she does. Then comes a surprise assignment—keep someone alive.

The tension, the psychology, the disguises—and Richards weaves it all together with often lyrical prose—creates an evocative protagonist, who is trending toward the dark side. And the assignment in *Exit Strategy* offers possible redemption. She's faced with instruction to protect this time—not to kill.

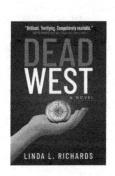

DEAD WEST (BOOK 3)

Rule #1 of being a hired killer: never get to know your target . . . and definitely don't fall in love with them.

"Linda L. Richards delivers yet another riveting entry in her hired killer series. Set mostly in Arizona desert country, *Dead West* is a dust devil of a story, twisting in wildly unpredictable ways and with a powerful emotional center. But this book isn't just a marvelously compelling thriller; it also cries out passionately for protection of the endangered wild horses of the West. Kudos to Richards for seamlessly weaving an important message into the fabric of a terrific tale."

—William Kent Krueger,
New York Times best-selling author

We hope that you will read the entire Endings Series and will look forward to more to come.

If you liked *INSENSIBLE LOSS*, we would be very appreciative if you would consider leaving a review. As you probably already know, book reviews are important to authors and they are very grateful when a reader makes the special effort to write a review, however brief.

For more information, please visit the author's website:
www.lindalrichards.com.

Happy Reading,
Oceanview Publishing
Your Home for Mystery, Thriller, and Suspense